ALL THAT LASTS

THE NAXOS QUARTET

PATRICK GARNER

AEGIS PRESS

First published in 2022 by Aegis Press
Northborough, Massachusetts

Garner, Patrick
All That Lasts by Patrick Garner.
Print & EPUB ISBN 9798354494262

Front and rear cover artwork by Patrick Garner.
Typeset in Baskerville.

AUTHOR'S NOTES

The cover image of the young ballerina depicts the goddess Gaia, who appears in these novels as a nine-year-old.

All That Lasts is the final novel of *The Naxos Quartet*, which chronicles the appearance of the ancient Greek gods in our world. All four books stand-alone, but the reader is encouraged to begin the series with *The Winnowing* (Book I), followed by *Cycladic Girls* (Book II), *Homo Divinitas* (Book III), and *All That Lasts* (Book IV).

Unattributed poems are by the author.

A glossary of Greek deities appearing in this volume is included at the end of the book.

The characters in this story are not based on living persons. Only the gods and goddesses are real.

Comments and feedback are welcome. You are invited to leave a review with Amazon or contact the author at patrickgarner@me.com

CHAPTER 1

... a man's life-blood
is dark and mortal.
Once it wets the earth
what song can sing it back?
—Aeschylus, *Agamemnon*

As she did on many mornings, Timessa scanned the sea from the upstairs deck of her house on Naxos. An hour after first light the waves were at rest. The surface was struck by early rays as if showered with shards of molten glass. A dolphin broke the scrim, hanging above the water, acrobatic, twisting in the air as if doing so might defeat gravity. As the goddess held her breath, it bellied into the sea.

The golden eagle, Aetos, appeared above the dolphin's eddy, gliding in a slow arc. One of the girls was hawking the bird from the promontory. From this distance she wasn't sure which of the nymphs had taken it out for work, but she guessed Delia.

The Olympic gods, Timessa thought, have never been as angelic as the girl. On the contrary, the gods are amoral, gray-eyed, aloof.

Amorality is their fuel, indifference to right and wrong their strength. Their compassion, were it measurable, would not be found. They are without affection, like the cosmos, like nature itself.

As she continued to gain divine power and understanding, she assessed the remaining divinities and knew that their reaction to mortals suffering was not as much nonchalance as ... as what? Obliviousness. Yes. She thought of Artemis's eyes — they were often as cold as the light glittering off the planet Venus.

Yet, Artemis had once saved a young girl from being sacrificed …

Timessa dismissed the memory. The gods, she thought, were detached, dispassionate. At best they observed. Now, although she dominated them, she had caught herself responding in the same manner. Once she had admired the trait of detached observance. It seemed principled and the highest mark of intelligence.

"But how can you let someone suffer if you can help?" her lover Iole (or Io, as she called her) had argued.

Timessa responded that intervention could have unpredictable results, especially on moral issues. "Morals are not static," she would say, "they change in every culture." The two had spent hours, weeks, in futile, circular discussion.

Unlike the austere Artemis, she often reacted explosively. Was such duality possible? Obviously so. Still, in this late era, only she struggled with the contradiction. The other gods had ceased to grapple, if they ever had, with any of this.

My fate, she sighed. She marked her fate as beginning when she ceased to be a simple nymph and began her transformation into the ancient Great Goddess, second only to Gaia herself. Her journey had been feverish, terrifying and lonely. When Io came into her life, she could share her pain.

Timessa now saw that Artemis the huntress and the eagle Aetos were essentially cold-blooded when they stalked their prey. They were effective because they lacked compassion. Without remorse Artemis killed fawns with her silver-tipped arrows. Aetos fell from the sky onto hares with a measured, careless fury.

. . .

Those two: their eyes were impassive. But Timessa's eyes were not. Hers were febrile, too often fiery. She *suffered*, as absurd as the concept was for a divinity. She suffered to the extent that her fever could only be quieted by Io, the heat passing from Timessa's bones to the joyous girl.

Yet despite Io's efforts, in the end, as the girl turned on her side to sleep, Timessa would lay awake in the darkness, the old fires mocking her, circling in a flickering heat, the conflagration demanding, clamoring for … something she still could not decode.

Often in this dreamworld the sea's waves would turn to flame — smoke rising, like low clouds, on the water. Often the images dissolved only in the dawn's light when she would step out onto her deck to gaze over the primeval landscape.

Hers was an enviable beauty. It was casual, stunning. Like dry tinder suddenly set alight, Timessa had burst upon the fashion world three years earlier, her face on magazine covers everywhere. Her allure was elemental. She had become famous, her eyes and lips and faintly aquiline nose an instant sensation.

Then she retreated from it all. The withdrawal was not one of giving ground. Rather, she changed her mind. There is an ancient Greek word: *katabasis*, which perfectly describes the turn she had made. *Kata* was downwards, as in going to the Underworld. The time to descend had come. She had been flying high. Yet modeling had become vacuous, mechanical, the predictability smothering all excitement.

A delayed yet innate realization of its triviality struck her one morning. She'd been drinking coffee in a Parisian hotel. A server had stepped close, asking, *"Une autre tasse?"* She looked up at him, startled at his varnished eyes, his slightly crooked nose. He was *mortal*.

At that moment all of it — the posing and the preening — seemed prosaic. The revelation demanded that she stand down. The repetition and routine, the monotony and emptiness — how could she not have seen it for what it was?

Yes, there had been months when the glamour had allowed her moments of triumph. In her defense, perhaps the realization had been delayed as she tried to beat back the fires that she saw almost every night in her mind's eye and did not understand.

Near the end — as the most photographed woman in the world — she knew that her celebrity was absurd. She had been naïve, believing that the work would, at the least, distract her from the terrifying changes happening inside her.

She could not escape. She continued sporadically to have the dispassion of a goddess. That divine coolness, rather than shielding her, fueled her sense of disconnection from the human world. On top of that, Gaia had filled her with the fearful memories of the first Great Goddess.

She eventually understood that much. And had escaped into obscurity. Now she lived with Io and a dozen nymphs on an island in the center of the Aegean.

Before purchasing the land, she had known it was once, many millennia ago, the home of the wine-god, Dionysos. Today the marble mansion he had shared with his wife Ariadne was only scattered blocks laying among the anemōnē and wildflowers that sprang up in the bright Greek spring.

Timessa had renovated a nearby 19th century house, as well as several outbuildings. From its upper deck she could look across the sea toward Delos and Mykonos. From the house to the sea's edge was a short walk interrupted by a promontory. One could descend from the overlook along a steep path to a long, crescent beach. That flat, washed shoreline had partly persuaded her to acquire the land.

But it was Dionysos's old claim to the entire island that had extinguished her doubts. Dionysos's ramparts! Unexpectedly, she felt at home for the first time in her life.

For all that, Timessa acknowledged that her evolution — her journey, however banal the term — was still on-going. Gaia, the primal Mother, had released her into the wild, placing her at a risk no different than that of the fragile anemōnē. whose flowers only opened to a breeze. Before Gaia's intervention, she had been one of Artemis's nymphs.

Yes, she thought, *I've been set free to face the wind. I face questions no divinity has ever been asked.*

Why can't I be content like Artemis and Athene? Their dispassion suits them. They struggle with nothing; their placidity acts as a shield. Yet ... she recognized (as she knew they did not) that imperfections shadowed their tranquil immortality.

For them, deathlessness had bred a complacency that had become its own limitation. None of the others could see themselves as Timessa did. (Once, many thousands of years ago when she was young, she had viewed them as flawless and golden, but no longer.)

For reasons she could not follow, Gaia had cut her free from her old life. She was no longer the carefree nymph under Artemis's protection, running through wildlands and serving the goddess. Everything she had recently experienced, all that she had become, was riddled with uncertainty and pain.

It was Gaia's doing; Gaia would not allow her the luxury of Artemis's placidity ... Instead, Timessa was given extraordinary beauty and unfathomable trauma. Now, in her transformed state, all she knew was that she had been chosen to reanimate old truths that had brought down the original Great Goddess.

Why?

She had not been aware of any of this years earlier on Delos. There she had inexplicably begun to dance the Dionysiakos, and doing so had brought back four of the gods who had been missing for more than 1,600 years. That moment had confirmed her metamorphosis.

In the months following the Delos incident, she would become acknowledged as the most powerful divinity of all.

Now, on her deck overlooking the sea, she knew that she was changing again.

CHAPTER 2

Because we smashed their statues all to pieces,
because we chased them from their temples —
this hardly means the gods have died.
—C.P. Cavafy, *Song of Ionia*

Io and Timessa sat at a table in the back on the marble-floored patio that extended half the length of the house. A single, flickering candle burned in the center of the table. Olive orchards spiraled backward over the terraces into the darkness. The flanking vineyards were rumored to date back to Dionysos. The starlight was unusually sharp and the two could hear waves lapping against the cove.

Io reached over and covered Timessa's hand, saying, "Nights like these ..."

"Seem eternal," the goddess smiled. "It's easy to imagine they have always been."

"And will always be," the girl said.

"There's no wind tonight," Timessa said, closing her eyes.

"There's been none for days."

"It's not my doing. I've just let sky be sky and wind be wind."

"That's kind of you," Io smirked. "Magnanimous. All the elements are grateful."

"I've taken a hands-off approach."

Io ran her fingers between Timessa's and sighed. "When you *do* intervene, how do you decide?"

"Usually ..." She laughed softly. "I just let things be."

Timessa looked at Io. "Lovely dress."

"Thank you. It ships out tomorrow. But I couldn't resist wearing it one time. The client's my size —" Io liked to call herself a simple dressmaker. In reality, she was a couturier whose clientele included many of the world's rich and famous.

When Timessa moved to the estate on Naxos, Io established her increasingly famous atelier in one of the renovated outbuildings. The clothes she designed were tailored to a client's specific needs, which often required Io to travel for consultations.

"There are times," Timessa continued, "when a subtle tinkering with the winds may alter everything. Even history."

"I can imagine. Conjure up a mega cyclone and you can destroy entire cities."

"Or the reverse," the goddess said. "Having no wind can destroy as well —"

Io waited, aware that her lover was setting the stage for a story. She lifted her wine glass and said, "When was no wind a threat to anyone?"

"When you're in a ship with sails."

"Oh, of course."

"Imagine when hundreds of ships are sailing to a specific destination. And they become becalmed."

Io frowned. "Sailing ships — this sounds like long ago."

"Something very old, although new to you."

"We have the night."

"You're always diplomatic, Io. I'll go on —?"

Io raised her hands head-high and fluttered her fingers with a half-smile. "Please. And here — I've started the winds for you, my love. Begin your narrative ..."

Timessa looked at the girl and said, "Many, many years ago in what we now call Greece, a war began. It was fueled by jealousy and theft. A barbarian prince wandered into a village beside the Eurotas River, and when he left, he departed with a king's young wife …

"The king was old, scarred from battles. He rarely laughed. The prince was handsome, charming. And he was twenty, the wife's age within a month ..."

"I see. She fell in love."

"Some say the prince kidnapped the girl. But that wasn't true: she left willingly."

"And the king was less than happy."

"Yes, and he raised a mighty force to secure his wife's return. He wanted revenge. He had lost his wife, and worse, lost face to this no-name prince …

"The king put out the word that all Greeks had been maligned. He demanded that each town, each city-state, each kingdom throughout the Mediterranean pledge ships and men. They would unite and revenge the banditry."

"You watched all of this?" Io asked.

"I was one of Artemis's nymphs. Some of this I saw; some I heard later. The king proved good at recruiting men and ships …

"Twenty ships here, fifty-five from another town, forty-two from the Peloponnese, seventy-eight from Crete. The king was admirably patient. In time, after arm twisting and threats, he gathered a thousand ships and ninety thousand men."

"All because of this woman."

"At the time it was the largest war force ever amassed. The ships gathered in Argos, the king's home, and set sail for the prince's city to the north. At first the conditions were ideal …

"A warm, steady breeze filled their sails. It was said that Zeus had given his blessings ..."

Io whispered, "At some point something happened."

Timessa nodded. "Needing a break, the force landed at a town called Aulis. It was coincidence, but many of us, including Artemis, were there in a sacred grove outside of the town. During a lull in the activities —"

"Activities?"

"Of the armada. Ship maintenance, restocking of food — that

sort of thing." Timessa paused. "The king's brother staged a hunt, entering Artemis's sacred grove. He was warned that it was protected, that all animals were consecrated …

"The goddess assigned several of us to keep an eye on the hunting party as it beat its way through the woods. I was hidden, but close enough to hear him when he exclaimed, 'Artemis? I can easily outshoot her — any of us can! There's nothing to fear. We'll hunt where we wish —' "

"Hubris," Io asserted.

"Yes. He thought a mighty force had his back. He felt invincible. I reported his words to the goddess. She listened without expression, telling me to go back and keep further watch."

"He should have known better."

"He should have," Timessa said. "But he didn't. Within a hour the king's brother scored a hit. One of Artemis's sacred deer went down. The party skinned and roasted it inside the grove. We were outraged."

"Did she summon a wind to destroy him?"

"No, she was more subtle. Great strategists act unexpectedly. She allowed him to return to the shore and brag about his exploits."

"I'm surprised," Io whispered. "She permitted them to leave?"

"No. She simply turned off the winds and imposed a terrible silence. The grasses grew still. The birds stopped singing. Even the waves lapping the shore flattened."

"So by stopping the wind … she … stranded them."

"Exactly," Timessa said. "At first the king and his brother assured their men that the change was temporary, that it meant nothing — and that the winds would return. But days went by …

"Nothing changed. The stillness became eerie. The men became increasingly restless. Rumors shot through the encampment that the gods were angry."

Io ran her fingers through her hair, puzzled by Timessa's words. "Artemis must have had a plan beyond just stopping the winds."

"Perhaps. She never said. But that one simple action threatened everything."

"I imagine they ran out of food."

"Yes. Weeks passed. Then suddenly, as all were becoming desperate, a seer announced that he had had a vision. That carrying it out would save the king's mighty force."

The girl looked incredulous. "A seer?"

"Every army brought several along. They were expected to fore-tell success and warn against failure, to bless a coming attack or advise against it. This one's name was Kalkhas and he was consid-ered unusually gifted."

"Was it true?"

"Apollo was said to sit at his elbow. I can't say. I do remember that he was a very old man — some said that he was hundreds of years old …

"The king, of course, was all ears. But what he heard from the oracle was shocking."

Io laughed delightedly. "Tell, tell!"

Timessa said. " A god required a sacrifice."

"A ram or a bull?"

"Something more precious."

"And after this sacrifice the winds would blow?"

"Oh yes — favorable winds. Good winds. A steady zephyr on the backs of the ships for every day they sailed."

"But sacrifices were normal, right?" Io paused. "What was shocking?"

"The sacrifice had to be human."

"Oh."

"Even at that time, only the most extraordinary circumstances could warrant such thing."

"Had Artemis made this demand?"

Timessa shrugged. "She has never said. But it gets worse. Kalkhas stated that the sacrifice … the *human* sacrifice —" Timessa drew out the word *human*. "— must be the king's oldest daughter."

Io whistled softly. "The payback."

"Of course."

"This is heartbreaking."

"Upon hearing the demand, the king refused. He was furious, first with Kalkhas, then with the prophesy itself. Several of his commanders, including his brother, had been on hand when Kalkhas spoke …

"In their excitement they spread the word throughout the troops. The men rejoiced. There was no escape for the king. He was cornered."

"Couldn't he have just said no? Said this prophet was a crazy man?"

"Kalkhas was respected. If he spoke, he spoke for some god. And the army now had a way out ...

"It was blunt, an ugly order — but no one could question a divine command. The king was trapped. He feared for his own life if he didn't act."

"Was his daughter," Io asked, "there, in Aulis?"

"No, she was back in Argos."

"Thank goodness. So it all fell through."

"Hardly. At first, the king put up a front and spurned the demand. Then his brother — the one who'd killed the deer — worked on him. After many hours the king buckled."

"The coward."

Timessa paused as if considering whether to go on. "The two came up with a plan. They sent their swiftest messenger down to Argos ...

"They concocted a lie. The sham was that the noble warrior Achilles had made the king's daughter a marriage proposal, that she was to come to Aulis immediately for the grand event."

"That is," Io said, "come to Aulis where we'll slit your throat."

"Exactly. So the young girl — her name was Iphigenia — and her mother arrived at the war camp with her wedding things. Both were excited, even ecstatic. To join the houses of Achilles and the king was an unexpected honor."

"Her father kept her in the dark?"

"At first, but within hours of her arrival the truth slipped out."

"And —?"

Timessa shook her head. "After her initial shock, Iphigenia embraced the demand, saying that she would do as Kalkhas said. For the sake of Greece ...

"All that she asked was that the sacrifice happen at high noon, in front of the soldiers and at an altar where all could see her blood flow freely."

Io grimaced. "I don't like this story. I can't believe that Artemis played along. Or that Iphigenia was so ... heroic."

"It didn't quite work the way you think. The stage was set. The sun was hot and afire — Helios, you know, had been watching and was always the showman ...

"Tens of thousands of troops lined the shore, chanting prayers without break to Zeus and Ares and Athene —"

"Not to Artemis?"

"They were afraid to speak her name. They worried she might change her mind. They wanted blood as soon as possible. They wanted to sail."

Timessa took a long sip of wine, set her glass down and went on. "I was there, along with others. We were disguised as village girls. Iphigenia was carried from the royal tent into the sun on a stretcher. She was wrapped from neck to feet in red-dyed sacrificial cloth, her mouth gagged so that she couldn't cry out."

"Who was to wield the knife?"

"Oh, Kalkhas had made that clear as well. The executioner had to be her father."

"The king."

"Can you imagine any man agreeing to kill his child?" Timessa picked up her glass and set it down immediately. "Yet he was terrified of appearing weak and stepped to the altar holding a long silver blade ...

"She was pinned down by the priests. The king flashed the knife in the sun, swiveling the blade before his men, showing his ... His what? His virility, I suppose."

"This really happened, didn't it?" Io stared at her.

Timessa nodded. "Yes. Iphigenia screamed in a muffled cry, 'Now, father!' And with a loud groan, the king raised his hand and brought it down toward the girl."

Io covered her eyes, exhaling. When she looked up, Timessa said, "But there was a final twist: as the blade came down, Iphigenia disappeared."

"I don't get it."

"No one watching got it either. In her place lay a fawn. The girl herself had vanished. And the king stopped his knife short. Then he stepped away, bewildered, looking left and right."

Io stood. "She simply disappeared?"

"It was Artemis's doing."

"I thought the goddess had ordered the killing."

"Remember, Kalkhas was the architect. Artemis was the supposed recipient. He probably made it up. And at the very end the goddess rejected it all ..."

Io said, "What happened to ... Iphigenia?"

"Artemis took her to a distant temple. A place called Tauris. There she served the goddess until she was old."

"And the army?" Io asked. "Did they turn on the king?"

"No, the winds returned. Within hours the ships resumed their journey toward the Hellespont. And the war began."

"I'm still confused. Why did Artemis save the girl?"

Timessa smiled. "Some say she would not allow royal blood to stain her altar, but I think royalty had nothing to do with it."

"Then —?"

"Since the event I've been content to say I saw it all. Artemis did whatever she did for purposes ... for reasons ... we may never understand."

Io paused. "Let me guess. You think she may have weighed divine right and wrong? And chosen right."

"It was odd," Timessa reflected, "watching it all unfold. Iphigenia, moments before she was to be killed, wanted what we call *kalos thanatos*, or a beautiful death ...

"Her father sought *kleos*, or glory. What Artemis wanted I cannot say. Right or wrong? None of the gods thought that way. They always just did whatever they wanted."

"Yet she opted to save the girl."

"Perhaps it was practical. Perhaps she needed a temple priestess and thought Iphigenia would do."

"Yet a deer was swapped for the girl."

"It was quickly explained away by those who watched."

"How?"

"Some whispered that killing the girl would be a *miasma*, a pollution. Something far worse than what the king's brother had done in the sacred grove …

"Others said that Artemis had had a change of heart. But none of that mattered in the long run — the *winds* were all that mattered.

"When the winds returned, a thunderous cheer arose."

CHAPTER 3

The evening was mild, the sky sparkling under its long ecliptic ridge of ancient constellations. Stars blinked in pinks and whites. The two women talked past midnight, occasionally beginning a new bottle of wine, one or the other infrequently standing and checking on the silent house.

Io shook her head, saying, "All of that ... the thousand ships and the crazy sacrifice ... was a prelude to war, wasn't it? One evil to ensure another."

"Yes," Timessa said. "The war went on for a decade. All because the Greeks believed the king's wife — who by then had been deemed the world's most beautiful woman — was hiding behind the walls of this barbarous city."

"Why did it take ten years?"

"Both sides had brave warriors. And the gods were involved, taking sides. The battles would go one way, then another. As the years passed, thousands died for this one woman."

"All regard for right and wrong," Io intoned, "seemed immaterial."

"Achilles's closest friend, Patroclus, died on the killing ground. The prince's brother, Hector, the country's bravest warrior, was humiliated, then killed. Then Achilles himself was taken down ...

"On the last day, the thieving prince, the man who'd started it all, was cut down. The Greeks got inside the city where the slaughter continued. Women with their babies were thrown off the city's walls. The few who lived were taken into slavery. At the end the citadel was burned to the ground."

"And after all of that, did the king retrieve his wife?"

"From the beginning to the end, all of this was propelled by the gods. At Aulis, Artemis set it in motion. Then the war itself attracted other gods: Zeus, Ares, Athene, Aphrodite, Thetis, Apollo, even poor Hephaistos — all became involved at one point or another."

"You haven't answered my question."

"The king's wife? Yes, they were reunited. But it was an illusion, a final stunt by the mightiest of the gods."

"Twists and turns."

"At every corner. Do you know the word *eidolon*?" Io shook her head. Timessa said, "From the Greek *eidos*, or form. Today it means specter."

"Like a ghost?"

"Closer to a phantom. Remember that the gods had their fingers in this from the start. The king's wife left her home willingly enough. The prince was irresistible — the gods's work, of course.

"She fled in the arms of this foreigner. But once the girl boarded the prince's ship to sail away, she was ... altered." Timessa paused dramatically. "*Zeus concocted a phantom girl to take her place,* an eidolon who looked every bit the same."

"What a tangle."

"Yes, and although the prince himself was fooled, the girl — the living, breathing girl — never made it to the prince's home."

"But this so-called specter *appeared* to be real?"

"Yes."

"What happened to the real one?"

"Hermes, at Zeus's command, whisked her away. One moment she was standing on the ship's deck, the next she was standing on a beach in a faraway land."

"That's crazy."

"She was beautiful. Zeus had had an eye on her for years. He thought his maneuver ingenious."

"So the war was fought for a ... for this *eidolon*."

"Only a few of the gods knew what Zeus had done. The warriors who were fighting and losing their lives had no idea."

"A nasty ruse. But why —?"

"Because he thought it was funny. Or because he wanted to make a fool of the prince. Or just because that's what gods did."

"But the suffering and carnage —"

"None of them cared. To the divinities, it began as grand entertainment, a sly joke. Then as they became more involved, it became personal …

"Ares practiced his battle shrieks as the sides clashed. Athene plotted to protect Odysseus. Thetis strove to save her son, Achilles. Warrior after warrior fell. Gods cursed each other. Oracles made grand predictions."

"And all the while, the king's actual wife was far away."

"Trick upon trick ... Once — unlike today — the gods were involved in human affairs. Once upon a time."

"*You* remain involved."

"In part. But the others have been detached for more than a millennium ..."

Gaia was, like the others, largely hands off. She had guided Timessa during her transition. She had set expectations but had remained ambiguous about what those were. The fact that the ancient fires were still shimmering in Timessa's recesses whenever she closed her eyes was telling: the dense smoke was Gaia's doing.

The fires, the smoke were a harbinger, a hot augury of ... something. Perhaps they had no more substance than the eidolon, the phantom that had, with a mocking beauty, sustained the ten-year war. Yet Gaia had planted the flames behind Timessa's eyes; they smoldered there since her metamorphosis.

The goddess knew that in Gaia's well-ordered universe, nothing happened randomly. The fires must be, she assured herself, signals, torches that, lit in succession as if down a path, led seekers to a final destination.

It could not have been coincidence that, two nights after Timessa had related the ancient war's chicanery to Io that Gaia strolled onto the patio at the same moment Timessa stepped from the house. She appeared, as always, as a young girl, incongruously dressed in a pink tutu, rising on her toes in the starlight, appearing delighted at what she saw.

She paused, swept her arms up into a half-circle and said softly, her gaze on Timessa, "Ah, the lovely one."

Timessa startled, quickly catching herself and closing her eyes as if in prayer. Gaia whispered, "Open your eyes. You wear the cape of creation and death, fertility and destruction. Never be differential."

Timessa was barefoot and the marble floor of the patio was cool. Opening her eyes, she smiled as she observed the usual slight transparency of Gaia's skin, the incandescence of her eyes. Nodding as if they were equals, Timessa said as smoothly as possible, "May I speak?"

"Of course."

"Time has passed since our last encounter."

"Are you well, Timessa?" Gaia never blinked and her gaze pierced those she interrogated.

"You know me better than I know myself."

"Wrestling, as you do, with contradictions is ..." The little girl paused and did a slow, flawless pirouette. "It's *annoying* after all this time."

"Annoying? You've infused me with all of this. I'm hardly to blame — "

Gaia raised her hand. "No arguing. All this grappling with compassion and morality. Are these things even appropriate for divinities?"

"I am what you devised. I was a mere nymph until —"

"You were not."

Timessa paused. "What brings you here?"

"Io. Is she on the island?"

Knowing that Gaia would know precisely where Io was, she said, "Upstairs. She wasn't in the mood to bathe in starlight tonight."

"I always enjoy the girl."

"Shall I call her down?"

She shook her head. "Timessa, when I chose you — when I recast you from what you were — I uploaded every act and memory from your predecessor. I made those yours."

The girl lifted her arm in a languid gesture, palm open. "That ancient Great Goddess was powerful but miserable. What an unhappy combination! Extreme power riddled with indecision ... it made for constant errors."

Timessa said nothing, watching Gaia advancing one leg and touching her toes on the marble, then shifting the same leg back, knees bent. A plié? Her ballet shoes matched the color of her skirt and appeared scuffed in the front and sides.

Gaia continued, "But you needed to know what she experienced, who she was ... You will be quite different than the old Great Goddess. I know I sound critical …

"It's not that she went astray … more that she reached conclusions that were disappointing …"

"Her decisions," Timessa said, "led to the deaths of countless mortals."

"Extreme disorder."

"You found it unseemly," Timessa guessed.

"You may not have found the exact words I favor, but we both desire what I call a well-ordered universe."

"Yes. Yet the universe I observe —" Timessa was careful to use a euphemism for Gaia. "— has no compassion for one species over another. *Things* spring forth and are extinguished. This is what I see. There is joy. But there is immense suffering."

"Birth and death are one," Gaia intoned. "Living things cannot distinguish joy without suffering. Exuberance would not occur if there was no pain."

Timessa shook her head. "Can't we do better?"

Gaia stepped closer. "Truth underlies all banality. What makes truth appear banal is its obviousness. It's easily dismissed. We feel we must work for what is given for free."

"But —"

"But I didn't come to debate."

Timessa hesitated. "My heart sings when you come."

"You are always careful with your words. That's admirable. But now you must deal with all these ancient memories. You ... and the antecedent to you ... must reconcile."

"How is that possible? I cannot go back 40,000 years."

Io was in an upstairs window, watching silently. She had seen the two interact before. Neither cast a shadow on the old marble slabs.

Their gestures were graceful, if that was possible between a tall woman and a nine-year-old girl. As she gazed down, Timessa took a half-step backward. Gaia reached out and quickly touched her arm.

Io squinted at the unexpected flash, then in disbelief, realized that Timessa had vanished. She gripped the window casement, filled with a sudden dread.

Instinctively, she screamed, "No!"

Gaia turned and looked up. Her face was expressionless. Io could no longer focus. Her eyes were full of tears. Without understanding what had occurred, she knew that Timessa had been sent away.

CHAPTER 4

Je t'ai libéré — I released you.

Timessa stood on the sandy bank of a slow, shallow river. Small gold-finned fish flashed in the riffles near her feet. The sun was high. Looking at herself she smiled at the thin wool gown she wore. The semi-gloss white of the seamless cloth fell from her neck to her ankles — it felt pleasant, and she recognized it as something of importance. She laughed at her own serenity,

A meadow of grasses fanned out from the river for hundreds of paces. There were occasional hillocks occupied by trees. Far beyond the meadow a low mountain rose in soft terraces. Everything as far as she could see was green.

Then as if instinctively, she knew: these lands were hers. Memories appeared. This was *Eurōpē*, ancient Europe, an endless territory that spread north from the wildlands of Thrace. There would be villages, scattered gatherings of humans beside streams, nascent hamlets at the intersections of the narrow roads that cut through the boundless fields.

As the river ran quietly beside her, she remembered facing Gaia only minutes earlier, hearing the words, "you ... must reconcile."

Surely she was not really in some past time. That era was her predecessor's. She knew only the memories that Gaia had breathed into her. Her impression when she recollected this strange time was shadowy and imprecise. What she *felt* was the primeval sensations of a long-vanished divinity whose passions had been preserved and ingeniously re-packaged for ... for some unknown purpose.

Yet she sensed that she was, in fact, in the past. She stood in a wide stance under a sun which hung at a familiar angle, feeling a breeze rustle her gown. None of these pleasantries reconciled with the dark memories she associated with this place.

She stepped into the grass, alert and waiting. Birds sang from a nearby hummock. There was no sign of humans, but she knew people lived here. A narrow path beside her wound into the meadow. Then she heard a muffled sound: a horse coming, almost inaudible.

She was certain it was approaching down the path. A reassuring power surged through her. Why try to conceal herself? She was indifferent to whom or whatever was approaching. This was her land. Of that she was certain. Let the encounter, if it were to be that, begin.

Hoofbeats became louder. Then she could see a single rider at a distance. A woman? Long hair flowed from the red cap on her head. Her cape was nut brown, tied loosely at her neck.

Timessa stood tall, pulling her shoulders back. As the horse came closer, the rider pulled the reins and slowed. A young woman slipped off the side, landing softly in the grass.

She shyly met Timessa's eyes, then knelt quickly, dropping her head, whispering hurriedly, "My Lady."

Timessa waited, saying nothing. After moments, the woman looked up. Timessa gestured for her to stand, aware of her name. "Anneth, you come with news?"

"Yes, my Lady. We have sighted the long-spears moving through the upper valley to the east."

"How many?"

"Hundreds. This time with supply trains and slaves."

"Has there been contact?"

"Yesterday their advance party burned our outpost on Singing

Ridge. All our people died — twenty-four total. The soldiers continue to approach."

As if watching from overhead, Timessa saw herself standing in the grasses, magisterial. The woman, Anneth, waited, thin sunlight washing her face.

Timessa knew somehow that the girl's mother had bravely wielded a spear and been killed brutally like the others. Now Anneth, without hesitation, had assumed leadership. Timessa observed a wound, a pink scar that ran from the girl's shoulder to her lower arm.

Even at her young age she had been in skirmishes and had cut down invaders as she wove her armored horse through screams and clashing spears — yet she appeared no older than twenty, her cheeks flush and eyes bright.

Timessa knew she was no more Anneth's imagined "Lady" than the eidolon had been the prince's wife. But Timessa was expected to assert command. Gaia had made that clear; the bar was high. The former Great Goddess had erred.

Now Timessa stood in her shoes in that same crusted time. This small rendezvous, this private moment with a woman dead forty millennia ago was likely to be, Timessa knew, the quiet inception of Gaia's trial.

She, Timessa, would be measured against the long-extinguished primeval goddess. Her predecessor's error? Simply, Timessa believed, that the divinity had tired of killing. Decades of warfare had worn her down. She had been called the Great One, Inanna or The Lady, and now her burnt, soured memories from those multiple summer wars rolled through Timessa like a torrent.

At first the Great One had proven to be a wily strategist, adept at protecting her people using ambush, avalanches, fire and, near the end, vast hidden pits deep enough to stagger dozens of the barbarians's horses onto sharpened poles as they savagely charged her villages.

Her successes had continued. But negotiations or conciliation with the marauders was impossible — they would not compromise, no matter how many she killed. Years passed; summer after summer the raiders swept into her fields, burning and pillaging. Each season she devised some new stratagem.

Then, without warning, she sickened of it all. Inexplicably, she turned against the carnage.

In a matter of days The Lady persuaded herself and thousands of her people that beating back the assaults had been a grievous mistake. Her brilliant tactics, their decade-old maneuvers, had been a miscalculation. She lectured that war bred war — that attacks and counter-attacks escalated violence.

The Lady faulted herself; she should have seen this from the start. To cries of protest, she said she was not suggesting surrender. On the contrary, she argued, she envisioned a gradual merger of the two peoples. Surely there would be common ground, traditions that, when shared, would enhance all lives.

She could not admit that the fields of dead had gradually broken her, that now, for days without cessation, the deaths nauseated her. In her bewilderment — in her incipient doubts — she became convinced that the killings could not go on. Almost overnight The Lady became a pacifist.

Timessa understood now that The Lady's conclusions had been tragically naïve. Európē was matriarchal. Men under her rule were laborers, procreators and, however nominally, fathers — but women owned all property and held all political offices. Command and control were female, and women above the age of sixteen made all critical decisions. No man argued that women were not more intelligent; men acquiesced and conceded the obvious.

Above them all, The Lady ruled with the same forbearance as her representatives, who were women in each village throughout her lands. But the abundance that characterized their rule for hundreds of years attracted intruders. The current invaders were hard men; their women, unlike The Lady's, were indisputably subservient.

To these nomads, equanimity was an absurd concept. Death came swiftly within their restless tribes, and peace was not just illogical — it was impractical. To annex richer lands, the raiders violently ensnared, enslaved or destroyed whoever got in their way. To control and plunder the rich lands of Európē became far more than an ambition — it was an obsession.

Timessa saw it clearly. But her predecessor had not. One hazy afternoon in July during the time of The Lady's dominion, a thou-

sand summer invaders appeared, expecting the usual defenses, fortifications which they might attack — advancing, yet knowing they were
likely to fail like their fathers and brothers before them.

None of them could remember how long the sieges had gone on.
None of that mattered as the men believed that eventually they
would prevail. But on this day there were no obvious defenses. It had
to be trickery.

They probed and met no resistance. At first they were disbeliev-
ing: The Lady, whom many called the witch, was infamous for
subterfuge. Yet they saw no barricades; the old ramparts that slowed
their attacks for so many years were not repaired. A road leading into
the sacred territory was not barricaded.

On the second day — after they had assembled in the open
meadows — the warriors were still unopposed. As the sun hit its
zenith, they raised a cry and streamed into The Lady's territory, their
banners high and spears horizontal. Gloriously, the valley passes were
open.

The first village they encountered was quiet. No one was visible.
The advance party dipped their spears into a flammable resin, set
them afire and, in unison, hefted them into the thatched roofs of the
homes.

As villagers fled their homes, the raiders hacked them down.
Then, exultant and increasingly confident, the warriors rode west
into the ripening fields of barley and toward the next small town.

The Lady followed the fighting precisely. After the first village
went down, she sent three women on horseback to intercede. From
their dress their status was clear: they were ambassadors of great
consequence.

The warriors met them in a semi-circular line fifty horses wide.
The Lady's envoys spoke respectfully, factually. They stated that The
Lady proposed their people merge. The warfare had solved nothing.
By joining as one they would be stronger. There would be immense
benefits for both sides. Any reasonable agreement would ensure that
the long conflict would end in amity.

A warrior in the center of the semi-circle nudged his horse
forward, then stopped. Speaking loudly enough for all to hear, he
demanded clarity on a single issue. Although he was difficult to

understand, they heard, "Who would preside over the ... merged people?"

The three women looked at each other. One said, "Our Lady proposes a joint committee, a commission of equality."

The warrior spat onto the ground. "This is your equality."

He raised his right arm high and turned to scan the warriors at his back. Then, without expression, he brought his arm down hard.

The men behind him lofted their spears and loosed a barrage of shafts. The women instinctively used their arms to try to shield themselves, but within moments they slumped forward over the long shafts that riddled their chests. They had not expected to live; they had gone out only in respect for their goddess.

To be asked to represent her was an honor. To die in her cause, if that was to be their fate, was to die in her grace. Whinnying, their horses bolted backward, shaking off their riders, spears continuing to strike their flanks and necks.

Pausing less than a minute, the men began to guide their horses around their bodies, proceeding by the tens and hundreds into the bright fields that lay before them to the west. Their march fulfilled a vow that each had made, that their fathers and brothers had made.

Now, standing by the river, Timessa watched it all replay as if in a dark cinema. The ancient images flickered in a bloody succession over the vast screen that was once a lovely Európē.

The Lady's decision to retreat had been ruinous. Her people faced death and enslavement. Yet even knowing this, the goddess would not act.

The old blood on her hands blinded her to what would be fresh blood. Fires, smoke and terror rose on the terraces and spread through the fields. Her sudden pacifism promised to obliterate a thousand years of peace.

She closed her eyes. When she opened them she heard the girl, Anneth, say, "My Lady?"

Timessa still stood beside the shallow stream. Her feet were bare and the sun warm. She looked at the girl's face. Anneth's trust appeared boundless.

The goddess realized that she had materialized at a time prior to her predecessor's improvident retreat. The boundaries of Európē had not yet been violated. The invaders had not ridden as far as the first village, or even managed to maneuver through the narrow pass in the valley. There were still options, particularly if the past could be replayed with Timessa as The Lady.

Anneth patiently awaited *her* command. The girl could not know that the goddess before her was not Inanna.

Timessa wondered: Was the girl herself a fake? Was any of this real? What had Gaia done — was Anneth more than a simulacrum?

Timessa concluded that it didn't matter. Gaia awaited. She, Timessa, was expected to issue commands and to protect these people.

And so she would.

CHAPTER 5

*Imagine the unimaginable
occurring after a long tail of stability ...
a rupture, as when what has been
long shortens abruptly ...
as when rainlight after rain
becomes unbearable.*

I o ran from their bedroom down the stairs and through the main house to the back. As she threw open the door to the patio, she stopped: Timessa and Gaia stood in discussion as they had before the flash.

She heard Timessa say, "My heart sings when you come ..."

"You're always careful with your words." Gaia replied as Io's ears rang. "... But you must deal with all these memories. You ... must reconcile —"

The two turned at the sound, Gaia smiling with apparent delight at Io's appearance. "Io! I was told you were avoiding the stars tonight."

Timessa scanned the girl, quickly saying, "What's wrong?"

Io shook her head. "There was a light — you disappeared. I had a dreadful feeling ... that I might never see you again —"

Gaia frowned. "The flash? My fault. But she's here. She hardly remembers being gone."

Io looked between them, catching Timessa eyes. "Where did you go —?"

The goddess remembered the sandy bank of the shallow river, gold-flecked fish flashing in the water near her feet. The sun had been impossibly close, the air dense. She turned to Gaia, saying, "I wore a white gown. It hung at my ankles —"

Gaia made a strange balletic move, shifting her left leg forward and pointing her toes in a small arc. "And you met Anneth, a lovely girl."

"Yes ... long hair, hazel eyes." As she spoke Timessa could see the girl's flush cheeks and the green fields behind her that appeared endless.

Gaia said, "Commingled with that exquisite beauty —"

"There was war," Timessa said in a trembling voice. "Fire, invasions, death."

Io stepped closer, taking Timessa's arm. "I don't understand. You couldn't have been gone more than seconds."

"Far longer than that," Gaia whispered. "Time slip-slides in peculiar ways when we play in the past."

Timessa watched the interplay between the two, marveling. In Naxos time she had been gone for seconds. Yet she was certain that she had spent hours, perhaps days among Anneth's people. She looked at Gaia. "You could have warned me."

"You would have objected ... Asked for time to pack a bag. Expected a picnic."

"Everything looked familiar. Like backlands in Provence ..."

"No, you were in the Balkans, your base at the time."

"What was I called by the people there?"

"My Lady, but referred to as Inanna."

"Moments ago … When I stood in that field … the girl knew me. Was I a likeness of … The Lady?"

"Anneth would not have recognized you otherwise."

"Gaia, why did you send me there?"

"Are you unhappy to have revisited those green hills … the lovely panorama?"

"The memories you implanted have been enough."

"You say you saw war," Gaia said. "And death. Didn't that jar your memories?"

"Her memories, not mine."

"You *are* her. What you call 'memories' are what you lived. Don't try to decouple from what you are. Her ruin came when she tried to disengage. Now, are you too trying to disentangle? One cannot flee to escape the fires that come at night —"

"You mean I can't run from my nightmares?"

"Precisely. You must face the flames, walk through them unharmed, tempt them to hurt you — while proving they cannot — and do so all the while with open eyes."

Timessa whispered, "Why?"

"You will be a useless goddess if you fear every shadow. Hubris destroyed the mighty Zeus."

"You told me once."

"He ignored my suggestions one gray afternoon … But it wasn't hubris that took down Inanna — self-loathing did —"

"How?"

"She lost her footing. Too much of this, too little of that. You remember now, don't you?"

Timessa shook her head. "You speak in riddles."

"Yes, if unveiling the truth is riddles."

"How am I to avoid the ancient errors you describe if —"

"If I'm vague? I'm not. You ask me to confirm what you already know. You run, Timessa, from what you did and what you were when you were Inanna." Gaia paused, her eyes never leaving Timessa's.

"Of all of us, you have a gift. Let's charitably describe it as compassion. Or with greater precision, an internal compass …"

Timessa grimaced. "Go on — "

"One might argue that, paradoxically, long ago, that kindhearted aptitude brought you to your knees, felled you like a lamb."

Timessa stepped away, saying, "Fine, I understand."

"Do you?"

"But it wasn't as complicated as you make it. Not at all. A compass? I'm not sure. I simply became appalled at the killing."

"Thousands had already died. Wasn't it that you no longer knew how many more you'd have to kill? Compassion — no goddess can afford that sentiment. Overnight, you went from one extreme to another …

"First there was killing to stop killing, something you were exceptionally good at. Then you drew an end to the killing ... which simply compounded the killing."

Io interjected, asking, "If there is killing to stop killing, is there its opposite?"

Gaia smiled and said, "Watch." She floated her arms out, saying, "Imagine I'm something lovely, perhaps a swan —" She turned her head to her shoulder, looking coyly at Io and performed a faultless pirouette. "Wasn't that sublime?"

Io nodded. "Yes, of course —"

"That perfection is due to one thing: balance. *Divine* balance."

Io said, "Only you are perfect."

The little girl looked down at her skirt, tugging a part of her tutu, then, ignoring Io, said, "Timessa, I have awakened memories, sharpened those that were vague, pushed to the forefront those that demand further deliberation ...

"And you will, when I wish, find yourself again in lovely Eurőpē. It's a pleasant climate. The people there adore you. And you will be useless to me if you cannot better Inanna's judgments. For, while you are not her, you undeniably are."

"I still don't understand —"

"As it will remain for some time," Gaia said. "*Mysteria, mystes, mystai*. So much must remain unspeakable. That is, until you break through your bewilderment."

"What we call *arrheta*," Timessa stated.

"*That which cannot be said* ... Yes, and I have already said too much."

"Then what am I to do?"

"You have been initiated — it was a quiet thing. You stepped from the river into the fields, remember? That was all of it. A simple thing. Now visualize the trail over which Anneth traveled: you too must travel that path to its end."

Timessa suddenly understood: Gaia was using the terms of the old *katharsis*, pointing her toward a purification. Perhaps. Pointing her down a path which might lead to some epiphany.

She wasn't allowed to know more. Gaia knew, but the mysteries had to play out at their own divine pace — which, Timessa sensed, was being measured in prehistoric shadows and by the fires that raked her sleep at night.

If she stepped correctly, perhaps she might stumble into light and find that which all initiates seek ...

Gaia touched Timessa's cheek. "Yes, you finally see."

Timessa nodded. She knew the time to probe had ended — and bowed slightly as Gaia turned and vanished skipping into the dark orchards beside the sea.

CHAPTER 6

Gaia's appearances seemed random, yet Timessa knew they were not. On the contrary, the visits, however infrequent, always signified a great turning or monumental change. For the last three years, Timessa's life had pivoted on these moments. On this last occasion, upon exiting, Gaia's words remained trembling in the night air like harbingers.

Timessa viewed her as a wise mentor, yet she knew that Gaia functioned equally as an augur. It was the old way. Her words were dispensed as portents. She spoke in enigmas, reveled in mysteries, and celebrated *mysteria* — the ancient μυστήρια — old Greek for mystic rites in which a certain induction was required.

Gaia had said near the end of this last visit, "You have been initiated." Timessa knew too well that initiates never celebrated their consecration — the event was simply the beginning, and the sacred had no value if it came too easily. In her case, Gaia confirmed that; she even implied that the stakes were extraordinary.

Timessa's path was set. That path wound through a bygone Európē — one lost in distant time. She knew she could not travel there without Gaia's prod. She had no coordinates to that winding stream. How could she possibly find the girl, Anneth? She wasn't even sure of the era, let alone the precise month and week she should appear.

With some dread, she knew that for this to continue, her mentor would have to participate — and, by necessity, be in command of the key machinations. For the first time in years, she felt powerless.

Several weeks slipped by. Timessa waited. Io left Naxos for a brief client fitting, then returned. She was effusive about Marseille and Monaco; she'd attended several off-season shows. Now she was glad to be back.

They ate a slow, late dinner on the patio under a pale moon, served by Asteria and Elissa, two of the older nymphs. Timessa said little, while Io described humorous incidents from her trip. Finishing languidly, their small talk winding down, they smiled.

Io whispered, "Miss me?"

Timessa laughed, nodding.

Io said, "You slept well?"

"For the most part. There were evenings when you could have been a friend."

"Nothing more from Gaia?"

"Not a thing. Perhaps she was waiting for your return."

Io shook her head. "I'm insignificant. And I'm not sure any of us matter a whit. Except you, of course."

Timessa frowned. "She leads me along, then vanishes. There are days when the slightest breeze takes all thoughts from my mind ... Those are the same days when the wind beats its wings and sends the asphodels trembling in waves ... I wish I could be one of those white flowers, a small bloom among the thousands."

After a moment Io said, "You know I love you."

"You indulge me. This dance with Gaia will end at some point. And when it does, we'll still be here, closer than before, beside each other, watching the stars move in the darkness overhead."

Anneth's horse reared back, and the girl clung to its neck. A snake lay in the path, its head raised. Timessa stepped forward, flicked her hand and it vanished. Continuing to retreat another moment, the horse finally quieted. Anneth stroked its neck and spoke gently to the massive animal.

Looking at Timessa the girl said, "She has such courage in battle. Then this."

"Serpents terrify many."

Anneth slid off the horse and bowed slowly. "My Lady, I have a report."

"More attacks?"

"Yes, but I come to report something different."

"What?"

"To report talk among our people."

She read the girl's face. "Some say I have become like that snake?"

Anneth looked down. "Some say you have lost focus, that you no longer defend our borders as vigorously."

"Surely you didn't come to tell me this?"

A small breeze moved Anneth's unkempt hair on and off her shoulders. She squinted, saying, "My Lady, you commanded that I tell you what I hear, both good and bad."

"Indeed. I do not fault you for that."

Anneth covered her face with her hands. "Every day, every week, the criticism grows bolder."

"Yet I am here."

"Yesterday, a man two villages away saw me riding through. He stopped me and shouted, 'Inanna once was powerful. Why does she look away? We'll all be killed!'"

"And you said —?"

"I said nothing." The girl's face flushed, her fury evident. "I took my spear and ran him through."

Timessa woke in bed. Dawn was hours away. Beside her, Io slept heavily. The goddess slipped from the covers and walked to a seaside window, looking into the darkness, hoping to shake her dream. It had been far too graphic — her heart was still racing. Then she understood that the dream had not been one at all: Gaia had spirited her backward without warning.

She paused, looking around the room, half convinced that Gaia might be hidden, lying in wait. A small nightlight glowed in an orange rectangle. She turned back to the window, the memory of Anneth still fresh, the girl's outrage remarkable.

A villager killed over a mere complaint ... The massive horse rearing at a snake ... Her own voice defensive ... And around them, the verdant fields, the shallow stream flashing with its small fish ...

She was being allowed to taste the darkness there. In the lush fields, there was an acridity, a bitterness. Timessa felt too that the girl, Anneth, existed in that time, not as a woman who had lived then, but as an invention, an allurement, a snare — perhaps even a substitute for Io in that forgotten time.

But Timessa wasn't certain. The setting was Gaia's, the stagecraft impeccable. What was she to conclude from all of this — and from Anneth's apparent centrality?

She looked over at the bed, at the shadowed girl who slept thoroughly. Io had not come to her by accident. Gaia had arranged their alliance, selecting Io from countless women. Timessa had never questioned the circumstance or choice. Gaia had chosen well: Timessa had immediately fallen in love.

Now she wondered, inevitably, what was artifice and what was not. She would have to remain on alert to ... what? Detect further guile? Chicanery? Certainly to be alert to intrigue. Gaia reveled in speaking like an oracle. But she would not hesitate to use contrivances.

Then there was *Anneth*: long, bronzed hair and brilliant hazel-green eyes. The girl was of average height, although tall for her time. Her cheekbones were high and her cheeks flush. She qualified as lovely, but her beauty was restrained by her palpable wildness.

And yes, Anneth's savageness was softened by her obvious loyalty. Timessa remembered with amusement the girl's shyness and how quickly she blushed when questioned. Timessa wondered whether the girl was mated, partnered with what would have to be a subservient man. Anneth appeared unlikely to submit to anyone's demands ... except to hers: the girl's fealty was beyond doubt.

As she replayed the dream that could not have been a dream, Timessa heard Io turn.

"Goddess?"

"I'm here. Everything's fine."

"You couldn't sleep?"

"A dream. Or a brief journey into the past — "

"Oh." Io pushed the cover back and left the bed. Without speaking she tiptoed to the window, slipping an arm around Timessa's waist.

Continuing to look out the window, Timessa quietly said, "Last night Gaia sent me back to the nomads."

"So she's returned?"

"Gaia, here? Who knows. She could be anywhere, pulling levers as she wishes."

"Was it a nightmare?"

"I'm not sure how to describe it. There was the usual landscape, a rider on a horse. The entire dream lasted five minutes, perhaps less."

"I remember Gaia saying that, there, you are called The Lady."

"To my face. Inanna to my back."

"I've never heard of Inanna."

"The name's an old one. There was an Inanna in Sumer six thousand years ago. The Sumerians called her Ishtar. She was young and widely venerated. Lions were always at her feet. But to find her in *Europē* 35 millennia earlier ...?"

Io giggled. "Does The Lady complain? You seem venerated here, there, everywhere —"

Smiling, Timessa said nothing. Far over the Mediterranean she could see the lights of a small plane. It was moving slowly and was low over the sea. The lights on the wings reflected onto the waves.

She turned to Io. "You should try to sleep. We're still an hour from dawn."

The girl nodded and returned to bed.

CHAPTER 7

I call to the mysterious one who yet
Shall walk the wet sands by the edge of the stream
And look most like me, being indeed my double ...
— Y.B. Yeats, *Ego Dominus Tuus*

The Lady, Inanna, Goddess, the Great One — her names were as innumerable as the flowers in a spring field. She had also been called Cybele, Lemnos and other, now largely forgotten names. And too, it seemed, she had once been Ishtar. Regardless, to Io she was simply, blessedly, Timessa.

Looking over the sea from the upper story deck, Timessa smiled. When she had dominated the fashion world, she was referred to as *T*. Now, in this year, in this place, to those who knew her intimately, she was commonly called, Goddess.

Gaia had once grown impatient at Timessa's inquiries into her past names, saying, "Why does it matter what you were called?"

Weeks before during Gaia's visit the two had used the word, *arrheta*, or "that which is unspeakable." There were times that she would prefer her own epithet to be exactly that — a title so dangerous that no one dare say it.

Hades had achieved that distinction. Millennia ago Greeks so feared the god of the Underworld that his name was never uttered.

Hades: saying it might draw his attention, elevating any speaker foolish enough to voice his name from obscurity to a person of interest. Better to be unknown.

Names and honorifics, she thought masked so many things. Labels too often blurred the reality of that which was named. She caught herself, thinking, *Mortals give benign labels to those they fear*. Titles like 'The Lady' allowed them to overcome their dread. The designation seemed so grand, even majestic, while Inanna and Cybele implied power, blood and — however subliminal — rang with foreboding.

The sun began its ascent behind her on the east side of Naxos. Her estate was to the west. There the Mediterranean remained inscrutable, an ebony salt flat that she knew, intellectually, to be sea. In another thirty minutes it would begin to reflect sunlight, and the temperature would rise.

She heard a small noise: Io appeared, still in her cotton top and shorts. Without speaking, the girl climbed onto her lap, straddling her lazily.

"Over your dream?"

"Long ago. I've been calculating the exact position of the moon overhead as it will appear in 535 days."

Io smiled softly. "No you haven't."

Timessa pointed over Io's shoulder. "It'll be there, shining in the dark. At precisely 11:33 p.m."

As they bantered Delia brought a tray with tea and fruit, setting it quietly on a rattan table near the door. Timessa reached over and took the nymph's arm, saying, "I want to join you this morning when you take Aetos out."

Delia brightened. "Yes, Goddess. Shall we meet downstairs?"

"That's fine."

Delia had become the eagle's keeper, hawking it off the promontory at mid-morning every day, regardless of the weather. Timessa had taught her the art a year earlier, and the bird had bonded with her within days, as it had earlier with Timessa.

She groomed it, and fed it squid and raw chicken after sessions. Now, having Timessa join her for the morning was unexpected. She said, "Ten o'clock?"

Timessa smiled. "Bring a gauntlet for us both."

Delia half-bowed, beaming as if she'd been complimented, and left the deck. Stretching, Io stood and took a chair beside Timessa. "Tea?"

The two chatted, then Io left. She had blouses to finish, pieces to complete. Timessa allowed herself to daydream briefly, then decided to swim before she hawked. She chose a dark bathing suit, pulled a kaftan over her shoulders and left the house.

The sun was rising and a soft humidity accompanied the light. She jogged down the path toward the sea and reached the old promontory, stopping for a moment as she always did at the spot where Artemis had shot Ariadne so many millennia before.

The killing was an event she would never forget, seeing, every time she passed, the arrow strike Ariadne's neck … watching the girl slowly reel backward onto the path … hearing Artemis as she told the girls who had accompanied her to turn away, that their work was done ...

Timessa accepted the memories without question. Only seconds passed as she stopped. She broke away and continued down the path onto the long crescent beach, pausing in the sand to assess the waves, then plunging into the water.

The cove was framed with massive volcanic rocks at either end and spanned a length of slightly more than 500 feet. She usually swam ten laps paralleling the shore — this morning was no different and she quickly ran off the time before stepping from the sea.

Standing barefoot in the sand she thought briefly of Gaia, then of Anneth. Was the girl from Európe an invention, or was she as alive as she appeared? If the latter, then time could not be linear. Or there was another possibility: the past and future were a poor explanation for what might, instead, be manifold existences, all running at different speeds, each having begun at random moments ...

She laughed, aware she was describing chaos. Or at least disarray.

Mortals were insistent that there was a single time — that which they inhabited. For them time never meandered or stopped; instead, it ran in a straight line, at a fixed beat.

But what if their notion of time was inaccurate? What if it was no deeper than their knowledge of life? The mechanisms that drove birth and death, the gears that spun all the majesty of life — the whole of it was a mystery to even the cleverest of men and women. If they could be so ignorant, why should their premise about time be right?

She frowned, choosing to welcome the pandemonium. Given her theory there were multitudinous existences. There was no singular time: there was a cacophony of overlap, of fountainheads and of genesis. Death too was always prowling, probing for weaknesses, seeking unprotected openings in the cells of the living.

Of course, she thought: Hades never closed his doors; the Underworld welcomed all. Artemis too was always poised, ready to loose another arrow, Yet, in this stew of being and extinction, worlds spun noisily beside other worlds.

Timessa met Delia beside the house. Both wore Greek-style chitons, woven from exceptionally fine wool. To a modern viewer, their clothes might have appeared classic or daringly chic. Io had cut the patterns from ancient designs and sourced the material locally.

On this morning, heat swept the estate, with wind beating its wings in gusts, bending the lush grasses on the promontory landward. Delia tied her hair back and pulled a watchman's cap over her head. Timessa shrugged at the conditions, saying only, "Aetos will get a workout."

She wore a golden necklace that Hephaistos had originally given Artemis, who in turn gave it to Timessa. Each gust, whipping off the sea, pushed their chitons against their backs as they walked toward the sacred grove where Aetos waited in its cage. Then the wind slackened, vanishing when they took the narrow path. In minutes Aetos had hopped from its cage onto Timessa's arm, its mottled orange claws gripping the bullhide gauntlet.

" 'Tos, 'Tos," Delia whispered. "You'll be flying soon —"

Timessa removed the hood that blinded the bird, and Aetos silently shifted its eyes from woman to woman. They walked the bird to the high bluff beside the sea and stood for a moment, watching the chop of waves against the shore. The low roar of the rollers and hiss of salt-spray was sublime.

Then with a hard, downward swing of her arm, Timessa released Aetos, its wings wide and coffee-colored, blurring as it rose against the gray sea. The bird swung in a low arc, then soared sunward.

Delia whispered, "I always think of a pterodactyl when it does that."

"Indeed, it's magnificent —"

Timessa felt the slightest tremor under her feet and braced herself. Naxos, like all the Cycladic islands, was subject to earthquakes. As she scanned the horizon, for a millisecond the aether seemed to compress, or coalesce. There was a slight flash. Then she stood beside Anneth on what appeared to be a high ridge along a mountain range.

She was dressed like Anneth in sewn skins and leather sandals. The girl pointed and Timessa saw thousands of birds spilling over the sloping tree tops. They swirled and tumbled as they flew toward a valley below.

"Hawks, My Lady," Anneth said loudly so that her voice carried over the wind, "Too many to count. They're leaving for the winter ... Going, I think, to the big sea."

Timessa marveled. After a moment she looked away from the turmoil and studied the girl.

"Have you ever seen the big sea?"

Anneth shook her head. "Perhaps one day."

As Timessa smiled, Anneth pointed. "Look! Vultures too!"

Timessa could make out larger birds, black, awkward-looking and flying below the hawks. As she scanned the waves of raptors, rising and falling in tandem, something below, in the valley, caught her eye: a river coiled like a chrome snake between wide banks. A roadway paralleled the river. She saw movement: horses were advancing shoulder to shoulder in a line.

Men. They rode silently. Spear tips shimmered in the light. Her first reaction was that there were as many horses and men as hawks in the sky. She bumped Anneth. "Horsemen!"

The girl paused. "Barbarians —"

"Why have we not been alerted?"

Anneth looked at her curiously. "My Lady, you asked that we come to the farthest reaches of the frontier to see the birds. On this ridge we're a two-hour ride from the closest outpost — and the first to see these men."

Timessa nodded. She guessed there were hundreds, perhaps thousands of them. From their tight order and uniformity, the men projected an imposing force. "Is there a trail that intersects the road below?"

"Yes," the girl replied. "Not far away."

"Let's mount and ride. I want to be there before they arrive."

Anneth nodded, a fierce elation crossing her face. She picked up a long spear she'd leaned against a tree. Timessa noticed her arm and the long scar that stopped at her wrist.

Holding the spear in both hands, the girl looked at her and grinned. "It's a steep slope, wooded. The trail is packed. We'll raise little dust. Come —"

The two leaped onto their horses, Anneth suddenly looking grim. As she took the lead, she constantly looked behind her, checking on Timessa. They descended the slope rapidly, taking the narrow switchbacks effortlessly. Their horses were trained for this and seemed to revel in the mayhem.

After minutes, they entered a gentle terrace. Anneth slowed, raising her hand in warning. "We're close."

The horses turned their heads back and forth in protest, eager to continue the mad run, but Anneth would have none of it. She caught Timessa's eye. "The trail meets the road there —" She pointed.

"Shall we dismount?"

Timessa shook her head. "Quiet!"

A light breeze stirred the nearby pines. Crows circled at a distance, cawing noisily. But the warriors were still at a distance, the sound of hooves not yet reaching them.

"How many years have our people fought them off?"

Anneth assumed the goddess was testing her. She said in an

undertone, "Four of our generations. The elders say the warriors first crossed the frontier 402 seasons ago in this same month."

"More than a century."

" 'Century'? "

Of course, Timessa thought, she counts time in seasons. "A word for many seasons, Anneth. And yes, your knowledge of our history is ... admirable."

"My Lady, when I first began to ride as a warrior —"

Timessa guessed. "You were twelve."

"Yes, and you personally gave me this spear —" Anneth lifted the hardwood shaft, smiling.

The goddess was swept with images of battles, of women on horseback hacked down by howling warriors swinging axes, of extraordinary bravery that allowed her people to overcome the hoards. She said quietly, "I cannot lose you, Anneth. I expect you to be by my side for many years —"

The girl looked rebuked. "Have I acted poorly, My Lady?"

"I am reminded of the village man you killed last week."

"He insulted you!"

"He could have had friends. You could have been surrounded and attacked."

"I am protected by your amulet —" Anneth lifted a necklace, fingering a fat rectangle of lapis lazuli.

The goddess remembered giving it to her on her fifteenth birthday. "Now no one dares to harm me, as you know."

"Yes, but still I worry."

The girl turned and looked toward the intersection. "For as long as we have been attacked, you have vanquished each attack."

"The dead are now countless. The savages have no end."

"May I speak?"

Timessa knew the girl wished to do so frankly. She nodded, opening her palms. "As my hands are open, may your heart be as well."

The girl bowed slightly. Before she spoke, she lifted a finger, listening.

"I hear them approach. We have a few minutes still ..." She closed her eyes as if weary, then opened them, saying, "You speak of my heart. I worry about yours, My Lady. Forgive me for what I'm about to say. You know my love for you is endless."

"Anneth, speak your mind."

"The talk I have mentioned in the past, the rumors —"

"That 'Inanna once was powerful' but now is not?"

"Yes, but what those who speak so carelessly mean is that Inanna no longer acts as decisively."

"The killing part, Anneth, is easy. And particularly easy when it becomes mechanical."

"I don't understand."

"Don't you see the blunder? We kill to avoid more killing."

"But we die if we don't fight back."

"Yes, and I do so. I defend these lands. I push them back. Once I counted how many died at each attack. I took pleasure seeing bodies scattered on the fields."

"As you should!"

"But ... I've begun to wonder if ... if there's a better way. Death, you see, compounds death. Anneth, your mother died in battle. She was but one of hundreds of our best warriors, our finest women who have fallen these many years …

"Now you, like her, sweep across the killing fields as if you think you're immortal. And you're not."

"I cannot fear my death and fight fearlessly."

"Oh, you're as brave as the greatest of our warriors." She paused, grimacing. "I don't question that at all —"

"Then what?"

"Yes, then what?" Her tone hardened. "You may meet your mortality. As for me, at the end of each new attack, I have to wash my hands longer and longer to get them clean."

Anneth put a finger to her lips. "My Lady, they come —"

Timessa nodded and slipped off her horse, commanding, "Don't dismount. Stay back. I won't be long."

With obvious vexation the goddess strode around Anneth's horse and down the narrow trail to the dirt road. Standing in the way, a small figure, she faced the increasing rumble of the approaching army, her arms at her side, a slight smile on her face.

CHAPTER 8

Tribes once blessed
by violet-eyed Inanna are now gone:
dark eddies, girls once timeless
twisted, vitreous
like paper planes felled in rain

As if weightless Aetos glided toward the promontory. Delia reached out and the bird pulled back as it landed, its legs forward, its wings beating against the salt air, touching down gently on the nymph's leather glove.

Timessa smiled, stroking the hawk down its back, between its wings, as it waited for a treat. She said, "We worked it hard. Two hares and a rat."

"Goddess?"

"Yes?"

"There was a moment as we stood together that you seemed ... detached."

"By which you mean —?"

"When we hawk together you're always ... completely engaged.

For a moment I sensed that you were off somewhere. Do you remember me asking you whether 'Tos was out too far?"

Timessa hesitated and the girl said, "You didn't respond. I don't think you even heard."

"I wasn't aware."

"It's okay. After a couple seconds you said 'What?' " Delia giggled and Timessa nudged her. They turned from the sea and walked the bird to the grove.

Hours later Timessa sat with Io. The goddess gestured toward the marble blocks scattered between the house and the sea, saying, "Every morning, seeing these, I think of Dionysos and Ariadne, their grand house, and their long lives."

"To think they live quietly in Eleusis. An hour drive from Athens and no one knows," Io said.

"They've promised to visit us again. I suspect we'll see them soon."

"Such a low-key life now. Dionysos has ratcheted everything down."

"That won't last," Timessa said. "He's too restless. And intoxicated with himself."

"Why do you bring them up?" Io asked.

"The old marble still gleams. Sometimes at night I think I see a glow."

Io smiled. "He'd have rebuilt the mansion if you hadn't taken over the estate."

"I know. He's better off away." She paused. "When I hawked with Delia this morning, she said I'd 'detached' for a minute. It was an odd observation."

"Did you?"

Timessa scanned the sea. There was a mist low over the waves. One could just make out the humpback of Delos to the west. Several gulls hovered overhead along the shoreline beside the estate.

She looked into Io's eyes and said, "Yes. I uncoupled. I found myself in Gaia's Európē. At first I was watching a vast migration of hawks. There seemed to be thousands. But then I saw men coming on horseback. There were thousands of them as well."

"Yet you were on the promontory."

"With Delia ... Where she said I'd tuned out for only a few seconds."

"How long were you in the past?"

"Over an hour." Timessa did not mention Anneth or the whirl-wind descent by horseback off the mountain. "I wore animal skins and was addressed as My Lady."

"And the men you saw — who were they?"

"I'm not sure. They're always called barbarians. Or nomads. As I watched I knew they were invading. That seems to be the pattern, the scheme Gaia has set up. Invasions, assaults. I'm still uncertain if it's real or some sort of theater."

"If it's theater, it's complex."

"Gaia's capable of that."

"But why?"

Timessa paused, then smiled faintly. "The first Great Goddess made disappointing choices. Apparently I'm to adjudicate right and wrong."

"That meshes with your preoccupations."

"All probably driven by Gaia as well."

"You could decide it's exciting. That you're leading multiple lives."

"Yes, but I feel obsessed rather than freed."

Io noted, "When I was about thirteen my mother took me to a movie. Something called *The Three Faces of Eve*. A shy housewife suddenly discovers she has multiple lives."

" 'Hope it turned out well for her."

"All I remember is that there was a wild Eve, and probably a dark one."

"So far I've not found my party side. Inanna, Ishtar or whatever her name, seems to always be ... imposing and fearsome. It's a theme. If you met me on the road, you'd fall to your knees."

Io took her hand. "But that's who you are." Timessa shook her head.

Io continued, "What I find fascinating is that when you're here, but then there, you're only gone for a millisecond. But hours go by wherever you go."

"I presume there's some logic. So far it's inscrutable. It was easier when I reacted like Artemis and the others. I simply observed. My refuge was detachment."

Io whispered, "You're on a mission."

"What a noble word: *mission*." She stood, majestic, yet Io knew her well enough to know she was vaguely fatigued.

"My 'mission'," Timessa said, "is to figure it out, whatever it is. But why? Divinities have never cared about such things. So much of it seems absurd —"

Timessa knew too well that what mortals called morality was in constant flux. Thousands of years ago a philosopher named Heraclitus wrote that one could never step in the same river twice. All was movement, whether atoms or the edicts of man.

Was Gaia demanding she find something that contradicted that? Discover that there was an immutable rightness?

She had been on the patio beside Io, complaining, but was now, without warning, again blocking the wide dirt road awaiting the nomads. A thunder of hoofbeats swept the corridor beside the river, and then the column of men appeared, slowing as they saw her. A tall man in stained leathers led the procession and raised an arm to stop the advance.

He halted about fifteen paces from the goddess, saying nothing, his horse restless and snorting impatiently. A second man maneuvered to his side and leaned closer to speak. Timessa could hear him say, "It is *Inanna*."

The tall man nodded, pushing the second man away. He prodded his horse forward slightly. His face was scarred and his eyes cruel. He addressed her, saying simply, "Out of our way, witch."

He was used to commanding. His tone was steady and indicated that he expected her to obey. She read him well: he found it inconceivable that a woman, however celebrated, would block his way. His horse reared back, impatient and intentionally dangerous.

The goddess raised her hands above her head and opened her palms. The gesture was one of surrender, or acquiescence. Yet her stance widened, her eyes narrowed and she hissed, exhaling with an almost imperceptible grimace.

With the sound, the air above the river suddenly became clotted with horseflies. Their noise was deafening. Some of the men instinctively raised their arms in defense. The tall man jerked his head sideways toward the river.

Timessa lazily turned her left hand counterclockwise and stepped back slowly. The flies were as fat as a man's thumb with bright green heads. As far away as the men were from the winged chaos, they could see the insect's eyes shimmering kaleidoscopically. Then before any of them could retreat, the flies had covered them.

There were so many that men could no longer be discerned as humans, and beneath them, the bodies of their horses undulated in endless silver wings that clogged the animal's eyes and nostrils. The flies knew to ascend up under the leather garments and between the horse's armor, biting furiously as they rose.

Screaming men were bucked off the animals and trampled underfoot. Those who could, crawled and stumbled into the river to escape. There the velocity and depth of the current swept them underwater, spinning them like broken trees, rifling them through the bouldered runoff.

They hurtled downriver, descending soundlessly toward their encampment hours away. Every horse had bolted at breakneck speed back in the direction they had come, followed by a dark froth of maddened flies.

Quiet followed the chaos. The road lay littered with spears, leather helmets, gloves, satchels and blankets. Timessa turned at a sound: Anneth. The girl dashed into Timessa's arms, clinging to her and crying. "Goddess, goddess —!"

Timessa wiped Anneth's tears. "It's over, Anneth. Once again ... Finished ..."

"No one will believe what I saw!"

"Perhaps, when the hundreds of bodies wash ashore, those who survived, seeing the carnage, will think twice before sharpening their spears again."

CHAPTER 9

Over 400 men had died. Less than a hundred had survived, but many of those were blind or deaf. The horseflies had filled their eyes and ears, entering their mouths as they screamed. Any warrior who had been on the scene and lived was, at the least, covered in countless welts.

The loss of men and equipment was unimaginable — the catastrophe had not been anticipated. Previous conflicts with the valley people had been face to face, spear clanking against spear. Had the witch caused the disaster, or was the confluence of the war party with the nightmarish flies at the river a horrific coincidence?

The encampment lay an hour away beside a wide stretch of riffles, a quiet straightaway where the river became gravel and slower, shallow water. Bodies had begun washing up within twenty minutes of the attack, flies still active and attached to arms and necks and distended faces. Those at the camp were almost entirely women and slaves — with several older warriors left behind to guard the enclosure.

As bodies began to appear, women washing clothes at the river's edge screamed. Inert, sodden forms tumbled up against boulders, the women's voices keening in lament. No man was recognizable; the flies over their faces had not drowned like their victims and now, back in the bright sun, continued their frenzied work.

At first, the older warriors pulled bodies from the river, laying them in rows along the shore. But after dragging out dozens, the men quit. Flies jumped from the dead to the living.

As hours passed, a few survivors staggered into the camp, incoherent and in shock. Horses wandered back as well, but all brought additional flies, and soon there was no one — warrior, horse, slave or woman — who had not been bitten repeatedly.

They abandoned the camp. Night fell, visibility waned, but a three-quarter moon allowed the shattered group to retreat eastward, traveling by foot, winding back through the forests, returning to where they had begun. As they made headway, the flies dissipated. Before dawn the nomads were rid of the swarm.

Yet eighty percent of their warriors had perished. Hundreds of horses were lost. The few witnesses left — that is, those who had seen the incident — whispered about a single woman, the Inanna witch who had started the contagion with a flick of her hand.

They feared that upon their return no one would believe them. Worse, they would face accusations of cowardice. Only the numberless pustules covering their faces would lend plausibility to their claims.

Timessa knew to the man how many had perished, and how many horses had been lost. Her use of flies had been spontaneous. The thought of duplicating the thousands of hawks she had watched with as many horseflies had felt inspired.

The flies though had been unusually savage: once she'd multiplied their numbers and loosed them to attack, their frenzy had effectively severed her contact. She, like Anneth, could only watch the violence.

Afterwards, as Anneth clung to her, she pushed the girl away, saying, "I know you'd rather have fought."

Anneth shook her head. "Too many."

"We were not prepared …"

"Goddess —?"

"I only intended to drive them away —"

"But what you did was better!"

"Hundreds were killed."

"My Lady, it was glorious."

She looked up, watching crows arc from pine to pine. Their cries seemed oddly forlorn. When she turned again at Anneth, she marveled at the girl's zeal. Putting her hand on her shoulder, she said, "There's something I want to try. Stand still —"

Timessa lifted the girl's oiled cape, exposing her arm. She continued, "No wincing."

She held her eyes as she ran her thumb lightly over the long scar that ran from the girl's shoulder to her wrist, stroking her where the lesion was fiercest, then cradling her arm as she smiled. The old spear wound slowly vanished.

"That's always bothered me —"

Anneth stepped back and examined her arm, then instinctively dropped to her knees, bowing her head. "I don't understand."

"Perhaps we both seek perfection, in our own way." Timessa took the girl's hand and raised her up.

Anneth asked, "What will I say when people ask?"

"Say whatever you wish. Whatever comes to mind."

Seeing the girl's confusion Timessa embraced her, running her fingers through her hair. As she stroked Anneth's back with her other hand, the goddess absently watched the circling crows. They never hunted together. A dozen stayed within view of each other, but each worked independently.

The birds were beginning to pick through the litter scattered for a hundred paces along the road, flitting into the debris and cawing loudly. The crow closest to them, hopping from piece to piece, glanced at her, its eyes orange.

Timessa shifted her attention to Anneth, who whispered, "The barbarians ... We may never see them again."

"They'll return."

"I don't know."

"We'll have snow soon. But spring will bring them back. Our fields are too rich. Our women too tempting. There will be no end."

꙰

She had erred. She knew she had. Her spontaneity, although well intentioned, had cost lives. How to proceed remained an enigma. Peace was impossible — the eastern tribes had made that obvious.

But far worse, she knew now that killing led to more killing. Numbers never decreased. The nomads accepted the losses; she increasingly did not.

Negotiation had not simply been declined — it had been rejected violently. As a consequence, her people faced endless attacks. Thwarting them was not difficult, but the inevitable destruction was wearying.

Too, she knew that she must keep her own people involved in the constant defense. If she did all the work, they weakened. Like Anneth, thousands of her women would sacrifice themselves without hesitation. She also knew that their ardor would melt away if she mismanaged the wars.

As Inanna, she admitted that in the beginning she took some satisfaction, even cheer, in seeing the slaughter. Attackers would brazenly raze fields of barley weeks before harvest. Cherished orchards would be felled.

In response, the goddess would attack their flanks, scattering their forces, then surround the panicked men. Time after time the women would ride in and finish what The Lady had begun.

Reason would argue that constant defeat would dissuade the attackers. Instead, they returned, stoically. Sometimes they struck once a year, but increasingly, they pushed forward whenever weather would permit. And with each new assault, a small percentage of her own warriors would be grievously wounded. Or killed.

She could protect them to a degree, but not entirely. The bravest ones would fall, dropped by error, by a crippled horse or a lucky spear. The losses were now anticipated and hardened the women's courage. They were good people, and the goddess would continue to protect them. But the savagery on both sides was escalating.

As she was flooded with memories of the years of carnage, Anneth nudged her. "My Lady, you were off somewhere. I just asked what we should do next?"

Something about the question seemed familiar. 'You were off somewhere. Do you remember me asking ...'

The girl was enthralling, her eyes fierce, yet as innocent as a fawn's. Behind Anneth a crow noisily dropped from a branch into the road, hopping randomly.

"My Lady —!"

Then, just as Timessa was about to reply — as she smiled at the absurdity of it all — she found herself sitting beside Io. One of the nymphs was pouring them wine.

CHAPTER 10

Immortal /ɪˈmɔːtl/
living forever; never dying or decaying
— *Oxford English Dictionary*

Io had been Timessa's lover and confidant for over two years. Their story was too fantastical to have any credibility, but nothing that had happened was untrue.

Only after the fact did Io realize that almost everything in her life had been planned for two decades. In many ways their relationship was indistinguishable from an arranged marriage — but in this instance, it was a coupling devised by Gaia.

Long before Timessa was being groomed for her chrysalis, Io was being protected for the time the two would join. Artemis, guided by Gaia, began to monitor her in her teens. The girl, of course, knew nothing of her destiny. And on those occasions when she would "accidentally" encounter Artemis (years before meeting Timessa), she would be oblivious to the extraordinary nature of the rendezvous.

On reflection Io was sure that Gaia, while Io was still a child, had matched her preferences, even her sex pheromones to Timessa's and had paired their desires. Otherwise, she thought, how could they have such rapport? Io could without fail sense Timessa's thoughts and anticipate her wants — such aptness was, she believed, a key to their attraction.

As they drank wine they had been talking somewhat aimlessly about Dionysos and the scattered remnants of his ancient home and how the goddess had seemingly returned to the past while hawking with Delia. Yet even as they spoke, Timessa tuned out again.

"Goddess —!"

The voice: Timessa heard it moments before, but then it had been Anneth, pleading, 'My Lady —!'

Now the voice was Io's. Timessa focused, took the girl's hand and kissed her palm. "Sorry. I obviously was daydreaming."

"You never daydream."

"Then ... I was having a vision."

"Of what?"

Timessa smiled. Io was irritatingly psychic, or at least intuitive. She replied, "Nothing uplifting. Of a battle line. Of destruction, death."

"Oh —"

"There were biting flies, a woman ready to give her life."

"So you were in Eurṓpē. again." Io paused. "My goddess, you're going back and forth. Not weekly, but —"

"Daily. Perhaps more often. You know I don't will these trips."

"How can you be here and there at the same moment?"

Timessa laughed. "You're right. It's not possible, is it? To be in two places."

"I'm worried. What if you leave here on one of these 'trips' and don't return?"

Frowning, Timessa said, "I'm far from understanding any of this myself. For instance, I'm here now, talking to you. But am I also ... back there ... functioning ... as Inanna?"

"You mean, there while you're here with me?"

"Yes ... I'd have to have a replica, wouldn't I?"

"Remember the word you taught me?"

"Be specific."

"*Eidolon*," Io whispered. "You said it meant a specter —"

"Or phantom. "

"You said they couldn't be told apart."

"It's true. But phantoms trick the mind. They're ghosts. It's one thing to trick others and something else to trick yourself."

"So you're convinced that when you're there, it's you."

"I remember the old stories of the eidolons. They were so ingeniously made that the eidolon itself knew nothing of the fraud. They believed in themselves."

"So then you wouldn't know for sure?" Io asked.

"Gaia would have no point in sending a close likeness of me into the past. As I understand it, I'm supposed to learn something from this, or experience some breakthrough."

Io watched her in silence.

"When I'm there," Timessa continued, "I'm no different than when I'm here. The only distinction is my name, and superficial things like clothes." She paused, then went on excitedly, "I *know*. It's so obvious: the best explanation is time."

"Time?"

"What if it's ... not linear."

Io tapped her watch. "It is according to this. Or —" She pointed at the sun. "— to Helios, who drags himself through the sky each day."

"We're being unimaginative. What if there are multiple times? Not worlds, but realities. And if there are, what if each has its own chronology? They'd be different — oblivious to each other ..."

"If that was the case," Timessa continued, "there could be countless sequences, and clocks in each dimension. And everyone in each location would believe that time, as they knew it, was the *only* time, the only reality —"

"You're saying that this magical Európē you go to is not really in the past."

"Possibly. Far-fetched, isn't it?"

"I half buy it. But there *can't* be multiple Timessas."

"I no longer know." She winked. "Maybe I'm nothing but multiple eidolons. Maybe there's no real me."

Io made a face in return. "Am *I* there ... where you go?"

As Io spoke, Timessa imagined Anneth, and accepted for the first time the similarity between the two. Their common adulation left her uncomfortable. They were not indistinguishable, yet there was more than a resemblance.

Timessa remembered Gaia saying weeks before, "*Mysteria, mystes, mystai.* So much must remain unspeakable." Yet *mysterious* simply referred to things one did not understand.

She touched Io's cheek, saying, "No, if you're there, I haven't found you."

"Then take me next time. Take me when you go!"

Timessa shook her head. "I can't. I don't even know what happens next. I may stay here. I may not. Perhaps this has all been intended to bring me down a notch ..."

As she spoke she heard her own reassurances, her quiet words to Io, believing none of them. She knew she would return to Eurṓpē, whether it existed millennia ago or was disentangling itself in the present. Did the dimension's whereabouts and its synchronicity with present time even matter?

Anneth was there. What had Gaia said? Timessa remembered: "Visualize the trail over which Anneth travels: you too must travel that path ..."

Timessa knew now that remaining solely in Naxos was an impossibility. Yet she could hardly see past the next hour, let alone know how this would end.

She found herself becoming impatient. A day and a night had passed, yet she remained on the island. Her beloved Mediterranean seemed mockingly inert, its waves mechanical. The world had become colorless, placid. She was becalmed. So she waited, remembering Aulis and Artemis.

She was acutely aware that she had lost her ability to control events. The previous night had brought dream-fires, roiling smoke over the dark seas of her mind. The haze lingered like a dirty fog until dawn brought its usual sunrise.

That morning, alone on the patio, she knew that the season was changing. The summer waned. Still, the changes were imperceptible in comparison to those in Európē. There, she thought, late fall was compressing daylight and cooling the nights.

She was certain of it. She wasn't there, but she imagined the people in the villages thrashing barley and repairing roofs for what were always harsh winters. Even when late afternoons brought early snow, women trained in small troops on their covered horses, charging at targets of rolled grass, spears straight.

Timessa knew that Anneth was among them, perhaps organizing the maneuvers. What she did not know was whether Inanna was there, manifest and sibylline, mysterious and two-edged like a bright spear point.

Io had flown out a day earlier to hold private shows for select clients, first in Tuscany, then Monaco and finally Paris. She could slip in a brief visit to Charleville. Her uncle had died weeks before, leaving her title to the small building where she had opened her first shop.

She'd been born and raised in Charleville. The city was famous for being the birthplace of the French poet, Arthur Rimbaud. It was also there that she and Timessa had met on a gray afternoon when the world's most famous model had wandered into her shop seeking a dress. She found those memories joyous. Now, settling the inheritance felt ill-timed, given Timessa's difficulties.

Charleville was two hours from Paris by car. After her last show Io would drive there in a rental. She hadn't decided what to do with the building, and thought she'd seek the opinion of a realtor she knew. The trip would be short and she'd return to Naxos within a week.

She called Timessa while in Marseille, surprised upon hearing about the slow pace on the island. The goddess had swum in the cove, then hawked briefly with Delia. The weather was quiet. Timessa described the sky as looking like one painted in a mural — flat clouds against a peeling azure. They missed each other and agreed to talk the next day.

When the call ended, Io broke into tears. She could imagine the goddess setting her phone down and looking without expression toward the sea. And the sea itself would be gazing back, equally impassive.

Io imagined Helios overhead, moving as if propelled by giant, hidden gears. The girl shivered, swept with dread. She knew the goddess would assure her that none of her fears made sense.

She considered, for a moment, cancelling her trip and returning as quickly as possible.

CHAPTER 11

There was no burning bush,
no burnished boys caught in bed
arms entwined,
no revenge for tawdry crimes
or audacious joy.
Dawn simply rose in blood .

"My Lady."
Timessa knew at once where she was: Europē. She turned to the girl. "Yes, Anneth."

"You just spoke of a ruse."

"A ploy."

"Ploy. Like a trick. Why?"

"To learn more. Our enemies pour in. We repel them, repel the invasions, calling the riders on horseback 'barbarous savages.' "

"Beasts," the girl said. "We fight them, kill as many as possible. Otherwise they would take everything we have, turn us into slaves."

The Lady said nothing.

"And your ploy?" The girl was deferential, her eyes afire, her loyalty clear. "You called me here. Will I play a role?"

"Not yet. But I will tell you my thinking."

"My Lady —"

"We don't know why they come, do we?"

"For us! For our crops!"

"Do we assume that there is constant famine a mere day's ride away?"

"Why do we care? We have fought them forever."

"Yes, your mother and your grandmother died wielding spears."

"Nothing changes. The seasons turn ... the warriors come ..."

"Yet we have never left our own lands, have we?"

"You have provided us with riches, My Lady. Our lands are green, our rivers clear."

"Perhaps we remain ignorant, know too little."

"About the men?"

"Indeed. To us they are dangerous and bizarre. They are strangers."

The girl paused. "You are saying that even strangers are driven by certain needs."

"Yes. And now I want to know what drives these men."

"But if we meet them face to face, they throw spears."

Timessa took a deep breath and said without expression, "I'll go to them, mingle, spend time and observe."

"That's *impossible*, My Lady. They already fear Inanna. Imagine if they find you there."

"They'll never know."

"They'll know you instantly."

"They will never mistake an old woman for Inanna."

"Old woman? Then you'll be disguised ... I see. But I won't let you go alone."

"I won't need company. While I'm there, I'll be here as well."

"I ... I don't understand."

She would play Gaia's game, send what appeared to be a duplicate Inanna, except this one would be disguised as elderly, infirm. "A gray-haired Inanna in rags will raise no one's suspicion."

Anneth paused, absorbing the news. Finally she said, "And what will you gain by this deceit?"

"Only by going will I learn where I've been."

"Yet you — the real Inanna — will remain here ...?"

"Yes."

"What will you call your duplicate?"

Timessa grimaced slightly. She knew that ingenuity was too often the sister of arrogance. She had to step carefully.

Anneth came closer, waiting, her eyes curious. Finally the girl said, "You cannot call this copy Inanna."

The goddess slipped a hand behind the girl's neck and stroked her hair. The girl closed her eyes and Timessa said, "No, my lovely Anneth, this thing, this shadow of an old woman that will appear as if alive, can never be called Inanna. Its name will be *Eidola*."

After Anneth left that afternoon, Timessa selected an old horse that would suffice for the eidolon. As dusk arrived she led the animal east down the single trail along the river. They passed over the detritus left behind after the fly attack, the horse skirting the debris nervously.

To save the animal the indignity of carrying her weight, the goddess walked beside it, whispering as the darkness grew. No one watched. Hours passed as they penetrated the unfamiliar territory. She passed no travelers and saw no settlements.

They paused near a bend in the river. Night obscured the banks, but she could hear water moving against the far side and assured the horse that they would rest. Within minutes as she brushed the long mane on its back, it fell asleep standing, its neck lowering imperceptibly.

Timessa stepped away, inhaling sharply, silently, her eyes on the dark bulk of the animal. As she watched, an old woman appeared, standing beside the horse. The goddess watched her gray-haired doppelgänger place a hand on the horse's neck.

The crone leaned closer and whispered into its ear, "Wake up, you old thing. We have business ahead ..."

At the same moment, the woman turned and looked directly at

Timessa. She was veiled as were all the women of the eastern territory. Her eyes, the only part of her face not hidden, flashed silver and
her face was expressionless. She raised her hands high, palms open.
Then she turned away and effortlessly mounted the horse.

The goddess had imbued the phantom with attributes that
matched her own, while giving the wraith more than enough age to
protect her from suspicion. The old woman tapped the horse's flank
and guided it toward the road. They turned east and were quickly
out of sight.

In the same way that Timessa in Eurṓpē could not communicate
with anyone on Naxos, the old eidolon could convey nothing — nor
could Timessa contact her. The eidolon understood its mission, and
its intended duration. It contained Timessa's intelligence and could
draw upon an array of her strengths, if required ...

Timessa wondered what she had unleashed. Eidolons were never
perfect copies. The old woman had been given a commission, a
mission. The goddess remembered telling Io with a trace of bitterness
weeks before that having a mission was noble work. She had immediately regretted saying so.

In Eurṓpē claiming anything had nobility was dubious. Tonight's
undertaking seemed more fraught with mysteries than magnanimity,
more shadows than light. Yet she had proceeded.

She had launched her eidolon but would know nothing of its
activities for days. Timessa also knew that her double might not
return. It ventured now into unknown lands, ignorant of what lay
ahead.

As Timessa walked back to her temple she observed the fields: all
were scythed, the stalks cut symmetrically at ankle height. She knew
that the threshing floors were swept clean and that the barley was
stored in buildings scattered throughout the land. In the last weeks
deciduous trees had begun to shed, and the occasional breeze, still
mild for the late season, blew dry leaves against the sides of barns
and livestock enclosures.

Anneth waited. Dawn had come and the sun was climbing. The

goddess's people, spotting her, fell to their knees, bowing their heads. The women whispered, "Inanna," rising only after she had passed.

The few men she encountered fell face down, immobile and pliant. Since she had first run with Artemis millennia ago, she had no use for males. She ignored them now, aware they were needed for procreation and labor. Women in the valley had always outnumbered them by eight to one. She guessed those numbers were reversed in the eastern territories.

Anneth's fear that she and her sisters would be raped and enslaved by the nomads was realistic. Women there were subjugated — in their decades of warfare, a female barbarian wielding a spear had never been encountered. They were never more than slaves.

Hours to the east in the land of the barbarians, the terrain was different. Subsistence was unavoidable. The eidolon struck the horse's flank, increasingly their pace. She began to pass primitive compounds scattered randomly along the road. Smoke rose from the center of roofs. Spears leaned against open doorways. Horses were tethered outside. She saw no women.

Farther along two men stood outside a small stockade, and turned idly to watch her pass, one calling crudely, "Hello, Granny. Too bad you're not younger." In their twenties, they were dressed in oilcloth capes and brimless caps.

She continued and soon heard dogs barking in the distance.

The sound became louder, shifting perceptively from left to right, the yelps becoming high-pitched. Then she saw them. Seven large dogs lurched over a hummock coming toward her. Their heads were all teeth and their eyes the color of dung. Their speed increased as they approached.

She had no weapon. Besides, there were too many of them even if she had been armed. She knew her old horse would go down at the first jaw clamping onto its ankle. She felt it panicking, beginning to rear backward. She raised a hand, turning her fist counterclockwise with sudden force. The ground before her began to boil.

The pack entered the sudden inferno at speed, each dog instantly bursting into a howling torch and skidding sideways, subsumed by the hellfire she had conjured. Her horse whinnied, stepping away from the chaos and heat. The old woman whispered reassuringly and patted its flank. In moments the dogs stopped convulsing, their eyes rolled back. She sat atop the horse in the silence, watching impassively as they died.

With another gesture she snuffed out the flames. Smoke clung to the ground. She steered the horse back to the road, thankful no one had seen the interaction.

Additional settlements lay ahead. Perhaps she would seek shelter at one — that is, if they extended cordiality to strangers.

CHAPTER 12

Timessa tried to grasp the events swirling around her. Had Gaia created an eidolon of her for Európē? (She had suggested the possibility.) Timessa knew at the very least that she — or her new apparition — had created an additional eidolon.

Was the Európē Timessa actually a dual being comprised of the ancient Inanna and Timessa? Or was the Naxos Timessa in two places at once in a multi-timed universe? Regardless, there now appeared to be multiple linked entities, all similar and co-existent.

Further, if the Inanna-Timessa entity was not an eidolon, then Gaia had not recreated that ancient time — she had somehow tapped into it. If so, Európē wasn't some arcane theater set built to serve obscure purposes. Instead, Gaia had inexplicably connected the contemporary goddess Timessa to the old goddess Inanna. The wizardry would be a cryptic compression of time, which — given the evidence — seemed most likely.

Dismayingly, Timessa knew that none of these entities, including herself, communicated directly with any other. They appeared sovereign, while at the same time, mirrors of each other. Timessa, Inanna and Timessa's veiled eidolon — each was autonomous, yet connected.

All were, in effect, sisters. The bloodline was blindingly clear. Yet Gaia's grand purpose — her goal in all this — remained obscure …

Timessa stood on her promontory in Naxos. An occasional bird passed, breakers soundlessly lapped the shore and she reveled in being the ruler of all she saw. Without having to act, she governed merely by observing the sun's bright arc, by being aware of the wind moving invisibly across the waves.

She thought: *The wind weaves the wind. I and I.*

During these moments alone, her anxieties vanished and her disquiet was easily dismissed. She was serene and answered lazily when Io called her cell phone. The girl said, "I'm in Monaco! I thought you'd never pick up."

"No, I'm here."

"My show went well. New orders. I saw a couple old friends. And I miss you."

"When do you return?"

"I'm in Paris tomorrow, then I drive to Charleville. So probably three days."

"Is the weather good?"

"Overcast and cold. And I didn't bring a coat."

"Buy one before you leave for Paris. It'll be colder there."

Io smiled. "Yes, goddess." She hesitated, then said, "I wish you had come."

"You know how I feel about that. But I want a full report when you're back."

"Of course. So … I'll try you tomorrow?"

After the call Timessa widened her stance slightly, feeling the thin grass under her feet. In parallel, she also felt *time* as if it were a *thing*— not time in progression, but time as an entity, almost as if it were an organism, breathing, its eyes blinking, its entirety moving in an erratic stagger-step.

Time. She thought of how Gaia seemed able to compress it, condensing forty millennia into a space of seconds. *Now* became *then*, the past insinuating itself into the present. Or the present into the past. It was all uncommonly strange and, even so, felt familiar.

Time took other twists as well. She thought of the Underworld, Hades's domain. There time did not move predictably, or compress or violently expand — on the contrary, it simply ceased. All who entered its gates entered a place where energy ended.

There, air stilled and life imploded — there all sequential movement stopped. There, there was *no* movement. The Underworld's occupants were those for whom time had been stripped away.

Stepping back, she scanned the sea's long horizon. Was everything today a paradox? During her call with Io, the sea's rhythm, its cadence had changed. Or had it? Was what lay before her today's sea, or was it the heaving brine from an ancient world?

Time's tricks, she thought … time acting timelessly on the material world.

She turned away and laughed. Gaia: what a strange trap she'd set. And today Timessa had fallen for it, or fallen into it. She had tried to outwit Nature itself.

By now she should have known better. One did not outsmart a sphinx. *She*, Gaia, remained the ultimate enigma, a time-conniver.

And undeniably, Gaia had spun a paradox that Timessa — at least one of the Timessas — was expected to unravel.

Anneth saw the goddess approach the temple. *Things must have gone well*, she thought. *The old horse was gone.* Watching, the girl noted that Inanna never changed.

Without exception, the goddess walked with authority, her eyes flashing, her long hair untied. No one spoke of it, but all knew that she was the one woman in the valley who traveled without a weapon — and that The Lady feared no thing.

Smiling when she was within hearing, Anneth said, "I've waited for hours —!"

Time, Timessa thought. *No one thinks of its meaning. Time veils and unveils truth.*

She caught herself, returning Anneth's smile. "You knew I'd be back."

"I wanted to wait ... in case you needed anything."

She took the girl into her arms. Doing so was something she'd recently begun. When she broke their embrace, Timessa said with a slight smile, "My double is now exploring the dangers that lie to our east. With luck she won't be skewered and roasted for someone's dinner."

"You should have given her a better horse."

"Then she'd be suspect. The more tattered the two of them appear, the better."

"When will she be back?"

"There are no conditions. But I left it with her that four to five days would be ideal."

Anneth hesitated. "Can she defend herself?"

"She can. But she knows that's a last resort."

As they spoke Timessa tried to communicate with the eidolon. The apparition did not respond. Nothing had changed.

She said, "Anneth, I saw no warriors, no forces when I traveled into the disputed lands. Have there been any reports of activity on their part?"

"None, My Lady. But that's typical for this time of year."

"I am concerned there'll be a surprise."

"How could they mistake what happened?"

"They may convince themselves that the war party encountered nothing more than a mass of angry flies. That it was a one-off thing."

"And so they'll be back?"

"Well, they have always come back. Those who saw me on the trail died in the river. Those behind them couldn't have known. It's possible that it'll just be written off as some crazy insect attack."

Anneth said defiantly, "Let them come! We've always beaten them back."

"We can't just 'beat them back' forever."

"We can! We have. We've always stopped them dead."

"Yes, but 'dead' is the problem. They die, we die. I'd like to end the ... butchery."

"It's always been like this."

"No, Anneth. Long before — before even your grandmother's time — there were no wars. And no invaders. We lived on these lands in peace."

"Of course," she said. "I know, but none of us are left who remember."

"I do."

The girl fell to her knees, her head bowed. "My Lady —"

"Stand, Anneth. You focus correctly on what you see — constant invaders. What happened long ago was long ago."

The girl rose contritely, whispering, "I would love to put away my spear."

"As I wish you could. Let's wait for now. Perhaps the eidolon will return with some revelation."

The air cooled as the sun set. The veiled specter appeared ancient. She rode unsteadily, sighing as the horse picked its way. A complex of irregular lodgings lay ahead.

Buildings appeared cobbled together, some homes tied to each other and others sharing roof beams cut from branches. Roofs themselves were thatched and blackened from smoke. The eidolon pulled up and stopped, her eyes flickering from stables to outbuildings.

A man stepped from one of the buildings. "Stop! What do you want?"

"A place to rest."

"Your name?"

She half-bowed, patting the horse, allowing her voice to crack. "Eidola, a traveler."

He approached carefully. "Why here?"

"Night falls. I seek shelter from the wolves."

"Leave."

"Have mercy," she said. "I have nothing. I am a nobody."

"Women do not travel alone."

"I am old. I lost my husband days ago when our house burned."

"Let your children save your life."

"My only child, a boy, is dead."

"His name?"

She put her hands over her face. "Eidos. A fine boy."

Another man stepped from an animal enclosure. "You're being rude, Helmut. You're always rude. She's an old woman. What's the harm if she's given soup and a place to sleep?"

The first man grunted. "I'll have Boda look after her." He pointed at Eidola. "Off your horse. Tie it up —"

The eidolon eased herself off the old horse, half-stumbling as she touched the ground. She looked around in a apparent confusion. The second man said, "Your husband died but you did not."

"His cloak caught fire. I tried to beat off the flames. Look —" She opened her hands. "My palms are burnt."

The man shook his head dismissively, "Boda will get you water."

The men left and she tied off her horse and waited. She could hear arguing in a nearby compound. Men and a woman. After a moment, a woman came out and looked at her.

"You're too old to be traveling alone."

Eidola lowered her head. "I only seek a place for the night."

"Follow me." The woman gestured and turned. Eidola walked behind her and the woman took her to a back building. She pushed open the door.

"Over there. No heat but you'll be safe."

The eidolon nodded. "I am grateful.

"Are there other women here?"

"I am owned by eight men here, three brothers and the rest like a pack of dogs. The next woman lives a half hour ride to the south."

"You are shared?"

"Taken as they wish."

"I'm sorry."

"You have more to worry about than me," Boda said. "At least I'm fed."

"At least."

"I'll bring you soup."

Eidola nodded.

The woman grimaced. "All of them leave tomorrow for some expedition. Stay here until they're gone. I'll feed you better then."

CHAPTER 13

Premonitions? It is the unimaginable
occurring, even after warnings,
things sudden and unspeakable.

At dawn the eidolon could hear men in the yard assembling, cursing and packing horses. She smelled rain. The light was dim and the horizon red. As Boda had requested, she stayed in the back shed, watching from a crack in the mudded wall.

She could see spears being hefted. One of the men issued commands. Horse hoofs clomped restlessly against the beaten dirt yard. Then with a hand signal from one of them in an oil cape, the men rode off. She counted eight.

Eidola waited before she pushed open the door. Waiting under the eaves a moment, she snugged her veil, then stepped out. Light rain. She walked with an affected limp to the house. "Boda?"

The woman stepped out of a building. "I told you to stay inside."

"I watched them leave."

"Now you'll say you're hungry."

"I eat little."

The woman looked up, squinting. "Rain."

"Yes, it'll be heavy by noon."

The woman looked at her carefully. "Now you're an oracle."

Eidola laughed lightly. "Weather. Somehow I always know."

"Well, they took all the remaining food. All of it. If you stay, we'll both starve."

"I'll move on."

Pointing, the woman said, "Your horse is there. I fed it earlier."

"The horses eat and the women go without."

"Isn't that always the way?"

"Where did the men go? I don't want to run across that lot."

"West, toward the valley. They're meeting the others."

"The valley?"

"Where the witch lives."

"Oh ... The one called Inanna."

"Yes. Helmut found a secret trail that bypasses her sentries."

"Why would he care?"

She shrugged, then said bitterly, "With luck half of them will not return."

The eidolon paused. "And if they don't return?"

"There'll be four less men." The woman was no older than twenty-five. "You should leave. There's no protection."

Eidola bowed awkwardly, feinting pain. "Yes ..."

Within minutes she was on her horse, slowly heading back toward the valley. When she was out of sight, she struck the horse, bellowing, "Now! There's little time!"

Gray-maned and in its last years, the horse flared its nostrils and tripled its speed.

The men had assembled at the juncture of where the river spilled into a pond. From there, a road meandered toward the west into Inanna's valley. It was along that road, at various places, that the witch's forces had always stopped the men.

Now one of them had found a secret trail. It wound, he swore, around and above a pinch point in the valley that they had never circumvented.

One of the trail's advantages, he noted, was that it could not be seen from the valley's outposts. He called it a rabbit trail, a coyote run — he had explored it from end to end by foot. Just wide enough for horses, the trail would, he emphasized, allow a force, if patient and stealthy, to spill unseen into the witch's lands.

Cold rain fell. Eidola slowed her horse and hid in head high brush near the pond. From there she could see the mass of men on their sodden horses clustered at the road. If the men took the circuitous route up the mountain sides — fighting brambles and downed branches, side-stepping rocks, following each other in a slow line of hundreds of men — their journey, she guessed, would take three-quarters of a day.

She would take the direct route: a hard ride down the open road beside the river to the first outpost was only ninety minutes. Leaning close to the horse's ear, she whispered, "Are you up for another run? I might kill you on this one —"

The horse snorted quietly. The eidolon immediately pointed the animal away from the men and steered it through the brush beside the pond's edge. Stopping every thirty or forty paces, she could hear faint arguing: bombast from several of the men.

Whatever the disagreement, it seemed to have slowed them. Let them quarrel, she thought. Within minutes she had moved around and away from the force and was now beyond their sight. She guided the horse onto the dirt road. Nothing lay between them and the valley ahead.

She bent down again, grasping the horse's mane. "Now we're off. This'll be the run of your life. Just last another hour —" She popped the horse's flank and they left at a gallop, well beyond the reach of anyone who might have seen her emerge from the wetlands beside the pond.

They rode west beside the river for an hour, stopping once at a shallow for the horse to drink, then rode again at a faster pace. Fifteen minutes from the outpost, she was stopped by six women on foot. Emerging from the woods in a semi-circle, they pointed spears.

The eidolon slowed; she had already pulled off her veil. One of the women stepped closer, examined her and said, "Your destination?"

"The closest outpost."

Clearly, Inanna had alerted them that an old woman might appear. The woman said, "We didn't expect you for days."

"Hundreds of men are approaching."

"Behind you?"

"No, over a trail." She pointed behind her. "Through the woods."

"Go." The woman pointed in the direction of the outpost. "Tell them everything."

The eidolon nodded, drew the veil back over her face and nudged the horse. It bolted down the road as if it knew their destination, froth building at the sides of its mouth. If the horse failed along the way, she thought, she'd finish her trek by foot. But the horse went on.

In a quarter hour they pulled up at a large building off the road. While she was still a hundred paces away, a dozen women emerged in battle gear. She cried out this time, "I am Inanna's envoy!"

She was allowed to dismount and led into the outpost. There she described what she'd overheard — the plan of attack, the location and timing, and the number of men. "They're bypassing the ravine, going up the mountain. They're a half day away, armed in single file."

As she spoke she saw women outside lighting a pyre. The smoke bellowed up in a high black spiral. She was aware that the signal would be picked up in moments down valley at another post, which would light a similar pyre. A succession of signals would convey the news to The Lady. Rising smoke always meant an imminent attack.

On this occasion Timessa knew even before her eidolon had arrived that an attack was at hand. She could read the apparition's thoughts as if they sat across from each other. Communication had not been possible, and now it was.

Well before she saw the signal signals, Timessa began to issue commands. Given that a small force could surprise and overwhelm the attackers, fifty women mounted their war horses and rode toward the terraces that, at the edge of woods, became steep mountain terrain.

The women would be outnumbered ten to one. A local woman knew the path and would show the women the trailhead. Their goal was to stop the men before they spilled onto the plain.

Anneth led the party. She vowed they would lose few, if any, warriors. She had staged ambushes in the past — this would be no different. Fire tended to skew the outcome of these aggravations.

Inanna outlined strategy. Anneth understood and simply nodded, raising her arm to the assembled force and led them east on a run. Each warrior carried multiple spears tipped with a dark resin.

They rode through long plains of cut barley that rose into soft terraces, each terrace slightly higher than the next, until the highest butted against a wood line of forest that ascended steeply up the mountain slope. The party of women arrived early in the afternoon and Anneth was shown the trail.

"It's just an animal run," the woman who farmed a vineyard on the nearest terrace said. "Almost impossible to walk."

Anneth dismounted and climbed the slope. The run was littered with small, sharp rocks. What she found most remarkable was that a mass of impenetrable green briars rose above her head on either side.

The oaks and pines that grew up the slope were thin enough to allow sunlight to penetrate the cover, and dense brambles had invaded the transition between terrace and woods. The trail itself rose steeply, then veered hard right and continued its ascent in a long curve. Maneuvering a horse would be challenging — the run was so narrow that a large animal could not be turned without tearing itself against the barbs.

Anyone going down on horseback, who suddenly turned right to make their final descent into the open plain, would be trapped between the wall of briars. In moments Anneth confirmed Inanna's strategy, wondering how Inanna was so familiar with this obscure trail.

The goddess had said, "You've seen us do this in other locations. They'll be snared. Pick them off."

Anneth had said, "A dozen of us can take them on."

"Be careful. Make it our surprise, not theirs."

"Yes, My Lady."

As the women waited on horseback for Anneth's return, warily watching the upper slopes, the rain lifted and a thin, warm breeze swept through the umber-colored plain. Anneth strode from the woods and began to issue crisp commands, her long hair whipping in the gusts, her eyes shimmering.

The preparations were brief and the plan simple. Horses were to be tied up and muzzled on the terrace. Below the trail's turn, thirty of the women would climb trees on either side of the trail. Each would be camouflaged, have multiple spears at ready and be hidden on branches well above the riders.

Their spears had been dipped in a thick, flammable tar. At Anneth's signal, burning shafts would be thrown down into the line of men. Anneth herself, with two lieutenants, would begin the ambush by straddling the trail midway down the final descent, facing the riders as they appeared.

A scouting party of two young women had been sent ahead. They spotted the men an hour away; the men were steadily working their way through the upper ridge. When the women returned, one of them said, "Impossible to count them all. The line winds back as far as we could see ..."

Anneth laughed. "Good. Can you estimate a time?"

"To arrive? An hour before dusk. The sun will be in their eyes."

"And on our back. May Our Lady give us strength!"

The circle of women clamored and hooted, hugged each other and then scattered to their posts. Anneth remained at the trailhead with her lieutenants, each carrying spears tipped with razor-edged points. She grinned, barely able to contain her excitement.

The three mounted the trail, stopping fifteen paces below the turn. They scanned the surrounding trees — with effort they could see several of their own warriors, but the horsemen would have their eyes on the trail. Small wrens and sparrows flitted among the shrubs, oblivious to the coming event.

The women waited, aware of the declining sun and the lengthening shadows. The trail was still wet from the earlier rain, the rocks glistening and slick. A chilly breeze blew in. Then voices could be heard, men cursing, horses's hooves tromping against stones. Anneth instinctively spread her feet and hefted a spear over her shoulder. The birds quieted.

A minute passed. The first man who turned the corner had his eyes on the trail. A second man and then a third followed closely, heads down, navigating the wet stones. Their spears were lashed to the sides of their horses.

Before any of them had looked up, Anneth cried, "*Aiiieeee!*" and released her spear.

It struck the lead rider in the center of his chest — he roared against the shock, both hands grasping the shaft before he slumped sideways, eyes open, onto the trail. The women behind her each released spears almost simultaneously and struck the riders behind him.

As they too reeled sideways off their horses, the women above the trail lit their spear tips, throwing them into the sudden chaos. Anneth and her lieutenants had rearmed and were now running up the trail between bodies, plunging their spears into any rider who had managed to remain astride.

At first, men behind the lead riders desperately tried to untie their spears, but lines got tangled or caught in brush and they resorted to turning their horses to escape. The animals lurched backward and sideways, caught in the wall of briars, astonished at the flaming spears. Riders were shaken off only to be trampled, kicked by their own horses or caught in the melee of falling spears.

Almost half died in the confusion. Dozens more were wounded. Those in the rear, stunned at what was happening ahead, managed to flee, swearing at their leaders, at their luck, and at the loss of their brothers and friends.

The melee was over in less than a quarter hour. None of The Lady's warriors fell. In the aftermath the women herded the scattered horses onto the terrace, counting them as spoils. The finest animals were culled out to be given to Inanna. Otherwise, inspecting the men's bodies, they found nothing desirable. The women left debris where it had fallen and reassembled on the terrace.

Anneth said quietly, "For our victory we give thanks. The Lady again prevails —"

CHAPTER 14

"... what seem'd corporal melted
as breath into the wind."
— Shakespeare, *Macbeth*

Anneth's war party, hauling dozens of captured horses behind it, rode back through the cut fields. Minutes from the trailhead they intersected a lone rider: the eidolon with her ancient mare. Anneth knew immediately but said nothing.

The women welcomed the crone. As the band wound back toward their homes, the old woman said nothing about her journey, only noting that she was traveling from north to south. She appeared grateful for the company.

The warriors split off one by one, turning down trails that led to their homes, until the party was reduced to Anneth and the eidolon. They said nothing as they rode. When the river near Inanna's sacred grove came into view, the eidolon stopped.

"This is where we part."

The girl looked surprised. "But we're almost there."

"You, not me."

The eidolon leaned down to her horse, whispering, "May you live for years. You saved my skin, old girl, and proved yourself courageous."

As Anneth watched, the old woman straightened and smiled, becoming disturbingly transparent before fading away, leaving her clothes jumbled on the horse's back. Her old cape slid to the ground. Only a second had passed since she had spoken.

Anneth paused, frowning, then scoffed at her own reaction, saying softly, "Of course. Nothing is ever as it seems."

The girl looked behind her, viewing the three black stallions tied to her own horse: still there. Then she turned to appraise the eidolon's old horse. It appeared restless and uncertain after its rider's disappearance.

Anneth spoke with a half-scoff, "So you've been abandoned ... Let's get you a meal, a blanket and return you to The Lady. She awaits us and our good news."

The girl looked ahead. The river glistened. She guided the horses forward, using the ancient path that meandered lazily through the fields and ended at the water's edge. Dusk had begun and night was drawing near. Thirty paces away she saw Inanna beside the river.

"My Lady!" she cried out.

Timessa motioned for the girl to approach. "Success. Isn't it sweet."

Anneth nodded, sliding off her stallion and tying the collection of horses to a post. She stopped at the bank, dropping to one knee. "My Lady."

When Inanna gestured, she stood deferentially and said, "Warhorses. For you ... from our victory.

"A triumph once again."

"Yes, as you predicted."

"Did you count the fallen?"

"Three hundred and eight."

"Wounded?"

"A similar number."

"Then we beat them back, didn't we?"

Anneth stood tentatively. "We did, My Lady. No casualties on our side."

"In the past we would lose warriors."

"I felt you were looking over our shoulder."

Timessa looked away. Was she? She wasn't sure. She only knew now what she experienced in each instant. For the first time, she looked directly at Anneth. "Was it good?"

"The fight?"

"Yes, the fight."

"Glorious. They were full of themselves, and then full of our spears."

"You used the fire shafts?"

"Yes," Anneth replied.

Anneth had the sense that Inanna already knew, that their conversation was merely obligatory. She said quietly, "They became torches, falling on the ground afire. The flames had them howling. We used our spears to stop their cries."

Her Lady seemed lost in thought and in a profound silence. It was one that Anneth found inexplicable. The war party had succeeded. Yet The Lady hardly rejoiced.

The river at their feet rolled over its gravel bottom and slid sideways into endless eddies along the grassed bank. A lone crow swept down from a pine and landed on the far side of the stream, stalking its shadow as it walked back and forth, mechanically bobbing its head. Anneth became impatient, threw a rock at it and watched as it skittered off, cawing loudly.

"My Lady?"

Timessa said, "Anneth?"

"I rode back with the one you called … the eidolon."

Timessa watched her carefully. Anneth continued, "We stopped when we came into view of the river … and she vanished. She was just sitting on her horse, then —"

"Eidolons, Anneth," Timessa said, "come and go."

"How? Was she ever real?"

"Do you mean, was she corporeal?"

The girl whispered, "Yes —"

Timessa sat closer and put her arm around her, saying, "You know the image you see when you look into still water?"

"You see yourself."

"The eidolon *was* more than that, more than a likeness … She was flesh, but not flesh. Her blood was what we call ichor …"

"Then she wasn't real."

"She was, but she wasn't … It's best to say that she was an *echo* of me."

"But so much older."

"Anneth, look at me."

The girl turned and met her eyes, drowning in the kaleidoscopic violets of her irises. Suddenly, she felt the goddess filling her with fire. Her thighs burned and she softened, feeling her fierceness wane.

Timessa said, "You feel what I've done?"

Anneth nodded. The goddess prodded, "Speak to me, girl."

"What did you do?" she whispered.

Timessa smiled. "What you feel is vivacity. It's what I poured into the eidolon. That same fire gave her … *animation*."

Anneth felt an overwhelming silence as if she were alone in a vast forest of sacred oaks. She desperately wanted to respond, but the part of her mind normally full of speech felt hollowed out. Something like music filled her instead, long vibratory sounds, a living wind. She opened her mouth, able only to voice a small whimper.

The goddess drew her closer, whispering, "That fire that moves through you like this river beside us … that fire is your *spirit*, Anneth. It usually sleeps, a mere shadow. But I've awakened it. Can you feel its strength? Its energy fills you. And this animation you feel is the same fire I used to make the eidolon."

The girl had begun crying and hesitantly, Timessa used her thumbs to wipe her cheeks. She said, "Close your eyes —" and kissed her forehead.

To Anneth, barely conscious now, the kiss was not sensual as much as it was sensational. She was flooded with a warmth hotter than the burning pitch the women had used hours earlier. Their victims had burst into flames — now she, too, burned. If only she could find her voice.

Laughing at the girl's predicament, Timessa stood, taking her hand and pulling her upright. "Come, we'll cool you off —"

To Anneth's shock Timessa led her barefoot into the center of the river. The cold water was only a hand's width deep. Timessa kept an arm around her waist, walking her over the rounded pebbles, letting the water wash over their ankles.

The goddess moved her hand up the girl's side, running a finger down her ribs and over her waist. "Are you back?"

"With you?"

"Yes."

Anneth nodded.

"Speak."

Her voice half-returned. She said, "Was I about to become an eidolon?"

Timessa laughed. "You're far more alive than any apparition."

"What's the difference?" Anneth could feel flickering through her muscles. Her lips burned. Her forehead was hot where The Lady had placed a kiss.

Timessa said, "Eidolons feel nothing. They observe and record. They're methodical — they measure and compare. They can even judge within bounds. But no eidolon can love or cry."

They stopped in the flow where the water suddenly deepened, the dark, washed stones smooth on their feet. Daylight had gone and a low, rose-salmon sunset sent a flush of color over the horizon.

Anneth frowned. "My Lady?"

Timessa turned to look at her. Anneth's eyes were black, her pupils as vast as her innocence. "Will you always be around?"

"What do you mean?"

They looked at each other. Anneth rose on her toes and kissed the goddess. Her lips were soft, the kiss brief, and she said, "The fire. You've let it burn in me and I see it burning in you as well —"

CHAPTER 15

Magic is the transposition of the properties of a deity,
person or object into a different object, person or deity.
— Jan Kott, *Black Sophocles*

Io returned to Naxos. Her side trip to Charleville had proven uneventful. The old building she'd inherited was fully occupied by two businesses and she revised the rental agreements to have monthly payments sent to her account.

She was surprised at how little nostalgia she felt seeing her childhood home. Her mother had died years before. Now her uncle was gone as well.

The town seemed frozen in its old glamour. She smiled as she drove past the Musée Rimbaud with its collection of remembrances. The river Meuse flowed in a long arc beside the brick mills. She was relieved to return to Paris, where she took an immediate flight to Athens, then a ferry to Naxos.

Timessa met her at the dock. The goddess was dressed casually and wore her usual dark sunglasses. They hugged and she said, "You've been gone too long."

"Only six days," Io smiled.

"Six too many, but you're back."

They got into her convertible, and Timessa drove fast, taking the high northwestern route that zigzagged along the Mediterranean. Io grinned as the hot air pushed her hair back.

As they motored through the small village of Agia Ayia on the northern end of the island, she commented, "You don't have a driver's license do you?"

"Of course not."

Io giggled, but said nothing more. Timessa glanced at her occasionally, finally asking, "What do you think? I want your every thought. Those were awkward calls last week."

"You hate cell phones, don't you?"

"I always have."

"I think Marseilles is overrated, but Monaco has good restaurants. A client took me out to a lovely restaurant."

"Nice?"

"Chi-chi. She paid a fortune to impress me."

"Oh dear. Did she know you couldn't be impressed?"

"I didn't let on. She wants half a dozen gowns."

"You've become quite practical, my dear."

Io laughed. "I suppose —"

As they arrived at the estate, Timessa pulled the car into the old garage and turned off the engine. She looked at Io. She had not put on a seat belt for the drive and was hugging her knees, looking at the garage wall through the windshield.

"Please act glad you're back," Timessa said.

"There were times on the phone," Io said, "when you sounded so distant."

Timessa frowned and Io continued, "I actually wondered, during that call I made from Monaco, if you'd be here when I returned."

"You mean, easy come, easy go."

"There'd be nothing easy about it."

"I go nowhere without you."

"That's not true —"

"I admit to rarely traveling these days, but when I do —"

"Europē? I hear it's become a mecca. The most divine women coming and going constantly."

"No, it's a land of blood and invasions. You wouldn't want to go."

"Were you whisked away while I was gone?"

The goddess nodded her head. "Repeatedly."

"And the visits became longer and longer, didn't they?"

"Why do you ask?"

"I called two days ago when I'd returned to Paris. Delia told me you couldn't be interrupted. I asked why and she said you had been in one of your zones for hours."

"Was I? I wasn't aware —"

"It's midday." Io opened her door and stepped out. She gave Timessa an appraising look and said, "Let's eat. You can confess all you want."

After sandwiches they dawdled on the beach at the cove, each reluctant to say too much. Or set the wrong tone. They sat on a bench, not touching, looking west toward other islands. After a minute Io said, "Remember the day Dionysos sprang from these waves while we swam?"

"Dionysos, the dolphin. You thought he was a shark."

"He sort of was," Io said. "What a swagger."

"An escapee from Poseidon's fishbowl."

"He didn't expect to run into you."

"He was an innocent. I'd turned into what I am while he was imprisoned."

"Poor man. He came back, you said, to reclaim the past."

"Yes," Timessa smiled. "His ancestral home."

"Then he found *us*. Two girls on the beach."

"I'm afraid I was the first woman who'd ever disobeyed his commands."

"I'd forgotten," Io laughed. "He stood right where we are and grabbed your hair."

"I was to be another conquest."

"You put a quick end to that ."

Timessa shrugged. "He'd always had an eye for me. But I straightened him out."

Neither spoke for minutes. The sea broadcast white noise —

waves sweeping landward, breaking, raking backward in a repetitive shuffle.

Finally, Io spoke first. "What will you do?"

"About *Eurōpē*?"

"Yes."

"I do nothing willingly."

"What do you do *unwillingly*?"

"Wrong word choice, Io. Let's say I do nothing *consciously*."

"Whatever happens just happens …?"

"Yes," Timessa said. "Like these waves. They come and I'm swept away."

"And once you're captured on this time machine, then what happens?"

"You mean there?"

Io nodded.

Timessa continued. "I find myself standing in that green valley, in vast plains."

"Are there people?"

"Oh yes. Those who live there and those who want what's theirs."

"And what part do you play?"

"That of the ancient goddess. The one who struggles with decisions, who destroys, who destroys more as the months pass —"

Io interrupted, saying, "Blood on your hands."

"Yes, that."

Io kicked some sand with her toes and sighed. "I'm having to pry information from you."

"You could tie me up and hold a knife to my throat."

"If I did, you know what you'd say?"

Timessa said lightly, "No —"

"You'd say, 'I'm immortal. Don't bother.' "

"I'm being that difficult, huh?"

"You hold it all in. You disappear — not bodily, but mentally — and when you return from wherever you've been, you say next to nothing."

"Io, you can't understand. *I* can't. It's all vivid and real when I'm there. But back here, I remember events as if they were a dream."

"Do you remember *anything*?"

"I remember that I created an eidolon, an old woman. I think she succeeded."

"At what?"

"She had a mission. She returned. There was some sort of skirmish. Burning spears. And there were women, warriors almost like Amazons."

Io shook her head in disbelief. "And what do you do while these Amazons defend the world?"

"I watch. I observe. And accept the adoration."

"Oh, they adore you there as well?"

"Yes. I'm Inanna. I'm sure of that. And I'm called The Lady."

"Gaia's doing."

"She doesn't seem involved."

"Oh, I'm sure she is."

"Then you know more than me."

Io hesitated. "There, in Európē ... do you have a mate?"

Timessa made a small face. "Like you, your counterpart? No, I think I'm more like a virgin goddess ..."

"Well, let me know if I have competition."

"If you do, it was pretty long ago." Timessa gave Io a dazzling smile. "Gaia said thirty or 40,000 years ago."

"Still ..."

Timessa nudged the girl, taking her hand. "We can kid about all of this, but it's terrifying. I have no control of when, or where, or even what to expect. And it all has something to do with time and morality. If I could only remember the details when I'm here —"

"It sounds like a history lesson that's taught by taking you back to the actual event."

"Fair enough."

Neither spoke, then Io said, "I'm sorry to have been difficult. You say little about what happens and I'm left wondering."

"It's partly that I return in a fog. *Now* becomes *then*. When I'm there the past becomes present. I'm *there*. And what I see seems familiar, like something I've seen before —"

"I think you overthink what you call ... time."

"No, but I am conscious that Gaia seems to compress it. When

I'm *there*, time doesn't move predictably … and the women who come to me, who call me Inanna, are like shadows on a wall, flickering, speaking in echoes …

"I keep waiting for my old friends — those nightly fires that have always appeared in my sleep — to suddenly arise in those vast fields of barley and burn it all away. To *save* me for once."

"But they don't."

"No."

"Because there's something there that you're expected to discover."

"Or to unravel."

"I'm envious."

"What —? I wouldn't wish this on anyone."

"Don't you see? I'm just a couturier, a stupid dressmaker."

"And I'm glamorous?"

Io hesitated. "Yes. Fascinating and smart, bewitching and … ridiculously complex. Plus, Gaia whisks you away to exotic locales."

"Yes," Timessa said. " 'exotic' places. And perhaps, in the end, I'll survive whatever this is."

Io squeezed her hand. They laughed, stood and started up the path to the promontory.

CHAPTER 16

> *… what splendor.*
> *It all coheres.*
> — Sophocles, *The Women of Trachis*

To be dream-burnt meant being on fire, being ablaze, being hot, aglow, seared, afire every night. To be burnt in dreams meant standing in the sun's corona — facing flames dancing on the dark horizon. When she tried to imagine being back in Eurṓpē, she instead saw a movie screen of conflagrations, sudden firestorms. There was greenery, but too often as she viewed the wide landscapes, the underbrush burst into flames.

She could picture a young woman there but couldn't remember her name. When she, Timessa, was in Eurṓpē, was she there for *her*? For this *fawn*, this nameless girl?

Yes, perhaps, yet that afternoon, merely remembering the girl's innocence had caused her a paroxysm, a *paroxusmos*. She had suddenly begun to cry, then caught herself: goddesses do not react with tears.

Timessa had time to reflect, hours to think. Io was occupied in her small atelier. As she sat alone, one or another nymph would stop in occasionally, bringing a drink and at others simply being solicitous. They were watchful, even anxious.

And time seemed suspended, as if the goddess had been gifted an eternity. She laughed to herself. *Absurd: eternities have no end.* Her thoughts were precarious (she searched again for a word): *Mercurial. Erratic. Or, at best, subject to droll calculations.* And what was the point of endless analysis if it led nowhere?

She suddenly pictured herself as a divine calculating machine incapable of ever breaking the code or unraveling the threads of the cosmos. Yet, each morning she returned to her task.

Then she remembered: *Anneth.* There: the name she could not recall. It appeared without warning as she sat on the deck in the sun making fun of herself. *Anneth.*

It's so hard, she thought, to connect here to there. Everything was utterly real wherever she was. As real there as here. Or so it seemed. But wherever she was, the details of where she'd been moments before were elusive.

Time was beginning to overlap, to leak from one dimension to another. Yes, the moments that did overlap were random and far from illuminating. Yet, she sought clarity.

She sought not so much to untangle as to simply remember. If, while in Eurōpē, she could be *this* Timessa, then while on *Naxos*, similarly, she should be able to be the fully cognizant Inanna …

With the slightest reflection, so much seemed absurd.

She paused … She could be critical of herself, but she *had* conjured the girl's name.

Anneth. Her face was bright — Timessa could not see her clearly. She was manifest, striking, authentic. *Anneth.* But … Timessa sensed graveness, gravity — and beauty. There was fierceness and a naïve passion. Yet that was all … And Timessa knew there was more.

Once when she was young, Artemis had accused her of what she called woolgathering, which Timessa had concluded was similar to having reveries. But *this* analysis she was doing now was hardly daydreaming: it was grasping for what *was*, what had existed and what was now real.

There was a reality in Eurṓpē as well as here, on Naxos. And now she needed to connect the two.

Why was it so difficult?

Another thing that Artemis had said was that she "should be at one with the thing, the place and the time, all of which are constantly changing." The advice had seemed superfluous, a typical *bon mot* that the goddess was known for tossing out to the younger nymphs.

She grimaced, knowing that while she lorded over her estate in Naxos, at any moment she could be thrown into primitive Eurṓpē. The timing was always at Gaia's discretion … and without Timessa's consent.

Perhaps she should be content to be wherever she was, regardless of control: "Be at one with the thing, the place and the time."

Behind Gaia's stratagem there was, she believed, an overt purpose — and even an elegant design. Here on Naxos there was never conflict and she could burn her days languidly.

In Eurṓpē lives were endangered. And from what she could recall, there was constant death. The anatomy of the two places was skillfully differentiated. Both were real — and she now believed — both were devised toward some mysterious end.

Was Artemis in league with Gaia? She didn't know. Artemis was a lesser goddess. Now she, Timessa, following her chrysalis, had overwhelmed Artemis in every way.

Artemis was composed and cool … whereas Timessa *reacted* to situations. Timessa appeared unable to solve problems. Artemis hardly bothered to become engaged. Whatever arose, she observed the event — poised and at ease — then walked away.

Perhaps, Timessa thought, she too would achieve that equanimity. It was enviable. And from it flowed immense power.

But she wasn't seeking power. She had power. Instead, she sought tranquility.

She sought escape from the nightly fires. Artemis, on the other hand, appeared to desire nothing: she was detached, always dispassionate. And at best, she observed.

Athene had once said that neutrality — the skill of detached penetration — was the highest mark of intelligence. Now Timessa wondered if such detachment wasn't simply emptiness masquerading as something grand.

Gaia had started it all when she began to turn the wheel. Timessa knew that she was tied to that grand wheel. But why? She remembered a quiet dinner she and Io had hosted at the estate a few years earlier.

Artemis and Apollo and others had attended. Near the end, as plates and glasses were taken away, Timessa had drawn a card from her pocket, passing it around for each guest to observe. It was an old, tattered tarot card depicting the Wheel. On it a man was being thrown off, his arms flailing. A naked, blindfolded woman stood turning the wheel. And a couple clung to each other at the top.

When the card had circulated and been returned to her, Timessa held it up, saying, "It assumes all happiness ends in ruin."

Io took the card from her and said, "Not for us," thrusting it into a candle flame.

Timessa knew better. Since the start of time all happiness ended in smoke and conflagration.

§.

Timessa would not glorify her ascendence. Her unexpected appearance as the Great Goddess coincided with the return of the old divinities — that is, those who had survived the passing millenniums — but the reappearance of the gods was hardly celebrated... or even known among the general populace.

Zeus, once the greatest of them all, had been the first to go. Gaia had taken him down with a glance. Ares, too, was lost, brought to ruin with his satyr devotees on a summer afternoon in Charleville, the same day Timessa first met Io at her little shop. The rest of the divinities were prospering, though their appearances were more circumspect than in the past.

Still, there was excitement among them from an expectation that she, Timessa, would amount to more. Why they would celebrate remained unspoken. Each was differential, but she was aware of their quiet machinations. She was also certain that much of the maneuvering, however subtle, was Gaia's.

Be that as it may, Timessa thought, at some point the veil would be pulled aside. There would be disclosures. The maze would be deciphered, the bushes ripped from their roots.

❧

The sun was high and the sky endless in its expanse. A large rectangular stone was mounted on two hewn pedestals as an altar. It was twenty paces from the bank of the river, and its surface glistened, polished from repeated applications of animal fat and beeswax. A long obsidian blade lay to one side. Grasses at its base were beaten down.

In the distance, a small group of women approached through the cut field toward the sacred space. Anneth was among them. All wore deerskin singlets over thin dresses that ended mid-calf. Several carried spears.

When they came within sight of the altar, the closest pointed, saying, "There. The snake."

They drew in their breath and slowed. Atop the flat stone was a coiled python — a snake so long that its tail dropped off the back of the slab. Its neck was erect, its head high and its eyes aglow. It gazed at the women, and as they drew closer, it began to move and sway. Its scales were slick and its eyes hypnotic.

All knelt in unison, saying, "Inanna!" The snake rocked in a grave silence.

"Inanna! Inanna!"

The women were now on their stomachs, arms stretched forward, foreheads against the grass. Undulating atop the altar, the snake slowly rotated its head, its yellow eyes unblinking.

The women cried out together, "Inanna, Inanna, Inanna —!" their eyes closed. As they chanted, oblivious to what was before them, the snake changed. There was languorous stillness, then the snake was the goddess they called Inanna.

She wore a long, rose-hued gown. Her face shone as if she had absorbed the entirety of the sun. Several of the women looked up, gasping.

Timessa chanted,

I am an emanation of dominion,
No being may compete.
My light burns those who come unbidden —

She continued, "You are the chosen, my defenders — those who believe and are blessed —"

There were seven women, none older than thirty years. All stood attentively, mindful of her eyes and aware of the never-varying ritual. Looking at each other, they slipped off their singlets and shook out their hair, half-smiling with their eyes low.

Timessa spoke. "Euthalia, come to me." The young woman put her hands together as if in prayer and walked closer to the goddess, head low. Timessa placed a hand under Euthalia's chin, raising her head just enough to touch her forehead with her own. After seconds, she said simply, "Yes," and Euthalia stepped away.

"Agnes, come …" Mirroring the first woman, Agnes stepped forward, waiting. Their foreheads touched, and then too she retreated.

Aneka, Hebe and the others repeated the ritual, leaving Anneth standing alone, the only one of them passed over. The girl looked up and into Timessa's eyes, seeking an explanation. The goddess was expressionless, then said, "Anneth, remove your dress."

Without hesitation she pulled the garment over her head and tossed it aside. She stood beside the others in a thin underslip, her arms at her sides.

Timessa said, " Anneth, you are virginal?"

"Yes, My Lady."

"Your thoughts are pure."

"Always, My Lady."

"And you, among all of these devotees, are unmated."

"As all know —"

"Anneth, this is because you shall be my priestess, my chosen, my bravest warrior. When I am absent, when I visit my other lands, you shall speak for me and I shall be the whole of your thoughts and you will know secrets unknown to others."

Timessa continued, "Close your eyes."

As the girl did so, Timessa reached over and lifted a red robe from the altar top. "See what I hold?" The girl nodded with wide eyes. "Then come to me."

Anneth stepped forward, her palms open. Timessa said, "Turn and face away."

The goddess slipped the robe over her shoulders, cinching a belt at her waist. A black python was woven into the back, its head high and tail worked into a spiral. "Wear this when you attend to my affairs ...

"Euthalia, Agnes, Aneka, Hebe and the others are witnesses to your empowerment. Let no one stand in your way. Let no man enter our lands without meeting your fire and rebuke ..."

She paused, looking at the women standing in a semi-circle. As she met their eyes, she cried out, "Do you favor our new priestess?"

The women raised their arms, fingers outstretched and shouted gleefully, "Anneth! May you live in glory! May you strike fear in the heart of every man!"

Aneka and Hebe lifted her up and onto their shoulders, beginning a slow dance that paralleled the riverbank. Euthalia, Agnes, Nastka and Isidora joined. All sang as they leapt and spun, Anneth laughing and looking constantly from the goddess to the women, her eyes sparkling.

Their voices grew hoarse chanting *Anneth, Inanna, Anneth and Inanna!*

When it was over and the women exhausted, Timessa said, "Leave us now. There are private things I must share with my new priestess."

Moments later Anneth stood alone, watching as the others left, then turned to Timessa. "My Lady, I am honored. And I am yours forever." She dropped to a knee. "To use as you wish."

Timessa whispered, "Stand and come here."

Anneth rose, then broke out into tears. "My Lady, my legs won't move. I cannot obey."

"Is that so?" she whispered.

"Yes. I am afraid."

"Of being my priestess?"

"My awe is too great."

"Your awe —?"

"My ... astonishment."

The goddess let a moment pass. "Have you dreamt of me at night?"

"Oh yes, My Lady —"

"And those dreams, when they occur — describe them now."

Anneth hesitated. "I cannot."

They stood close and Timessa hesitated to touch the girl. Finally, she said, "You cannot walk. You're afraid. You can't describe the simplest of dreams. And how do you respond when asked? You say, 'I cannot.'

"Now I'm the one in wonderment," the goddess said. "I lionize you before all the others, and look what happens! You are our greatest warrior, yet you stand before me like a lamb."

Anneth lifted her head, her eyes tearing. "My Lady —"

"Anneth?"

"What if I'm incapable? What do I know? How shall I speak for you?"

"Were you in fear of the python?"

"No ... I know it's you."

"Yet you fear me in this form?"

"I ... feel differently about you ... when you're Inanna."

"When I appear as a woman."

The girl nodded slowly. "Yes."

Timessa turned toward the river. "Shall we wade? Take off your boots. We'll go barefoot —"

Anneth looked at her and giggled. "The water's cold."

"It'll clear your head. We'll hold hands."

The girl blushed, but removed her boots and straightened. Timessa held her by the shoulders and said, "First, off with your sacred robe. It's not to get wet."

Anneth waited patiently while she was disrobed. The goddess folded the garment and placed it on the altar. Her underslip was perhaps too long to go wading, but Timessa could imagine the girl's fright if she removed it.

The goddess took Anneth's hand and led her into the riffles. The black pebbles underfoot rolled and shifted as they stepped across the stream, the water almost reaching the hem of the girl's slip. To keep it dry Anneth reached down and bunched it up.

Timessa smiled. "I forget how young you are. Is it twenty-one or twenty-two?"

"Twenty-one, My Lady."

"And you have wielded a spear since you were —?"

"Twelve." She raised a hand suddenly, covering her mouth and sneezed. "Cold feet."

"Then let's sit on the bank and dry off in the sun." Timessa steered her to a small rise beside the stream where they had rested in the past.

"When you first rode against the nomads, were you afraid?"

Anneth shook her head. "I was excited."

"Yet you could have lost your life."

"I never believed it so."

"Why?"

"My mother had told me I was consecrated."

"I haven't heard this story. 'Consecrated'? To whom?"

"*You*, My Lady. That you shielded me from being harmed."

Timessa took her hand and kissed her palm, then laced her fingers between Anneth's. "Your mother said those things?"

"Yes, even when she was wounded, when she was dying on that field and I held her in my arms, she said, 'Inanna loves you, child.' "

Timessa watched the tears begin again. "A month later when I rode against the men, my first kill was the barbarian who took her life."

"How did you know?"

"He alone among the dozens wore a red cap and carried a red spear."

"You were a mere girl."

"My own spear drew black blood, not red when I struck him in the neck. Our eyes met as he fell backward to his death."

"All mortals die, some more swiftly than others."

"My Lady … was what my mother said true?"

"That you are consecrated?"

"Yes, and that I am yours?"

"Have I not chosen you from all who live upon this land?"

"You have, but …"

"But what?"

"… Can't you see? I cannot serve you fully. I've failed before I've even started!"

"Oh?" the goddess said.

"I am … *mortal*. How can I serve you when I'm dead?"

The goddess exhaled dramatically and squeezed her hand. "You never worry about death when you're on the battlefield, do you?"

"No …"

"Because I protect you there."

"Yes, of course —"

"Yet you worry about death as you stand before my altar, as you serve me at my side as priestess? Do you think I protect you in one place and not another?"

Anneth looked at her, blinking. "My Lady, will I die someday?"

"I also ask myself about time," Timessa said. "Isn't that what death is? When time ends, so does life."

"Not time," the girl said, pulling her hand away. "*Death*. I'm talking about what happens when a spear slips like a branding iron between two ribs, tearing meat and cracking bones …

"*Death*." she said, "which happens when eyes turn black and roll backward into darkness … *Death*, My Lady, not the passing of the seasons!"

Like a hot branding iron, Timessa thought. *Fire*. She suddenly remembered: dreams, fire that races across distant horizons, always waking in a sweat … There was usually a girl beside her, in a bed, shaking her arm. She couldn't picture the girl's face…

She knew too that, night after night those fires would taunt her, ridiculing her divinity, like Furies with burning eyes. Was that dark, smoking dreamscape here as well? Was the girl who woke her nightly the one beside her now? *No*, she thought. *Impossible. I'd know …*

Time, she thought, had slipped through a membrane as thin as Anneth's underslip. It had accelerated forward, then with great stealth, woven backward like breath passing through a veil. Negative time, she thought, was like a black hole pulling her into Gaian contrivances such as this, such as Európē — pulling her through the caul that separated *there* from *here*.

Anneth said, "Goddess —?"

"Yes," she caught herself. "I was thinking about what you said." To the girl's shock, the goddess ran her fingers through Anneth's hair, then rested her hand softly on her shoulder. "Anneth, if I asked, would you walk through fire?"

"For you?" she said. "Yes, yes!" She blushed again, then said, "I mean, I'm honored to do whatever you ask —"

"If it meant you might die?"

"Yes," she cried out. "*Whatever* it meant!"

Timessa took the girl's hand again and said, "Anneth, I chose well. You'll be a fine priestess. And a companion —"

"A 'companion'?"

"Yes, that. But you must know that I can't predict the future as you think. I can't say I will live forever, or that you may not die on a certain day. Perhaps our roles will reverse. Perhaps you will outlive me. I control many things, but even as an immortal I cannot stop death for all time."

Anneth nodded. "As long as I live, if I am yours, I will be at ease."

They sat in silence. The river seemed to slow, stilled, then uncannily, almost imperceptibly, reversed its flow. Anneth quickly looked at Timessa who ignored her, then back to the river. "Goddess —?"

"Yes, as easily as I upend the flow of our stream, I can capsize clouds overhead, cause avalanches in the mountain passes and ..." She shrugged. "Revert to being a yellow-eyed snake ...

"But I cannot turn death on its head ... Watch —" She languidly flicked her hand and the stream returned to its natural flow. Marveling, Anneth shook her head.

As Timessa gazed at the girl, she thought, *Io*, then caught herself. No, *Anneth*. She knew no one named *Io*. There was a woman in a nearby village named Iole. So what? She struggled to comprehend the importance of the name. Then she knew, or thought she knew.

She remembered someone, at some point far away, saying, 'Time slip-slides in peculiar ways when we play in the past.' That was a quote. She was certain. But who had said it? She wasn't sure.

She thought, *The membrane that separates the memories of these places has been pierced.* She, Timessa, could reverse rivers at will. But she had not conquered time. And did not understand these memories which seemed, as they competed for her consciousness, to leave her astonished and dumb.

Anneth nudged her gently. "My Lady, when you disappear for days, where do you go?"

Timessa laughed, grateful to be distracted. "To another time. One far away."

"Are you happy there?"

"Happy? I don't know. I'm aware I go, but I'm not certain where it is or what takes place …"

"You're a goddess there?"

She smiled. "Although so much about that place is blurry, I am an absurdly mighty goddess there. As I am here. That much I know."

Anneth smirked at the description, saying, "Forgive my smile. I love how you portray yourself."

"Be careful, Anneth. I think it's not 'I love how,' but that you're *in* love."

The girl's mouth opened. She went pale and shook her head. "Oh no, I'm sorry if you think —"

As she stood to flee, Timessa took her wrist and pulled her down. The goddess's strength was overwhelming.

"Loving me, Anneth, is all that matters now."

CHAPTER 17

Creation cannot take place except from
a living being who is immolated.
— Mircea Eliade, *Myths, Dreams & Mysteries*

More than 600 women gathered on a late afternoon as they did yearly, in a field studded with uncut poppy pods. The petals on the poppies had fallen two weeks before, signaling the celebration's start, which was known as Offering Night. Those skilled in harvesting poppies had incised the swollen sides of a dozen pods. Opium secreted from the cuts for several nights, hardening into brown resin in polished clay bowls. The stemmed pipes used to smoke the drug had been reamed thoroughly and washed clean.

Dancing had begun. The ring of women, like a long snake's tail, wound tighter and tighter toward a center — a moderately wide wooden platform — then unwound to the edges of the field, then returned again in a tightening circle.

The young man on the platform had volunteered a year before, like the many men before him, and now swayed languorously to the

beat of multiple drums — one, two, *three*, four — one, two, *three*, four
— the rhythm unvarying. He had been the first to sample the drug.

Unlike the women dancing, he was naked and painted front and
back in white chalk spirals. For a year he had been allowed to couple
with selected women and been successful, fathering at least a dozen
children who had come to term in recent months. Given that he was
healthy, he might have bred another dozen in the last week alone.

Throughout his mock-reign he had been deliciously high, eating
when he wanted and mating with any young woman who took him
to her bed. In the last week he had been barely conscious and had
not spoken a complete sentence in days. Still, his appeal was his physical stamina, one that was enhanced by herbs — his erection, never
abating, was considered remarkable.

He was also the only man at the ancient ritual. No others were
allowed to watch. Sunset was less than an hour away, and the
dancing was amplified by singing that mimicked the beat of the
drums.

> *Awake, Inanna, awake! Tonight we sacrifice!*
> *Awake, awake tonight!*
> *Bless us, Goddess, with your milk and honey!*
> *Bring us fertility tonight!*

Laughter and a rare revelry propelled the weaving dance.
Torches on tall poles were lit around the field. A young woman
climbed the platform and danced, open-legged, bent-kneed before
the man. He took her wrist and spun her in circles and finally
dropped her onto her back and mounted her to the howls and
clamor of all watching. Other women followed, lewdly lifting their
dresses in an increasing debauchery.

Hours passed, the young man roaring with laughter, deftly
mounting women in the darkening night. These annual gatherings
were always the same. The dancing devolved into an orgy. Sisters
embraced sisters and women who had never known a man took their
turn with the sham king whose sovereignty was reaching its
denouement.

From a small hillock to the east, at the edge of the goddess's inviolable grove, Inanna and Anneth watched the event unwind. The goddess was in a pale gown and the girl, her new priestess, wore her sacred robe. They stood apart, and yet together, silent as the sound of drums and carousing, screams and laughter, echoed through the old oaks behind them.

Timessa said, "Our yearly revels."

"Our time to conceive," the girl replied, "a time when seed is celebrated."

"When all of those who have obtained puberty run wild."

"The poppy makes it good."

"Yes, recklessness, something we can rarely afford, is celebrated."

"As you have said, My Lady, chaos breeds order. The man's seed brings children."

"Anneth, you never danced on this night?"

"On Offering Night? Never. But it is said that you are always here, watching through the night, blessing everyone who dances —"

"Blesséd are they who dance, for they are purified."

"Yes, My Lady, so it is said."

"Yet you were already sanctified. You knew from an early age."

"I knew that my mother would not allow me to go. I found it confusing. She wouldn't explain. She called me 'immaculate.' I railed against her dictates. But even as I did, I sort of understood."

"That you were perfect as you were?"

"That I was a maiden. That I was a warrior. That one did not contradict the other. That I was somehow special. But I spent years half-resenting that."

"Purity is a strange burden, Anneth."

The drumbeats had become louder and insistent. The goddess raised her voice. "I differ from your mother on that count."

Anneth looked at her in surprise. "But is not my purity for you?"

Timessa appeared to focus on the chaos below, squinting at the constant movement. Then, barely loud enough for Anneth to understand, she said, "Yes, your purity is for me. To save or take. To claim or preserve …"

"Goddess —!"

"Anneth — these women who dance for me — look at their lack of restraint. All are making love to all. Yet, are they not sanctified?"

"You bless them all. But they … they're hardly pure!"

"Have I not ordained, 'Bléssed are they who dance, for they are purified.' ?"

The girl's confusion grew. "But how can …"

"Purity may arise from dancing, from fecundity, from saving oneself as *you* have done — or from making love like a lion, howling into the night in pleasure …

"In love, my Anneth, all is chaos, and all eventually comes to an end in order to be reborn."

She reached over and took the girl's hand, pulling her closer. "Yes, you are sanctified. In my name. Inanna's *priestess*. But … as my priestess you are always pure, no matter your imagined morality. As you are mine, those women —" She pointed at the mayhem. "— are mine as well. All are equally blessed."

"To be blessed is to be … pure?"

"No woman among my people is purer than another."

"But I am saved for you."

"Your mother's word was 'immaculate.' As you are. But tonight I want you to understand that, no matter your actions, under my shield you are always pure."

"My Lady, my behavior is beyond reproach."

"And what is that which 'is beyond reproach'?"

"That I am yours. That I'm not down on that field in —" She paused.

"In someone else's arms?"

Anneth felt increasingly disorientated, her breathing becoming unsteady. Timessa continued, "As you say — as you have always said — you are mine."

"Yes —"

"And however I use you, Anneth, losing your purity is impossible." She put her arm around the girl's waist, drawing her hip to the goddess's. "The time has come —"

The girl's mind was swirling — believing that Inanna was about to take her no differently than the women who were ravishing women on the field. Anneth was surprised as the goddess released her and instead pointed toward the platform below.

All but one drum had fallen silent and the young man stood alone on the dais facing the hundreds of women. He swayed slightly, his arms out as if embracing them all. Anneth couldn't see his eyes but imagined his pupils were wide and black.

As Timessa whispered, "Look!" a woman stepped behind the man and, holding a narrow strip of leather in both hands, whipped the dark tong over the man's head and yanked it tight around his neck, crossing her hands behind his back, cinching the strap.

He staggered, bewildered — then, as she maintained the pressure — dropped to his knees, trying with both hands to pull the strip away. The single drum fell silent and in the lingering, almost unbearable silence, dozens of women began to moan. Then in unison, all resumed their frenzied dance, singing and chanting,

Awake, awake, Inanna!
Bless us, Goddess, with your sight!
Bring us fertility tonight!

and with a grunt, the woman who had strangled the man cast him sideways, releasing the tong. He slumped chest down, arms out.

Anneth clung to the goddess, saying, "Every year's the same."

"From every death comes rebirth. Thus we procreate …"

"Must we watch what comes next —?"

Timessa ran one hand over Anneth's back, then opened her robe with the other. "No, we're done tonight. They'll quarter him at dawn, take the pieces and plant them in the newly opened furrows to bless next year's barley crop."

"I know. I used to help."

The goddess stroked the girl's side. "Then the remaining parts, bones and bowels, will be burned with prayers on my altar."

"The man will be forgotten."

"When he volunteered, he knew his end."

"Yet, each year," Anneth whispered, "a new man steps up."

"Their lives are brief. They have no glory. They groom our horses and clear the dung. To become king for a year …"

"Yes, I see."

Timessa abruptly pulled the girl's robe closed and knotted the belt at her waist. Then she took her face in both hands and kissed her briefly.

"And I have always taught that without these sacrifices, pestilence will come like a flock of birds and peck out our eyes. Thousands of us would perish. That man tonight did not die in vain —"

੪

The goddess met Aneka, Nastka and Isidora at her altar. They knelt before her, lowering their heads. The sun rose through the oaks.

She said, "Stand and look into my eyes." The women did so, all obviously weary. Anneth stood beside Inanna, holding a laurel bough. The goddess said to the three, "Is the planting done?"

Her eyes lowering, Nastka said, "Yes, in furrows in four directions. An arm to the north, an arm to the south, a leg to the east and a leg to the west."

Her words had been spoken without alteration for generations. The goddess continued, "Repeat the prayer you prayed upon completion."

Now grow green!
Now dance the dance
of the goddess!

Inanna nodded in approval. Following the ancient protocol, Aneka and Isidora stepped up to the altar, carrying a leather tarp between them. In its center was a small heap of gristle, fat and bones. On cue, Anneth raised her arms high and cried out, "Blesséd, blesséd are those who serve the divine Lady!"

Responding, "Blesséd, are those!" Nastka unwrapped a narrow bundle and held up a thick reed. She shook burning embers from inside the yarrow stalk onto a small pyre in the center of the flat stone. The kindling caught. As flames began to rise, Aneka and Isidora shook the body parts over the fire and stood back from the smoke.

Anneth opened her palms in an ancient hieratic gesture and said in a singsong voice, "It is done. It is done again. It is done as it shall always be —"

The goddess intoned, "Year after year —"

The three young women bowed, turned and left. Not a word or gesture of the ceremony had changed. The weather was favorable. The sun had hung like a golden crucible over their heads, its heat broken only in the cold wind that had begun long after midnight, long after as the celebrants had sought to sleep.

Timessa knew too well that winter, like the relentless attackers, was poised again, again, to lower itself upon her lands. Snow would cover the furrows and in time spring would return with its promise of milk and wine, poppies, honey and the fat heads of barley through the fields.

CHAPTER 18

Blesséd are those
who wear the crown of ivy.
— Euripides, *Bacchae*

Gaia waited, watching as Timessa wandered alone through one of the lower orchards that hugged the sea's slanted shoreline. As always in the last three years, Gaia was in a tutu, this one black. The goddess turned to ascend the path, saw her there and stopped.

"I thought we might speak," the little girl said loudly.

Timessa half-bowed. "Yes, you have me leading dual lives."

"Thus spake Inanna?"

"I'm on Naxos today."

"Not the ancestral lands?"

"No one there has ever seen a sea. Or a car or plane."

"These lands are ancestral too." Gaia put a leg out, straightening her foot, tapping the pathway. "Are you acclimating? To the here and there?"

"I wish to remember more. When here, *there* is a blur. When there, I barely remember who I am on Naxos. Or at least who I think am."

"It's like learning to dance: you have to find a balance."

Timessa took a deep breath and said impatiently, "Is that it? Is it balance? It seems a boundary exists … What is Inanna and what is Timessa hardly overlap. One divinity looks in the mirror and does not see the other."

"Is the experience dismaying? I mean, like a terrible disconnect?"

"You have no sympathy."

"*We* never have sympathy."

"Yes, I'd forgotten …"

"Could it be that you're not intended to remember?"

"Perhaps your scheme is fraying."

"Elaborate."

"Perhaps the tissue between now and then is weakening. At times I get glimpses of both …"

"There are many millennia between Naxos and old Eurṓpē."

"Indeed?"

"But perhaps I exaggerate the importance of time."

Timessa smiled faintly. "Yet … time grinds down every living thing."

"You're thinking linearly. Surely you're over that." Gaia was backlit, and her shadow trailed down the path, ending near Timessa's feet.

"Gaia, I have a question. We've never spoken directly about Io. Artemis told me once how you'd chosen her. Then Io filled in some details —"

"Chosen just for you. You're not having problems with the girl?"

"No. That's not where I'm heading." She paused and Gaia watched her silently. "Tell me instead about … Anneth."

"Oh, her."

"Did I get the name right? I think I did."

"She's your new priestess."

"Is that what she is? I only half see her face."

Gaia looked overhead, frowning lightly. "Are the seasons changing? The sun angle seems … different than the last time I visited."

"Gaia!"

"Are you still hawking that eagle? Aetos, right?"

"You're avoiding my question."

"Yes, Timessa, there's a young woman named Anneth. For you to know that here means that the membrane *has* been frayed."

"What am I to make of her?"

"She's mortal. You'll try to grant her immortality, as you did with Io."

"Oh." Timessa paused. "And you say she's my new priestess."

"New as in very, very long ago."

"Her face haunts me even as I walk around the estate."

"She has that effect."

"So she's real."

"Timessa, there are many pathways for each of us to follow. Here, there may be several. There, others …

"While in this place," Gaia said, "in this time, you have rediscovered yourself. When you ran with Artemis, you were like a roly-poly caterpillar. I left you like that for far too long …"

As she spoke, Timessa watched her enunciate. Gaia chose her words carefully, sometimes moving herself lyrically, using gentle arm gestures. Smiling, she continued, "You were my wild larvae, the girl who hardly knew up from down. Then your time came. You see, the gods who had surrounded you became exhausted …

"I called for your chrysalis. For a goddess, such a time is like pubescence — an explosion of hormones. Your consciousness expanded. Mortals call it metamorphosis. You became my butterfly."

"Yet since that moment, I have agonized."

"A lovely, amoral butterfly, yet still, a goddess with a conscience. Contradictions. You're vexed, are you not?"

"Exasperated, distressed. I'm rarely satisfied."

"Flying that eagle satisfies you."

"Yes, and there are nights when Io …" Her voice trailed off.

"Ephemeral moments, all —" Gaia toyed with a new position, an arabesque, straightening one leg behind her body, arms out and staring seaward without expression. Then relaxing, she said, "Timessa, you must learn to love these mysteries. Of course, they'll all play out or be revealed in time —"

As Gaia emphasized the word *mysteries*, Timessa could suddenly

see the all-female ceremony, the dancing and the mayhem and a
young man striding across a platform in his ephemeral moment. A
shadowed woman with a leather tong stepped behind him, raising
her hands, her face blank, the strip pulled taunt.

Timessa covered her face and took a deep breath. Gaia said
softly, "Did the veil come down?"

"Or the tissue ripped. For the briefest moment."

Death and love and bliss — peak moments, she thought, *obscured by deceit
and whatever else Gaia has conjured.*

She thought back a year to her worldwide tour with Dionysos
and the others. Then she had had a mission, which at the time had
seemed simple enough: to guide into bliss the hundreds of models
who belonged to her club, The Girls.

She had grieved at their disquiet and insecurity. Each was desirable, considered part of an elite spectrum of unusually beautiful
young women — yet, like her, none was content. She had recruited
Dionysos who, through his ecstatic dances — the raw, orgastic
Dionysiakos — opened girls to a rare rapture, however briefly.

Timessa had believed that she could seize that moment, with Io's
help, to infuse each girl with a startling euphoria. The maneuver had
worked. She had blessed each with a lasting bliss — but she knew
now that the stratagem had been merely trickery. The girls had not
sought elation: she, Timessa, had imposed it upon them as a salve for
her own suffering.

She turned to Gaia, saying, "Machinations, contrivances. It's so
difficult to see clearly."

"You see my conundrum," Gaia said. "Containing the entirety of
here, while there, could be overload. That is, for you … as is knowing
all of what happened there while on Naxos would be … let's say,
encumbering. Good rarely comes from standing downstream of a
splintering dam."

"You mean the old Greek *amnēsia*. Is that what you're saying?
That forgetting works in my favor —?"

"Nothing is lost. More accurately, nothing is *remembered*."

Timessa hesitated, then asked, "Gaia, will this ever end? Will I …
find my way?"

"I don't know … You're something new. I've created nothing like you before.”

The two watched each other silently, neither moving. Finally, Timessa said, “You speak of my chrysalis and call me a butterfly —”

“And you whine about the luxurious conditions.”

“Yes, I’m fortunate. Flutter my wings and …I’m here, there.”

“A unique gift.”

Timessa stooped and picked up a small shard, a piece of red pottery. “Look! This could be thousands of years old.”

“Unremarkable. Broken pottery is everywhere on these islands.”

Timessa shook her head. “We never resolve our differences, do we?”

“Our differences are my doing. Your *oscillations* are meant to prevent you from falling into hubris like the other gods. The fires you look upon as such a burden are quite the opposite —”

As she faced Gaia, Timessa suddenly imagined Artemis thousands of years earlier facing Ariadne, her bow drawn, her voice without compassion. The two had stood less than a hundred paces from where she was now. She could see the bow flinch as the arrow loosed, could see Ariadne stagger back a step. The scene as it did now always replayed soundlessly, slowly in her memory, drained of all color.

Gaia whispered, “We are hardly at that point. Ariadne strayed, whereas you have merely lost your way.”

The little girl fluffed her tutu absentmindedly, rose on her toes and did a quick pirouette.

Timessa said, “Must I relive Inanna’s mistakes?”

“Nothing from that time can be recreated flawlessly. The old Inanna destroyed herself in recriminations …“

“And I go down the same path.”

“No, I did not bring you back to be a parrot, or an echo of the old, failed Great One.”

“Then what am I to be?”

“Ferocious and unflinching —”

Then, like fresh snow caught in a warming sun, Gaia became translucent. As Timessa watched, the girl’s form became slightly, then entirely, transparent. The sun behind her flooded her body with a golden light.

❦

Timessa was aware — an indefinable and instant feeling that followed Gaia's disappearance — that she was in dual locations. That much her consciousness acknowledged: Naxos and Európē overlapped. She was beside a seashore and then — as if at a seance — in contact with someone dead who seemed alive.

There were sacred oaks. A sacred river, high and swift. Skewered, leafless hickory trees. Crows cawing almost within sight. And once verdant fields, now brown and cut at ankle height.

A small group of women recited a liturgy as they faced Inanna. She stood mid-river. Slanted in the late fall afternoon, the sun cast warm light upon her.

She was resplendent, her rose-colored gown pulled down over one breast as was the ancient custom. The women wore red ribbons in their hair and chanted,

O Holiness, queen of the chosen!

Hail, daughter of the shining season!
Goddess who brings us grain and honey,
Milk and rain,
Fertile wombs and victory!

As the song finished, the women gathered lustral branches from a cut pile of evergreens at the bank. The branches had been collected for the ceremony earlier from holly, pine, and laurels — trees that signified everlasting life. Each woman took a branch and held it high.

Inanna, knee-deep in the flush river, gestured to the women, now loosely lined up on the shore. "Make your way, you who seek immortality!"

One by one, they stepped into the river, taking turns, wading barefoot, arms out for balance. All wore identical white gowns. Once they reached her, they raised wet gowns to their thighs, bowed and were touched on their scalp. They nodded, smiled and turned to allow the next woman to take their place.

This was a ceremony of joy which, yearly, followed Offering Night. Only the fiercest warriors were invited, although hundreds of the valley's women watched as the blessings were imparted. Inanna's gift of grace insured their continuing victories. Her love was a light that protected all who rode out carrying spears.

Anneth was at the goddess's side, her hands cupping a censer which she held chest high. The fired-clay container held burning incense made from frankincense and amber. Sweet-smelling smoke filled the air as she sang,

O Queen, O Holiness,
Who comes on golden wings,
Blesséd is she who is touched today!

As the last woman turned to leave the stream, Anneth raised her voice, singing,

Blesséd is she
Who is happy in heart,
She who is touched by the Our Lady!

Once the rite started, the goddess had not spoken. Still, she scanned the landscape as she conducted the ceremony, watching faces, measuring emotions and guarding against reacting herself.

Tradition, she thought, *I know each gesture, each solemn word, the order of events, the precise timing of the liturgy, what words to emphasize, even the angle of the falling sun in the holy month of the holy celebration —*

The hundreds of women began to leave, scattering in different directions, many singing joyously. The cold water flowing over the goddess's legs sang as well. The river's golden trout were hidden, hovering under bank cuts and large stones. They would return in the spring to flash their metallic scales, showing off their flecked jewels, rolling their impassive eyes.

A rainbow arced across the fields, its bands of red, violet, blue and orange bending in the benevolent rays of the sun. The goddess was reminded of the ribbons the women wore. The custom was ancient.

Even Anneth's hair was aswirl with red strips of raw silk that twisted in the breeze like snakes.

CHAPTER 19

Heroes always have an hour of warning,
An hour of despair ...
— Jan Knott, *The Eating of the Gods*

Io watched Timessa as she drank water. "Feeling better?"

"The nausea was brief. I'm better now —"

Moments before she had left the orchard, walking toward the house and stopped when the feeling swept her.

"You never get sick."

"This was Gaia's doing. I suspect that as she winged off, she sent my double away as well. I've felt the nausea before, but never like this."

Pausing, Io said, "Would it help to get away from here? We could go anywhere. Monaco, or Geneva ... A trip might break the spell —"

"You mean to escape her grand design? Io, I'm surprised you'd even consider that."

Timessa continued, "Her parting words were something like, 'Be ferocious —' Those were orders. A challenge. I can no more run from her than —"

As she paused, searching for the right comparison, she was snared in a strange cinematic memory. A small band of horsewomen were charging to the left across an open field, heads low. They had spears tucked under their arms. Their hair was remarkable in that all had dozens of multi-colored ribbons tied on their braids.

The view changed to encompass a line of irregular warriors who stood crouched and waiting: men.

Then her view of the women intensified. Their faces were taut. She had never seen any of them before. Was this Európē —?

"Goddess?"

"Flashbacks, or flash forwards. A skirmish about to occur."

"These are all violent, aren't they?"

"Most, when I remember them, remain a blur. This was unusually vivid. At least as long as it lasted."

Io smiled. "We have a phrase, perhaps it was Rimbaud or something from Baudelaire." She laughed. "Or perhaps it just came to me while I worried about you. But it's about clarity, being in the moment."

"And —?"

"It's *lucidité poétique* — poetic lucidity. Nice, yes?"

"It's a lovely phrase."

"I think you should try to remember these ... events from the past. Be lucid. String them together. Gaia must intend for them to have meaning."

"Gaia's playing a long game. She always has. That's what I find terrifying. This could play out in a couple weeks or go on for years. Time means nothing to her."

"Does time mean anything to *anyone*?"

Timessa laughed. "To mortals time means everything."

"I wonder. We're told to live in the now. Those who succeed lose attachment to the past, right? And never worry about what lies ahead."

"Gaia is beyond these simple concepts. I think time to her hardly exists. Or what we think of as the *here* is really inconceivably long ago. Or we're wrong and it's already light years ahead, and she's waiting for us to catch up. Or even more likely, she's everywhere at the same time."

"Nothing's sequential?"

"In Gaia's world it's all just a façade. Every moment overlaps every other."

Io refilled her wine and frowned. "She's Nature, isn't she?"

"As mortals view her, yes."

"She's like an embodiment of the earth?"

"Not 'embodiment.' That not vast enough. It's more that she encompasses … the cosmos itself. She's wired into everything we know. For all I know, she *is* the cosmos —"

Io laughed. "Then, my love, you're in safe hands."

"I suppose. Yet it's all mixed up in mortality and morality, passion and indifference … and in an excruciatingly slow unveiling."

Io smiled charmingly. "And what are you to do?"

"Persevere. Be 'ferocious.' She implies that there'll be a great revelation along the way …"

"Do you believe it?"

"All I know is that she's watching."

Io's voice was thin. "You must have some glimmer of where this goes."

"Maybe I'm meant to collapse time. Like Gaia has done —"

"You mean, stop it completely?"

"Isn't it interesting that humans are the only species that worry about time? And it's only because they worry about the future."

"So then it's a mental construct?"

"What if it's identical to morality? Not real. You know the routine: somebody presents commandments. You must obey."

"Or you go to hell."

"Or the Underworld. Or prisons. But it's a fraud: time and morality are both irredeemably capricious."

"You mean inconsistent?"

"No, I mean what if there's nothing there? If time and morality are a mirage? If whatever we think they are, they aren't."

"It's complicated."

"Or ridiculously simple."

Io paused. "What happens if you succeed?"

Sweeping her hand out toward the sea, she said, "You and I and

Artemis will be able to sit around with a glass of wine in our little eternity."

"And laugh," Io said, "at how seriously we took all of this —"

❧

In the orchard Gaia had used the word *oscillations* as if it were a mark of respect — as if Timessa's fluctuations between extremes, all undisguisedly Gaia's doings, were some honorific — and would prevent her from falling into self-conceit like the other gods. Timessa saw the induced oscillations differently. They were far from admirable: they denoted wavering and self-doubt.

But Gaia had also said, Be ferocious, fierce, unflinching. She demanded courage, assertiveness. There could be no room for wavering.

Wavering was done. It had to be.

Yet it would all be so much easier if she could connect *here* and *there*. And she was certain that doing so was a matter of two things: One was remembering place to place. The second was consciousness, being aware of everything at all times.

And she suspected that the latter was more important. The former would follow if she were aware. She needed to know what had occurred wherever she was.

The barrier Gaia had thrown between the ancient and the now had to go. What was Io's term? *Lucidité poétique.*

Yes, rip down the veils! Nothing good came of barriers. Gaia implied that they were something protective, that she, Timessa, could not handle a flood of dual experiences …

Yet if Timessa agreed, how was she to initiate a live connection between now and then? Saying simply, "compress time" felt dishonest, even gratuitous.

As it was, she could barely remember what had occurred *there* when she was here. The distance between millenniums, physically and intellectually, appeared vast.

Then she knew. There was a commonality that she remembered wherever she was: Io and Anneth.

Perhaps they were the bridge. Timessa was now always aware of both, almost as if they were next to her at all times. In Európē Io never faded. Here, on Naxos, Anneth increasingly flooded her thoughts.

Her awareness of them as being the same was growing. Gaia had called them that. *One*.

Yet they were not. They knew nothing of each other. But Timessa could not contest the nexus: the two were linked.

Still, she knew she could say nothing about one to the other.

CHAPTER 20

Rain fell from thunderheads.
Whirlwinds moved from point to point
along a geometric path … switch to switch
diodes lighting as electrodes sang
the words the water-nymph sings
plaintively beside the sacred springs

The goddess inspected the sacred temple. Its foundation was on the far bank of the river, slightly upslope and overlooking the plains to the east. Excavation of the sandy substrate had taken weeks. Upon completion flat stones to support the structure had been set in the straight trench.

A dozen house carpenters, recruited from villages up and down the valley, framed the complex. All were men, valued above others for their skill.

The goddess had hand-picked oaks to be hewn, and assigned several of her warriors to supervise the work. Winter had proven to be the ideal season for construction as sap was not running, and many of the men would have otherwise been idle. She allowed occasional snow flurries, but anything more precipitous was delayed until the temple was weather-sealed.

To her immense surprise, Anneth had insisted on drafting the temple plans. Dimensions were roughly sketched on slate. The resulting symmetry was pleasing. The girl proved to have an innate sense of proportion, and as far as anyone knew, the building was the largest ever built.

The temple roof was finished with a high pediment above a portico of square columns. The entire building was painted white using a mixture of local chalk, oil and water. The compound had been boiled, then allowed to cool in large pots before application. Once completed the temple shone in the sun with a brilliance that befitted its purpose.

Even before it was erected it was called The Temple of Inanna. The massive original altar remained in front. The complex was surrounded on three sides by ancient oaks. Given that it faced east, the temple was flooded with light at dawn, washing the high portico and inundating the public area of worship with a ruby-tinged light.

A collective of women artisans from the villages had carved an immense snake figurine, painted it black and hung it directly above the wide doorway. Its spiraling tail mimicked the coils of the snake on the back of Anneth's robe.

Finally, a sacred statue said to represent Inanna was mounted on a square base in the central room. The pitted, cylindrical meteorite was half her height, and had fallen nearby like a thunderbolt during the temple construction.

Anneth had immediately declared it sacred. The holy stone, when it had finished smoking from its fiery descent, was revered as a simulacrum of The Lady. After the goddess herself touched it, smiling, all who saw it bowed and fell to their knees.

Rear rooms flanking the public area were private and reserved solely for the goddess, her priestess and the rare guest. They were furnished simply. Temple attendants maintained the facility, furnishing food, fuel for the temple fires and clean garments. They appeared at dawn to open the temple, and again at dusk to close the wide doors.

A small cadre of warriors — all women hardened in recent skirmishes — guarded the site. Men on horseback had been driven away on three recent occasions. In the latest skirmish, one of the warriors had been captured and taken as a prisoner. The decision to spare his life was unique.

The generational code among them had been to keep no prisoners. This was an exception: when the man was surrounded he had cried out, "I'm a follower of Inanna!"

He was disarmed, tied, gagged, hooded, slung over a pack horse and hauled to the valley. The woman commanding the small unit guessed he was no older than twenty. After a four-hour ride to a wooded area outside one of the central villages, he was pulled off the horse and roughly tied to a tree to await the goddess's orders. His hood was left in place.

Tasenka, a horsewoman from the unit, ran to the temple to report the usual event. She expected Inanna to order his immediate death, but was, regardless, obligated to report what she knew.

The goddess stood alone beside the altar in a red garment, a loose cloak over her shoulders. She raised a hand before the woman could speak and said, "Repeat his exact words the moment he was caught."

The woman kneeled, lowering her head — shocked that the goddess knew. "My Lady, a second before we were to run him through, he cried out that he was a follower of yours … of Inanna."

"And he is being guarded as we speak?"

"Yes, My Lady. The man is tied and gagged. Shall I execute him?"

"If so, Tasenka, for what purpose would he have been hauled off the mountain and secured?"

The woman knew not to speak. The goddess continued, "No nomad is a follower of Inanna. No man there utters my name without disdain. Bring him here at once."

Tasenka left and quickly returned with the man. He had again been slung over a horse and was guarded by three women. As the party arrived at the temple, the goddess now stood with Anneth, waiting.

She ordered the man taken down, and his hood and gag removed. As he was freed, he shook his head and rubbed his eyes, staggering in the light. Finally looking around, he saw her and fell to the ground, prostrating himself and crying out, "O Goddess! Spare me certain death!"

"How do you know to whom you speak?"

Half-groveling, he said, "No other being can have such radiance."

"Why should you be allowed to live?"

He shook his head. "I should be killed. I don't deserve this honor, Goddess —"

"When you were captured, you claimed to be a 'follower.' Why?"

"Some of us worship Inanna. Secretly."

"Why secretly?"

"When we're found we're killed. You are called the witch, the snake —"

"Your words are spoken to save your life. No nomad praises Inanna."

"Not just women believe, Goddess, but men as well."

"How many followers exist?"

He slowly raised himself onto his knees, keeping his eyes low. "I know of six, Goddess. And each of us knows others. All are afraid to speak."

"How can this be?"

"Word has spread of your open heart —"

"There is no communication between your people and ours. There are only raids and killings."

"Wherever there are mortals your name is known."

She paused. Anneth whispered, "What are we to do with him?"

The goddess spoke loudly, "Your name?"

Head down, he slowly said, "I am Adalwolf."

"An unpleasant name."

He said nothing. The goddess turned to the women who surrounded him, saying brusquely, "Gag him, cover his eyes. He may not be anything he says —"

She watched as the women secured him. The man made no attempt to resist their efforts.

"Take him away," she said. "We'll continue this tomorrow."

❧

Inanna, in her pre-Timessa incarnation, had made assumptions and had erred. Cumulatively over a century, thousands of barbarians had died at her hands. More damningly, hundreds of her own people had died defending their lands.

The two territories had nothing in common except their mutual distrust. That distrust had hardened into an irresolvable hatred. Generations of women had become efficient warriors, increasingly reveling in the bloodshed and victories.

Once they had been peaceful hunters, gathering food from site to site and roaming the wide valley in small family groups. Today they were predominately soldiers, worrying about the sharpness of their spears and the swiftness of their steeds.

Because of the constant raids, the goddess now focused on defense and fortifications … certainly not on thoughts of what the invaders might believe. Now she was hearing that there were secret pockets of her worshippers in the foreign lands. The thought was absurd. Was the news credible? She had made no attempt to impose herself there. She presumed the nomads had their own divinities. What was to be gained by exalting a foreign goddess like herself?

Anneth nudged her gently. "This seems an immense distraction."

"Or an opening. Isn't it all strange?"

"Yes. Better that we end this quickly."

"What if he is what he says?"

"How is any of this to your advantage?"

"Perhaps," the goddess said, "we have been naïve. Perhaps there are many who believe."

"Even if it's true," Anneth speculated, "there are many more who would destroy us at any opportunity."

"What if I send the eidolon back?"

"She warned us of an attack. What more could she do?"

"Assess how many followers are hidden among the enemy."

"And if you find more than you expect —?"

"We divide and conquer."

The girl shook her head and looked away.

At dawn heavy rain swept the valley but none of its inhabitants cowered — their work went on. Tasenka appeared as requested before the temple with the prisoner — she had forgotten his name, *wolf* something. Simply saying it was unpalatable. The women thought of him simply as *the man*.

The goddess stood waiting behind her altar. The rain was warm and she spurned any head gear. The squall was simply an irritant. When the small party arrived, Adalwolf was pulled from his horse and his hood removed. He fell immediately to his knees, facing in her direction, looking down, occasionally wiping the rain from his face.

Inanna said, "If I release you, how will you explain your return?"

He looked up cautiously. "You will not kill me?"

"I said 'if'. Will you not be viewed as a deserter who has come back home?"

"I would say I crawled through the woods, following the sun, praying to escape the women who killed all those they saw."

He paused, then said, "Goddess, why would you release me?"

"You say you are a follower."

"What if I'm not? What if I'm a spy?"

"You are not."

He stared at her, then broke into tears. "*No*, I am not. And I never believed I would be before you, that you're real …"

She frowned, showing distaste for his emotion. "You may prostrate yourself, but do not grovel."

He nodded. "Yes, Goddess."

She went on, "In your land, in your miserable villages, how many follow Inanna?"

" Maybe hundreds," he said, "perhaps more. None of us dare speak of what we believe. But peace … has an undeniable attraction."

"Answer simply," she said. "No opinions."

Her eyes flashed with a distinct melancholy, her face forbidding. "What, *Adalwolf*, would happen if Inanna rode into your land?"

"Without disguise? You'd be taken, flayed and crucified. There's a bounty on your head. Every warrior hopes to be the one to capture you and be rewarded."

"Why?"

"If you were taken from these valleys, the riches here would fall to our forces."

"Don't they know I cannot be harmed? I am not one of you. I have no interest in conquering, but I *have* conquered time and death."

He lowered his head, saying, "Only the divine do not die."

"If you believe, you know that."

He said, "If you suddenly appeared, and no man could defeat you, there are those who would applaud. Who would celebrate. Who would praise your might."

"I am interested in concord, amity and peace — not 'might.' "

Anneth appeared beside the goddess. She wore a leather slicker and a cap. Her hair below its rim was soaked. "Has the interrogation ended?"

"Yes," Inanna said turning to the girl. "I've no patience for this talk."

Tasenka stood behind the man, her spear ready. Stoically, Anneth commanded, "The goddess orders him taken back to the pass. Do not ride alone — expect a trap. If you find the woods to be empty, if the birds sing, release him there —"

Glancing at the man, Anneth said, "The goddess is through with you. Stand. You get to live another hour, perhaps another day."

He bowed. The rain beat down steadily and the goddess turned and walked into the temple, leaving the wide doors open. Tasenka pulled the leather hood over the man's head and yanked him up, saying, "On the horse!"

Anneth said, "If we have been deceived, kill him." She waited in the rain, watching, until the horsewomen and man were gone.

In the temple, the goddess stood, eyes-closed, in the atrium before the meteorite. These people — hers and the others — expected a harshness from her that increasingly felt wrong. So much of what she presented as infallible authority now felt dark. Worse, it seemed tinged with catastrophe.

Perhaps it was the season. Winter was always gray, bleak. But this winter seemed washed in a thin red over gray, like a claret-colored stream running over a freshly killed body. She thought of the debacle of the stinging flies. So many attackers had drowned that day. The once unspoiled river had run crimson for a day.

In retrospect the event was a harbinger. Month after month brought more forewarnings. Yesterday, she thought, a man is captured and I have allowed him to live. So what if he sang out my name? Was that enough to spare his life?

Being a goddess required certainty. Her authority sprang from unwavering conviction. Yet, now, in the days that ticked by, in the long months, in the repeating seasons, something enigmatic seemed to color everything around her.

A favorite phrase among her women was that such and such was a "sign", as in, "crows gathering in the field are a sign of an impending death ..." She had always staved off their unease with confidence. Doing so was easy; they were childlike in their steadfast superstitions.

Now she found herself swept with similar anxieties. Theirs could be easily dismissed; hers seemed inscrutable.

As she imagined portents that she knew might be imaginary — omens that might have no more substance than afternoon shadows — Anneth stepped beside her. After the two passed a moment in silence, the girl kissed her shoulder, taking her hand and said, "I've closed the temple doors."

"No, they should be open."

"Not today. There's a storm. No one will appear. I can moderate your apprehensions. My Lady, come. We'll dally in my room."

CHAPTER 21

As flies to wanton boys are we to th' gods,
They kill us for their sport.
— Shakespeare, *King Lear*

They untied the man and removed his hood. The heavy rain
continued, whipping through the stony pass on the mountainside where the barbarians had been ambushed a day before. Adalwolf found himself in brush surrounded by three women on
horseback.

Tasenka pushed the point of her javelin against his chest, piercing
the wet leather garment and breaking his skin. He stepped back,
muffling a cry.

"Your way is behind you," she said. "East, where the sun rises.
The goddess was indulgent. I am not. Run while you can —"

He knew not to speak. Without a horse his trip would take more
than a half day. The rain would slow him down.

He looked at the women. Their faces were unreadable. He
shrugged and began walking east. A hundred paces into the under-

brush he stopped and looked back. The women had not moved. One of their horses whinnied and stamped its feet impatiently.

The man continued at a faster pace. Perhaps the storm would abate. He was young and fit and thankful to have survived. Now he would have time to craft his story. And those who were his fellow followers would be incredulous when they learned he'd seen Inanna, that he'd spoken to the goddess and that she'd spared his life.

By evening he was on the back slope of the high terrain, bush-whacking his way downhill toward lights from fires in scattered homes on the distant lowlands. To his knowledge he had not been followed. And he had memorized a good story: his war party had been surprised by dozens of Inanna's warriors. Before his compa-triots could react, the women were throwing spears.

The attack had lasted seconds. Horses and men went down. During the assault a spear had hit his chest — *Look! See the wound?* — but his cloak had somehow deflected the point. He was left with the others as dead. Later he awoke on his back, his head throbbing. Finding no one alive around him, he had crawled in the rain, then run from the scene when he was out of sight.

Hours later he walked into the dirt yard near the house he shared, and stood silently beside the stables and outbuildings. A light flickered in the barn and a young woman stepped out, looking into the darkness. "Who's here?"

He stepped forward, whispering. "Boda, it's me."

She held the lantern high, gazing at him. "The Wolf. We thought you dead." He looked side to side. "I was captured. I saw her— Inanna! She's radiant, more resplendent than we believed!"

"Is it true?"

"Yes." Even in the dark he could see her eyes fill with tears.

He slept till dawn and was shaken awake. The older man standing over the bed ordered him into the common room. As Wolf stumbled in, the first question was, "How many others lived?"

"None. Not that I saw." He explained that the cadre of men had been ambushed — "dozens of the witch's warriors stepped out from behind trees."

He went on, describing the spears that flew through the air, noting that the attack probably ended in seconds — and that he awoke on the ground that night, his head on fire. His chest ached— "Look! See the wound?" — but he'd lived.

He'd found no one else alive. Although he had no weapon, he'd looked for enemy warriors, hoping for revenge. Yet the woods had been silent. He'd returned as quickly as possible, not stopping as he navigated his way through the rain.

His interlocutors listened, sighing or exclaiming at his words. There was surprisingly little pushback: no matter how elaborate their plans, Inanna's warriors always prevailed. It was as if she had a sixth sense of when their probes would occur and precisely how to counter them.

Their country encompassed a vast territory, and — although their losses from these clashes totaled in the thousands — they had new men to draw upon. One of those in attendance reminded the others that their growing numbers made the valleys to the west more attractive than ever.

They couldn't forget: famine was a constant threat. The soil in the valleys was more productive. And yes, eventually the tide would turn their way. The witch remained their one impediment.

The conversation went back and forth, but terminated quickly. Adalwolf was told to resume his work. His report echoed what they'd heard from others after other forays. There was nothing new.

When he was alone, he bowed his head and gave silent thanks to the goddess. Without her reprieve he'd be lying dead like his companions, carrion for vultures and — he smiled to himself — wolves.

As he stood to go outside, Boda appeared. Assuring herself they were alone, she said, "Now tell me how this miracle occurred. Of us all, Wolf, you alone have seen her with your eyes."

He squinted at her, saying, "Not here. The gate in the back pasture needs repair. I could use a hand."

The storm lasted two days. The river ran high and many of the lower fields were flooded. The path to the temple was almost impassable. As Anneth had predicted, no one came the first day.

On the second several girls braved the rain, coming with bunches of dried barley which they left as offerings beside the meteorite. The usual daily sacrifices were delayed. When the sun finally appeared, Inanna stood by the altar, her head thrown back and her arms up. No one saw her. Anneth slept.

The goddess held her position for minutes. Then she watched a hawk circling overhead. Its movements appeared effortless. When she lowered her arms, she felt elation: she had resolved her quandary.

Her plan was audacious. No matter. Audacity had always worked for her. Her recent waffling, her angst — the oscillations — had to end.

Oscillation? A word close to vacillation. *Vacil-, oscil-, oscillate, oscilla-tion, oscillations* — the word-sounds reverberated strangely, resonating no differently than when she looked into Anneth's eyes and saw the eyes of another woman.

Echoes, evocations. These ghost eyes were eyes she knew intimately but could not place. *Eyes, eyries, oscillations, evocations ...*

She shrugged it off. Incongruities had nothing to do with her epiphany. Now she would act. Her realization, like the best insights, was simple. And pleasantly dramatic.

She closed her eyes a moment, concentrated and felt a presence. When she looked, a woman stood beside her, her eyes sparkling. They were the same height, with the same long hair cut to their shoulders. Each wore an identical red cloak. The woman said evenly, "I return."

The goddess smiled. "Indeed. But no longer a crone. An identical Inanna."

At the same moment Anneth stepped from the temple, startled to see goddess standing beside a woman who appeared to be her double. Their backs were to her, and she cried out, "My Lady!"

Both women turned, their faces identical. Then she knew: one of them must be an eidolon. She panicked, unable to tell a difference between them. The woman on the right, raising her arm in a warm gesture, said, "Anneth, come down now."

The girl remained amazed. It was not an old woman beside the goddess, the specter who had appeared months before, but a beautiful woman indistinguishable from the goddess. Looking between them, Anneth felt lightheaded.

Then she saw movement on the path: Agnes, Aneka and Hebe approaching, carrying a basket. They stopped, clearly startled, when they saw the two women. The one on Anneth's right said to the girls, "Today there are two of us. You will welcome my sister, who visits at my invitation."

As if they had rehearsed, the three set the basket down, opened their palms and bowed. The goddess continued, "Now approach."

When they stood before the altar, Aneka said, marveling, "She looks just like you."

"Yes, we are twins in divinity."

Hebe frowned and asked quietly, "May I speak?"

Inanna nodded. Hebe turned to the second woman, saying quietly, "What's *your* name?"

Inanna's double glanced at Inanna, as if seeking permission, then turned to the girl. "I am Eidola."

Agnes whispered, "We come to make the morning sacrifice." The sound of birds moving and chattering in the wicker basket was constant.

The goddess nodded. "Proceed —"

She and Eidola stepped to either end of the long altar. Anneth, who oversaw the daily ritual, stepped to the center and lifted her hands, gesturing for the girls to start.

Two of them lifted the basket to the slab and opened the woven top. Hebe began placing the birds — all heavily mottled doves — on an oak board atop the slab. The bird's legs and wings were tied.

The birds rocked awkwardly on their sides, trying to free themselves, cheeping in protest. Hebe took the long obsidian blade that lay parallel to the edge of the slab and raised it high.

As she held it toward the sun, the other two cried out, "Messengers and auguries, these birds we offer daily —" Hebe completed the chant, singing, "— are gifts to … Our Lady!"

As she exclaimed '—*Lady*!' Hebe brought the long knife down, ecstatically, mechanically, cutting off their heads. She chopped twelve times, then rested, inhaling sharply.

Agnes and Aneka brushed the heads off the slab. Anneth extended her hands, holding a wide silver bowl.

The three girls held the birds upside down, draining blood into the bowl. When finished, the bodies were removed, and they bowed low, saying as one, "To the glory of Our Lady!"

Before they turned to leave, Hebe whispered shyly, "And *welcome*, Eidola —"

The eidolon smiled in response. The girls left. As they turned a bend in the path and vanished from sight, the goddess turned to Anneth and Eidola.

"I've had an epiphany."

Anneth replied slowly, "It has to do with why has Eidola returned?"

The goddess nodded. "Yes. One might say that."

CHAPTER 22

Goddesses and snake prevail
in ravines where locusts drone
where barberry tears her gown
where, one by one, the girls unveil

Timessa was awakened by Io midmorning. She rarely slept so late. The girl sat on the edge of their bed, stroking Timessa's arm.

She sat up, gazing at Io. "You spent time tying all those ribbons."

"My hair? For you." She shook her head for emphasis. Blue and gold ribbons cascaded to her shoulders.

"I was dreaming, I suppose. I remember far more than usual."

"Good dreams?"

"Eurṓpē."

"The dual Timessas."

"Yes, dreaming of *here* and there, now and then."

"When you're there, does it seem far, far away?"

"It seems," she said, "real. Almost as if it's not a dream."

"What happened last night?" Io asked.

"Same characters. Women against men. War. It was daytime …
three girls who repeatedly appear sacrificed a dozen birds."

"To what god?"

"Inanna. There, there are no other gods. Or goddesses."

Io half-smiled. "A few months ago you could remember almost
nothing."

"Now I remember more."

"But not everything."

"No, not everything. But there's something peculiar." Io waited.
Timessa continued, "Remember I've speculated about whether, while
I'm in Eurōpē, I'm some specter that Gaia whipped up?"

"Gaia's eidolon."

"Yes, that's it. Am I an eidolon she made to wander around in
ancient Europe, looking for *me*?"

"But your point?"

Timessa paused. "I remember enough from last night … enough
to know that there, as Inanna, I created a lookalike of Inanna. It
wasn't Gaia's doing. In the dream it felt ingenious, a brilliant move."

"Too confusing."

"Imagine, Io. There's me, here. Then Gaia creates a specter of
me, sending it back in time. Or I think she has. And the specter in
turn creates a specter of itself."

"Dominoes."

"No, closer to a hall of mirrors. But the eidolon there, the one I
created, is definitely a conscious thing. It seems to reflect Inanna to
perfection."

Io said, "Strange dreams, my love."

"Or not dreams."

"I hope you always return from wherever this is." Io smiled.

"I seem anchored to Naxos." Timessa took Io's hand. "What was
your phrase a moment ago? 'Dual Timessas.' "

"Better two-headed than three."

"Ouch. You mean like Hades's dog? Cerberus was three-headed.
An unfriendly bundle of teeth and growls."

Io looked out at the Mediterranean. She said, "We have to
presume that this will all lead somewhere, don't we?"

"What gives me hope is that it's not random. There's an agenda.

Me, Inanna, Inanna's Inanna — each of us is moving toward something."

"But still, you're Gaia's *tools*."

"Tools?"

"Finger puppets. Like it's all a game."

"No, I don't think a game. Perhaps a play. She set the stage. But I'm caught … there are no backdoors, or trapdoors. No way out. Or off. Worse, there's a theme, but no script."

"Then that makes me the audience."

Timessa laughed. "You may be the protagonist for all I know."

"What if," Io said, "that's not it at all?"

"If you have answers, you know more than I."

"I dreamed last night as well," Io said. "I remember I stood before a huge black snake. It was coiled atop some sort of altar."

Startled, Timessa looked at her. "There *are* such snakes in Eurṓpē, but not here."

Io said, "As I watched it, there was a golden flash, like one of Gaia's tricks. Then it was gone."

Timessa stared at her a moment, then got out of bed.

She remembered the carving of a python which hung above a temple there. And she could visualize a black snake woven into the robe worn by a girl … Worn, she knew, by Anneth, who looked remarkably like Io.

In a back area in the temple, the three sat in silence, looking at each other and saying little. Eidola looked like the perfect personification of Inanna. She remained expressionless, waiting. Anneth fidgeted, sensing a changed dynamic.

"Anneth," Inanna finally said, "have we made progress with the nomads?"

"Progress?"

"You are my priestess and you lead our warriors. Do you not have your fingers on all things? I am requesting a report on our state of engagement."

Anneth went blank. "But you know what I know."

"Your perspective differs. I seek *Anneth's* insights."

"Certainly, My Lady." The girl paused. "There have been reports of more intrusions, all southeast of the site of our last ambush. These probes are early-season and unusual. But each was repelled … I've ordered two forward outposts to be added. Also, twenty-four warriors have supplemented the eastern flank …"

"What else?"

"We have had no deaths in nine months, and no injuries in the last sixty-four days. Horses and weapons are in superb condition —"

The goddess cut her off, saying, "I asked about progress."

"In what way, My Lady?"

"In the way that might decrease or end the encounters."

The girl looked away. "Was I was tasked with such an assignment.?"

"You weren't," the goddess said. "I was hoping for initiative."

"How could I do such a thing? If we are surprised, we're killed."

Eidola interjected, asking Io, "There is no dialogue?"

Anneth looked at her, then turned to Inanna. "Am I to respond to … Eidola?"

"Treat her," the goddess said, "as you do me."

Anneth nodded slowly, then said to the eidolon, "Talk with these men is impossible."

For a moment Anneth thought the eidolon's skin had become translucent, then the impression passed. The goddess watched the interaction, and Anneth felt she had to continue.

"Once, generations ago," she intoned, "we were invaded by a large force. We sent three women out on horseback to intercede. They were ambassadors, the finest of us in word and deed —"

Eidola cut her off, saying, "I know these stories."

"Then you know," Anneth said angrily, "there's been no 'dialogue' since that day years ago."

"None?" Eidola said.

The girl shook her head. Silence prevailed. After moments Inanna stood, looking at them both, then said to Anneth. "Each of us here, through my skill, cannot be harmed. As you know, I see all that occurs, I anticipate what will come … The two of you, while under my protection, are like immortals. Their javelins, their hatred, can do us no harm."

"My Lady —?"

"I say these things because we can never die like those ambassadors from the past. I could have inoculated them as well, but I was naïve. I take all blame. They died because of me."

Anneth looked down as the eidolon watched impassively. The goddess continued, "That was then, generations ago. Yet shamefully, today, we know no more about these men than we did then —"

"We could assemble a force," Anneth said, "and take the initiative. As it is, we're always second-guessing, defending ourselves."

"No," the goddess said. "*No!* We're unsurpassed as what we are — resistance fighters. But they outnumber us a hundred to one. Face to face, we would be no match. We'd be crushed in any direct assault."

"Then we have no choice," Anneth said loudly. "We change nothing that we do!"

Inanna waited a moment, then said, "And go on like this forever? Do the deaths mean nothing? Are our bravest warriors no more valued than the man we kill on Offering Night?"

"Goddess, I can't see where you're going with this —"

"Listen carefully. *There are believers scattered among them.* Adherents of mine. What if we tripled the numbers of these followers? Or better than that? What if we turned half the nomads into devotees?"

"Devotees?" Anneth said incredulously. "The barbarians?"

"The prisoner we released was a follower. He said there were others —"

"He said five or six," the girl stammered.

"No, he corrected himself and said hundreds. Anneth, think: we could walk among these men. Those who wished to fight, we could ignore. Or crush. We could have —" The goddess turned to Eidola. "— a 'dialogue.' Perhaps, slowly, more would believe. Perhaps their will to fight would recede … No one looks forward to dying, even the bravest men. This represents an alternative."

The girl said, "May I speak?"

"Of course."

"They want one thing: our land and women. Yes, a number of

them might convert. Of course. But most are hungry. They want food and a woman for every man. They'll die to get these things. They've shown they'll kill all who resist."

"What if they're given no choice?" Inanna said. "Convert, consent or die."

"My Lady, a moment ago you decried death. Now you threaten to take lives."

Eidola spoke suddenly. "I could go there a second time. As you, Goddess. As I look today."

"And your purpose?" Inanna said.

"To execute your mission. I am invulnerable. You have made me so. If I succeed, we win. If I fail?" She shrugged. "I return and life goes on —"

The goddess sighed. "Yes and no. Almost but …" She paced a moment, then said, "No, the three of us will go."

Anneth said, "We ride as ourselves into the foreign land?"

CHAPTER 23

There were only hours
before they would lay without a sound
mighty walls to fall soon enough
scent of myrrh amid dust, the whirl
winds of time that scatter limbs

The apparition paused, then turned to her twin. "You should go as your snake-self."

The goddess said, "A savage thing to the savage lands?"

"A fabulous creature to intimidate."

"Our spears are tipped in poison," The goddess said. "Snake venom. And what do we call the compound?"

Anneth made a face. " '*Snake*.' We rub the tips in snake."

"It's unforgiving," the goddess said. "My intent is to encourage dialogue, not to intimidate."

Anneth half-smiled. "The toxin brings instant death. But you say that snakes *protect* life as well."

"There cannot be one without the other."

Eidola whispered, "Death and life. It's all so portentous."

The goddess said, "Don't get caught up in that. Life and death are one of many opposites. You, my sister, are neither one nor the other."

The apparition murmured, "So something in-between."

"What you are is irrelevant. You are no more than what I wish."

The eidolon looked away.

The goddess concluded, "The nomads almost always meet an untimely death. If we venture there, we'll offer longer life."

Anneth paused, then asked, "How do we even enter their territory? Isn't it guarded?"

"We ride in. As Eidola did before. Unarmed. Quietly, like any traveler might travel from town to town."

"But we're women. Women *there* go nowhere unaccompanied."

"I go where I wish. As I wish. We'll do the same."

The girl said, "We'll need the lay of the land. Beyond the pass, none of us knows anything."

Eidola said with irritation, "Except for me."

Anneth looked at her. "Of course. But you barely crossed the border."

The goddess said, "Enough! Yes, we'll have to be veiled. Imagine if we weren't. Then again, imagine if we rode in veil-less, topless, only in our boots."

The eidolon smiled. "Topless?"

The goddess continued, "You and Anneth looking like every man's dream. Outrageous, audacious, while I arrive as the Great Snake."

Anneth said, "We're treating this as something funny. I think it's terrifying."

"But Anneth, you'll be invulnerable as long as we're together. Besides, I envision immense success. Conversions, miracles, a breakout of peace."

"Just like that?"

"Probably not. But we have time. And patience. Perhaps we'll do multiple visits."

Eidola said, "Weather next week will be pleasant enough."

"Yes," the goddess said. "It all feels fortuitous."

She didn't act immediately. For all her bravado she was uneasy, which was itself unusual. Her anxiety, as vague as it was, seemed to point toward something inauspicious — which she found unnerving. She was used to knowing the outcome of events before they occurred. *Gaia*, she thought, *is orchestrating this, picking and choosing my faculties.*

Two days after her meeting in the temple with Anneth and the eidolon, the goddess bathed in the river, stepping down the river's center through the riffles as she dried herself, reveling in the texture of the polished stones below her feet.

The sun was high and cast short black shadows around the maples and willows that lined the bank. As she stepped out of the water, pulling on a gown, she heard hoofbeats and saw three women approaching at speed on horseback.

Nastka led the riders and leapt off as she slowed her horse. The other two dismounted behind her. Seeing the goddess walking toward them, the three bowed quickly.

The goddess stopped several paces away. "Welcome, Nastka. Explain yourself."

Her eyes tearing, the woman said, "Thank you for seeing us like this."

"You bring news."

"One of our scouting parties on the southeast slope near the upper pass —" She brought her hands to her face, covering her eyes. The goddess waited quietly, aware that this report was likely to confirm her apprehensions. Nastka went on, "This morning. Almost all were killed. A trap —"

"How many dead?"

"Eighteen."

"Led by —?"

"Tasenka." She choked. "I had been assigned the duty, but she stepped in as I prepared my horse, saying the day would be beautiful, that she needed a ride."

The goddess turned away, blankly watching the river as it danced and sparkled through its slow meanders. She had not lost a warrior in almost a year. Almost a generation had passed since more than a handful of women had died at any one time, and in that single instance, they had faced men on an open plain.

She turned back to Nastka. "You say they were trapped. Do you know the details?"

"Yes, Goddess. the party was its usual size."

"Twenty riders."

"Thirty minutes out, Tasenka led them through Goat Pass —"

"Where the rocks narrow?"

"The slot." Nastka nodded. "We've never encountered anyone there. Never. It's just where we ride to get from one place to another."

"Go on."

"Tasenka was in the lead. She took the first spear. In the neck. Then there was chaos. Men sprang out from the rocks above them. Two of the women in the back got away, and even then, they were wounded."

"How do we know there weren't more survivors?"

"We returned an hour later with a larger force."

"And —?"

The woman shook her head, struggling to speak. "Must I, Goddess?"

"You must."

"The pass was strewn with corpses. The dead had been beheaded. Tasenka had been quartered. Her parts were hung from a tree ..."

"An ambush. Our specialty," the goddess said, "turned on ourselves."

"Yes, a first."

"And the condition of the two who got away?"

"One is likely to die, the other may recover."

"Bring them here. I'll see that both live to ride again."

Nastka rubbed her eyes. "I apologize ... I just came from the scene."

"And this happened when?"

"Two hours after dawn."

She looked overhead, saying, " The barbarian raiding party has had time to return?"

"Yes. They would have expected us to hunt them down …"

"Do we have any idea why they attacked?"

"My opinion?"

"Your experienced opinion."

"Revenge for their last defeat." She said angrily, "A stupid move on their part. Now we must reciprocate!"

"No," the goddess said. "This has got to stop. Eighteen dead is eighteen too many."

Nastka looked down, shuffling her feet. "Then your orders, Goddess?"

"Bring the wounded to me, find any loose horses that were left, clear the pass of *any* evidence this ever occurred …

"Pick up every spear, every fallen cloak, every personal item. Then tomorrow, bring every woman here who rides a stallion in my name —"

Nastka nodded. "I'll issue orders immediately."

"There's more: bring the remains of the dead. Have a pyre built this afternoon before the altar. We will celebrate these warriors at tomorrow's dawn, in the old way."

The three women made obeisance, mounted and left. Anneth had watched quietly from the temple. In the silence she said, "I should shed my sacred robe and pick up a spear."

The goddess turned and looked at the girl. "No. I blame myself. I wasn't aware it was about to happen. I knew nothing until Nastka reported the attack."

The goddess was awake the next morning at four. She began an intricate purification ritual. Anneth attended her, holding lustral branches, pouring oil and lighting incense. Neither spoke to the other. Many of the incantations the goddess chanted were ones the girl had never heard.

Warriors began arriving at the temple hours before dawn. A massive pyre had been built before the altar, one which rose as high as the temple roof. Horses were corralled in a side field.

By sunrise hundreds of women had assembled and waited

shoulder to shoulder. Lamentations rose and fell in murmurs, in broken voices. Idyllically — and at variance with the solemn occasion — the eastern horizon turned increasingly from black to salmon to pink. Birds sang along the river, oblivious to the somberness of the warriors.

As the sun broke the skyline, the goddess stepped from the temple. She was followed by Anneth and six of the youngest temple attendants. In a white gown, the goddess stood on the upper front step, looking over the assembly, then walked slowly to the altar and mounted a low platform. The gathering grew quiet, and in the silence she spoke loudly, rhythmically, her voice carrying over the field.

"I need not explain why we convene at dawn today! In this land we celebrate admirable behavior. We applaud merit, and we honor those who defend and preserve our freedom. Here, no one dictates our behavior …

"No one decrees a woman's duties or prescribes where we go, what we must say and what we wear. Like the birds in this sacred grove, we make our own way, unencumbered by restrictions …

"As a united people our memories go back into hallowed time. Before any of you were born, before your mothers and grandmothers were born, all who lived in these valleys and plains lived in peace. War and conflict were only rumors of strange events in foreign lands. Violent deaths were rarities …

"But that changed. We abhorred the change. Decades ago we came under attack. In our struggle to defend ourselves, we learned the way of warriors. We became armed guardians of these verdant lands …

"In our need we assumed nobility. We were never the aggressor. Our actions have never encouraged or precipitated assaults …

"Instead, we have insisted that our lives go on in their simplicity. We have asked only that we be left to ourselves …

"But the invaders chose otherwise. They crossed our borders and set fire to our fields. Thus, we have learned to fight and ride swift horses and craft sharp spears. We resisted every attack …

"In that we can be proud. Because of our fierceness we became feared by all. Today those who dare to enter these lands know that they do so at great risk …

"By fighting for our freedom we have humiliated generations of invaders, men who want our lands, want us as women and want our wealth …

"They find our success insufferable. Why? Men do not tolerate humiliation, particularly when it is women who bring them shame. Consequently, the clashes we endure are increasingly about man against woman …

"It is a vile thing. And contemptible …

"Yesterday we lost eighteen of our finest warriors. No one here is unaware of this tragedy. They were on a routine patrol. Each of the riders had ridden the same trail hundreds of times …

"Then they were ambushed. Two escaped, but nine times more were lost. Their bodies were defiled. The attack was an act of reck-lessness …

"But I tell you today that their deaths were not *pointless*. They died like their mothers, their grandmothers and all of those before them so that you could live today …

"We honor them now in the old way. In moments their spirits will fly like eagles on the fiery smoke — their ashes shall fall on our sacred fields —

"And their exploits shall be celebrated by the sun, which watched from overhead as a witness to their extreme bravery …

"Their lives shall be sung by their children. We crown them without exception. We counted on their courage, and they held the course …

"All will be remembered by each of us —"

The goddess paused, raised her hand and Anneth struck a gong.

A line of women split the crowd, carrying the remains of the warriors on dark tarps, marching to the pyre. As the bodies were stacked on the tinder, a long moan arose from the crowd. Anneth struck the gong at intervals, and the moan from the hundreds of women became a tumultuous cry.

After minutes the goddess raised her arms, crying out, "*Aiii!*" and each of the temple attendants threw a firebrand onto the heaped branches. In seconds the heat was so intense that the assembly fell back, covering their faces, squinting against the flames.

The smoke, roiling in a chaotic surge, wheeled against the goddess's face. Yet she stood impassively, watching the conflagration, lowering her arms, allowing the heat and crimson flames to wash across her face.

She cried out over the crackling fire, "When each of you has mourned these women in your own way, you may leave —"

Then she turned, finding Anneth and took her hand, pulling her close.

In a third of an hour the pyre was reduced to coals, smoke and glowing embers. No one left until the goddess raised her voice again, crying out, "It is done! Mount your horses! Return to your homes! A new day has begun —"

The sun was now above the oaks. Almost reluctantly, the women scattered, finding their horses, exchanging embraces in the sharp morning light. After all had ridden off the goddess hugged each of the temple attendants, telling them how brave they were and that they should return to their duties.

Anneth's eyes shone, and the goddess said, "Your eyes are on fire."

"Goddess —?"

"Fierce and proud. Your loyalty is beyond reproach."

The girl said, "It is not only loyalty, My Lady. It has become far more."

CHAPTER 24

She joined with the raving ones
those in frenzy,
those who were god-intoxicated.

E idola had removed her gown and was bathing in the river
beside the temple. Two of the younger girls watched the
surrounding woods, and the goddess herself, half-dressed, walked
beside the apparition in the midday sun.

"You cannot allow the outrage to go unanswered," the eidolon
said.

"Are you qualified to discuss this?"

"You made me so," she frowned.

"I and I," the goddess said. As she uttered *I and I*, she recalled
oscillations, defining it to herself as a see-sawing of time.

She thought: *The oddity of words. Mere words are now functioning as
gongs.*

After a few moments of silence, the eidolon said, "Your comrades
have fallen — and we have not responded."

"We shall."

"Do you want my opinion?"

"Your opinion," the goddess said, "can only be my opinion. Your thoughts are mine."

"Of course. I am but your double."

"Analyze, if you must. I may ignore anything you say."

Eidola laughed. "Any word I utter is your own. My words are yours ... Better that I not speak."

They walked together for a minute, then the eidolon turned to her, saying, "You have no one you can talk to, do you? No one who really understands."

"Are you suggesting that we be confidants? I would be speaking into a mirror."

"As you wish."

The goddess stopped and took Eidola's arm. "That's enough. You cannot play the role of my conscience. You are only what I have created."

"Perhaps," the eidolon said, shaking free, "you are quite unclear about who you are."

The goddess pulled her gown up, and left the river. As she stepped onto the bank, she turned and said, "You are here at my discretion. I can as easily make you disappear."

Eidola spread her arms out as if to say 'whatever,' and laughed. As they locked eyes, the eidolon half-turned away — sunlight bathing her hips and long thighs, washing her breasts — leaving the goddess by herself.

Where is Anneth? the goddess thought. She always knew. Now she did not.

Her ability to control events seemed to be drifting from her reach. She had lost eighteen warriors and had had no premonitions. And the eidolon was right — no response was cowardice.

She glanced down the river: Eidola had vanished, which on its face was impossible. The goddess stepped into the water, looking in both directions. Two of the younger temple attendants remained in the area; otherwise, she was alone.

She smiled — these small things that distressed her were trivial. The sacred grove, here where she stood, could easily be the center of the earth itself. *Omphalos.*

Turning to the girls, she waved her arm in a vague gesture, saying, "We're through here. Back to the temple —"

Stars that evening were bright in an unexpectedly crisp sky. The goddess and the eidolon stood beside the blackened altar. In the dim light it seemed to be a sidelong monolith, a mirror of the leaden sky except that it lacked the glitter of the cosmos.

Running her hand over its surface, the eidolon said, "I should go back to the nomads. Probe further. We know too little to act."

"You will draw attention and be a distraction."

"No," she said. "I won't return as the old one."

"Oh?" the goddess said. "Will you go as a donkey?"

"It's good to see your humor return."

"Not humor, irritation," she said.

"Is that what it is?"

The goddess said nothing. Cutting through the quiet the eidolon said, "All people have leaders. Theirs is nameless. We must assume it's a man. But whom? None of us knows … And this chief, as I'll call him, either lives near our border, or faraway. We don't know. But we need to reach him. We need to know who to approach —"

The goddess said, "No, no 'approach.' My strategy will not be that. Diplomacy failed long ago. I have a simpler way: I will convert them all."

"To what?"

"Followers."

"Convert the barbarians? They probably worship dogs."

The eidolon looked overhead. A meteor shot lazily across the sky, drawing a soundless arc through the constellations. She grimaced, saying, "Then you won't send me as your ambassador."

"As I have said, you and I and Anneth will go together. We'll appear, and … things will happen. We'll react. And things will change. Perhaps I can turn their bloodlust into something else."

"Of course. The nomads won't believe their luck."

The goddess shook her head. "A mystery remains. Perhaps you have already guessed, given that you know so much."

"You mean, we go there, we get farther than I got the first time, and what happens then is —"

"That's it," the goddess said. "What happens is a total mystery."

"The gall of it."

"The annoyance is that until recently I never had to wonder: I always knew what would be."

"You had foresight."

"I had power. There were never surprises."

"That's gone?"

"The ambush," the goddess said. "I never anticipated it. Before that ... *incident* ... I thwarted every probe because I knew the details even before the raiders began ...

"No attack surprised us," she went on. "My war parties destroyed them before they rode into our lands."

The eidolon shrugged. "And then a dozen and a half warriors go down."

"If I were capable of anger, I'd be infuriated. Instead, I'm mystified."

The eidolon raised her arms toward the dark sky, crying out in obvious caricature of the funeral oration, "You constellations, you stars! Like the sun you watch all things. You have never withheld what you know or what you see —

"You are harbingers, forerunners who have whispered in our ear. Withdrawing from your ancient ways violates my laws! I want to know what's up! I call on you to re-engage!"

The goddess allowed silence to grow between them. The eidolon was taunting her. *Perhaps*, she thought, *I deserve the mockery. 'You constellations, you stars!'* Really!

The eidolon said, "We should walk through fire when we go east. Seeing that flames do not affect us, the men will fall back and cower at the sight."

"Making men cower is easy enough. But I want their hearts."

"Respect," the eidolon said, "is earned."

"Or not. But I won't debate. The three of us leave within the day."

❧

Anneth began preparations. Each of them would require a stallion chosen from the finest in their stock and provisions for a week. They would venture east without weapons.

There was nothing to be gained by being armed. The three would be invulnerable in any case, and the goddess had no intention of fighting back. Seeing that the women were unassailable might turn an assault into a conversation, as well as empower her followers, however covertly.

Their mission could not be diplomatic; the goddess was no longer naïve. Once, three of her envoys had been killed. No more would be sacrificed. Not again.

Although she had lost the ability to predict the precise events that would unfold, she knew mayhem was predictable. Her faux-sister, the eidolon, had suggested they walk through fire. Perhaps so.

She took some pleasure in anticipating a confrontation, but cautioned herself; revenge for the earlier assault, however arrogant the attackers, would blind her to a greater purpose. She must remain above reprisals. *Her sole purpose*, she thought, *was to turn their hearts*.

Preparations took the better part of the day. Nastka brought horses. She arrived with Hebe, who had been appointed by the others to argue against the undertaking itself. Their reasoning was uncomplicated: risks were extraordinary, no matter the goddess's confidence.

What if Anneth were somehow harmed? What if the goddess had miscalculated in some way? Besides, given the recent loss, they had made adjustments to strategy: an ambush would never again occur.

The goddess listened quietly, then dismissed Hebe with a kiss on her cheek. None of their concerns were valid. Divinities were more powerful than she knew. The three would be susceptible to nothing. The trinity, as she called it, would be at no risk. They needed no guards. In short, the mission would proceed.

Hebe stammered, "Then may I go? My horse is swift. And there is strength in numbers —"

"If that were so," the goddess whispered, "I'd bring you and all of my beautiful warriors. But we will not succeed if we arrive as an army …

"This business must be direct, personal and without bloodshed. No snake-tipped spears. I may return empty-handed. But before we leave them, they will know more of me and know that they can never triumph here—"

"Goddess, our recent loss was a once-in-a-generation thing. We will not allow it again. Our hearts break to see you put yourself at risk."

"We must, Hebe, end the slaughter. And the sorrow. Half of the eighteen women had children. Tasenka had a fine daughter who is just learning to ride. Agnes had two, both pubescent …

"They, like their mothers, will learn to sharpen spears. Is that what we wish for our children —?"

Hebe bowed, saying quietly, "We will escort you to the border."

CHAPTER 25

Sea foam, broken shells and ancient pottery were scattered across the sand. Timessa watched the waves form patterns, an embroidery, a brocade, rising and disintegrating in an orderly *oscillation*. The word still dazzled her, although she couldn't explain its allure.

Perhaps *oscillation* deftly defined the engine of an indomitable sea, one that was enduring and perpetual. It was Gaia's term. Was it word play or another instance of divine machination?

In the last week other, stranger words had begun to randomly appear in her mind: *Nastka, Tasenka, Adalwolf* … Were they names, or primeval lyrics, or passwords that might, if whispered, allow entry into Gaia's walled gardens? She shrugged. More mysteries.

Behind her the white promontory was green with plants, and flowering grasses, their stamens erect and proud. The grass reminded her of the hyacinth she had planted in long cedar boxes along the marble edge of the patio. The flower's purple-bluish color — and its fragrance — would be pleasant on warm afternoons.

That morning as she lay with Io — the girl's hair scented with a citrus wash — Io had said mysteriously, "Remove my veil."

She had replied, "Veil? You're not even in a gown."

"It's a way of speaking. I want you to always see the real me, not an imaginary Io —"

Unveil me, she thought. *Some wish to be hidden while others want transparency.*

The nymphs had a similar wish: *we want no secrets —*

Perhaps that was what *she* wanted from Gaia. To be rid of the mysteries. To obliterate the secrets, the veils that hung between them — as well as those between her and Io, between here and *there*.

Yes, she had continued to have glimpses into that ancient past. Yet Gaia had erected a barrier that she, Timessa, was expected to bring down. But she was yet to find a toehold, a bridge or even shallows that would allow her to cross from one side to another.

If she sat quietly she could imagine — she could *see* — her doppelgänger, Inanna. But the view remained unclear … and the portal between the two time periods steadily opened and closed like a heart's valve … or like the beating wings of a hawk.

Certainly she now knew much more. She knew the presumed era, her ancient name and that the place was Európē. The portal, the swinging gate, was an opening, but was it to be taken by force?

Portals were feminine by nature. They were doorways, thresholds to revelation, passages from place to place. They were *entirely* female.

Was that, too, a sign?

Remove my veil, Io had pleaded. Timessa had done so, turning the girl on her back. At the end, sighing, after endless loving words, Io had said, "Yes, yes. You alone see me …"

She thought unveiling Io was a simple thing. She was not at all the maze that Gaia had erected for Timessa. There were no brambles to beat back, no high barriers. The girl was easy, effortlessly uncovered. *Európē*, on the other hand, remained obscure.

Nastka, Tasenka … What were these words? Definitely feminine. When she had pinned Io to the sheets, dismayingly she thought, *Anneth*, a girl there, in Európē, whom she now recognized must have died millennia ago.

Or was Európē Gaia's invention? Then Anneth would be as well. Gaia, she who reveled in chaos and entropy. Gaia whose mischief seemed, ultimately, an unadulterated wisdom. Gaia who had set a trap as variable as Nature itself …

Timessa was aware that even as she made love to Io at dawn, she felt an uneasiness. Some *thing* was about to occur.

Gaia would know what it was, but Gaia had not appeared in weeks.

❧

Morning.

Eurṓpē.

The goddess had not slept. Anneth lay restlessly beside her, dreaming, having to be waken, having to be stroked to sleep again.

Shortly before dawn, she heard horses snorting, leather side packs being strapped on, gear being checked. She rose quietly and dressed. As she stepped from her room, the eidolon rose from a chair in the anteroom, saying, "Neither of us slept."

"Do you ever?"

"As much as you."

"It's not important, is it?"

"Sleep?" the eidolon asked. "There are nights when I'm exhausted."

The goddess looked her up and down. Anneth stepped from the room and the goddess said, "Let's go outside and check the preparations."

The three left the temple wearing thin leather cloaks over their field garments. The clothing was heavy enough to conceal their breasts, but they made no attempt to disguise their long hair. The back of the goddess's cloak was stitched with a large, spiraled snake. The air was thin and the predawn sky still crackled with stars. A half dozen women worked at the horses, and briskly bowed when they saw the three.

The goddess called, "Are we on time?"

One of the women smiled and raised a fist. Horse hooves were being checked, manes were brushed and claret-red ribbons were being woven into their tails.

"Ready, My Lady, when you are!"

"Then we'll leave soon. My thanks to you all —"

She returned to the temple's central room. The meteorite was shadowed and seemed aglow. She knelt, whispering, "The future was once clear, and is now unfathomable. But we will return."

When she stood she noticed the eidolon, who watched from the temple doors. The specter said, "It is said that those who speak to stones are not at risk."

"Why is that, my sister?"

"No stone," the eidolon said, "speaks when commanded to share secrets."

"Indeed," the goddess said. "I've found them to be, above all other things, trustworthy."

The eidolon shook her head. "We should leave."

"In minutes."

"Will we succeed?"

The goddess stared at her. "Will the sun rise today?"

"You are all bluster. We both know you can no longer see ahead."

"Does it matter what I see?"

"Do eidolons survive a hundred spears?"

"Am I immortal?"

The apparition winced. "No one questions your immortality."

"You are my twin. What I am you are."

"And the girl?"

"Mortal, but for now, she rides under my aegis. We are all, for the purpose of this venture, immortal."

"I'm getting restless. We should ride."

The goddess didn't move and instead cried out, "Anneth!"

The girl appeared as if waiting to be called. She wore her sacred robe, carried a small satchel over her shoulder and joined the two.

They left the building and found the women standing shoulder to shoulder in front of the horses. One of them said, "The horses are ready, My Lady."

Anneth took the goddess's arm and said, "Our strategy?"

"We have none. We simply ride."

The sun had just risen. The three mounted and the goddess nodded her head toward the east. The horses bolted. Within minutes they were out of sight.

As they approached a crossroad in the long roadway, they saw dozens of women waiting on horseback. Nastka raised a fist and cried out, "*Our Lady!*"

The three slowed and the goddess laughed. "Nastka, explain yourself."

"We heard you'd be riding east today. Do you object if we ride along? All of us here thought you might welcome good company …"

"Come," she said. "But only to the easternmost outpost. Then we part."

"Yes," Nastka responded, "and from there we will await your safe return."

"Fair enough. Now, no more of your drollery." The goddess nodded to her riding companions and they broke into a swift gallop. The contingent of warriors followed close behind.

Riding into a light breeze blowing from the east, the goddess felt an unexpected exhilaration. The sun was rising and in their eyes. She sensed Anneth on her right and the eidolon to her left. The horses behind them made a thunderous din and she imagined the throng raising a vast cloud of dust as they rode across the plain toward the terraces.

Within a half hour the women had mounted three low terraces and had turned onto the trail that paralleled the river. It wound lazily through the valley separating the western plains from the eastern desolation. In minutes they entered the shadowed woods.

The goddess knew they were now fifteen minutes from the outpost known as Broken-Hearted Way. At that juncture they would leave the horsewomen behind. Shortly after, they expected to encounter enemy sentries.

At the outpost they slowed long enough for their horses to drink from the river. When the goddess motioned that the time had come to leave, Nastka rode up beside her and said, "May you accomplish all you wish."

Anneth caught the goddess's eye and asked, "Do we veil?"

"Never." She jerked her horse toward the trail and the two followed.

They passed the bend where flies had forced the death of so many attackers. In another ten minutes they rode by the pond where the eidolon had slipped passed the men. The goddess expected to find border sentinels in the vicinity, but there were none. She knew they were entering nomad country. Although the sun was now high, there was a bleakness washing the land.

She signaled for the horses to slow. "Be alert. We may as well be three women riding naked in the sun. Everyone will gawk. No woman appears unveiled."

Anneth said, "And when we are seen —?"

"We will act depending on their reaction." The goddess paused. "Regardless, the three of us and our horses are safe. We cannot be harmed."

"Literally?" the eidolon asked.

"Spears, hands, stones — nothing will harm us."

Anneth smiled. "I may be recognized. I have killed many and wounded many more."

"But you come as my priestess, not my warrior."

The eidolon interjected, "My sister, I remain confused. To anyone else, you and I appear the same. To these men, we will seem to be double goddesses, twins —"

"Remember," the goddess said, "I am derided as the witch. Now there will be two witches. Double enchantresses."

"And which of us," the eidolon asked, "wields the actual power?"

"Both of us as we see fit. Our minds are merged. As my twin you will know what I know."

"I and I …"

"Yes, that exactly." The goddess turned to Anneth. "And you — we will not have to explain ourselves, but you will play the part of who you are."

"Which is, My Lady?"

"My priestess. You will not be otherwise."

CHAPTER 26

The red-shouldered hawk with scalpel eyes
spies a meadow vole, a mockingbird, a thrush,
checking off each
— finally sweeping down in a screech
to rest upon a branch.

As they rode out of the woods and swept into the arid plains, the goddess's elation grew.

She was surprised by her reaction. Men where she ruled were compliant, duteous. Here, from what she knew, they were arrogant tyrants. She was sure their response would be: take them down, subjugate, humiliate.

But at this moment the three rode as if they owned the open countryside. There were no impediments, no encumbrances. The sky was streaked gray and she could see low buildings far ahead. She urged her horse on.

The eidolon cried out, "Up ahead. Those houses. That's where I stayed."

"And what should we expect?" the goddess responded, leaning into the horse's neck.

"A single woman shared by many men."

"Her name?"

"Boda."

"These are outskirts to nowhere," the goddess said. "It can't all be like this —"

"I think it is," the eidolon shouted. "Everything's run down everywhere. No food, too few women to too many men."

The goddess grinned. She felt her deathlessness, as if the three of them were riding through an endless eternity. They slowed as they pulled into the first scattering of corrals, outbuildings and a house. Smoke rose from the roof center. Dry leaves blew against streaked walls.

Two men worked in a rear enclosure, their backs turned. They were bare-chested and wore oiled, conical hats. They swung around, one of them saying, "What the —?"

The second man grabbed a spear and pushed open a gate, advancing. The women had stopped their horses beside a packed dirt yard. The man yelled, "Identify yourselves!"

"We're only strangers," the eidolon said. "in need of rest."

The man appeared baffled. "Why have you not covered your faces?"

"Why would we?" the goddess responded.

The second man stepped around him, limping. He abruptly lurched for the reins to her horse. His arm appeared to hit an unseen barrier.

He cursed and reached again, then failing twice, angrily swung the side of his spear against the horse's flank. It ricocheted away before contact.

The goddess spoke commandingly, "Hands off. We are not what you believe."

The two men backed away as if watching snakes. The taller man cried out, "Helmut!"

A large man stepped from the house, immediately assessing the scene. He said, "Tie them up! — Take their horses."

"They have some strange defense, Helmut. I tried to grab her reins —" He pointed at the goddess. "She uses magic!"

Helmut bolted for the horsewomen, cursing. He, too, tried for the goddess's reins, hit an invisible barrier, then swung a stick toward Anneth's horse, to no avail. The goddess began laughing, and the eidolon pulled her horse back on its rear legs, threatening the man with its hooves.

He stepped back, shouting, "Unveiled whores —!"

Anneth, deceivingly angelic, said loudly, "My mistress demands respect! Your rudeness will lead to your ruin."

Helmut stood, shaking his head, looking at each of them.

"Surrender," he ordered. "Now. I'm losing patience."

As he spoke a small, fully veiled woman stepped from the house. She saw the horsewomen and gasped. Falling to her knees, she bowed at the waist and cried out as if seeing ghosts, or double goddesses, "Two Inannas!"

Helmut spun away from Boda and stared at the women. "What? *Inanna?*"

Boda looked at him, crying and said, "Fall to your knees, Helmut. It is the goddess herself. Doubled. Or worse, her look-alike specter come for revenge."

Rejecting her warning, he grabbed a spear and turned on the three. "Enough of this. Off your horses or we end your journey here. No more tricks —"

The goddess continued to look immensely amused. This had been predictable. She had not foreseen this precise event, but she had expected something like it. Anger, threats, undernourished men. A single woman alone among them who recognized the majesty of the visitors. The reactions were already tedious.

The goddess opened her palms as if making an offering and said, "A land that mistreats strangers is a corrupted land."

She turned to the woman who had remained on her knees and said, "Stand."

The woman did so, trembling, and the goddess said, "Your name?"

"Boda, My Lady."

" 'Boda' means to command or order, does it not?"

Helmut laughed. "She's a slut. She *takes* commands."

"You," the goddess said, "will say no more." She snapped her fingers. His sentences slurred, the muffled words staggered as he tried to speak.

Then he emitted a long howl which became increasingly inaudible. Anneth watched, remembering an afternoon when the goddess had become irritated with crows. A small wave of her hand had silenced them all.

This was — if the situation were not so dangerous — far more entertaining. "He's tongue-tied," the girl said. "Dumbstruck."

The goddess said, "It could have easily gone another way."

"They appear," the eidolon said, "to be brutish men without exception."

The goddess caught movement from the side of her eye. A lone horseman approached over a field and slowed as he saw the group. She knew immediately: it was the one called Wolf.

Before she could react, Boda cried out, pointing at the women, "Wolf! Look!"

Adalwolf reacted like the woman, bowing as he straddled his horse, then sliding off and onto his knees into the dirt. "Inanna!"

The goddess realized that she had stumbled onto a cabal of followers, however small. That this clique existed so close to the border was one more unforeseen and fortuitous event. She said, "You live here?"

"Yes, goddess, if it can be described as that."

"Stand. Tie up your horse. No more words."

The young man leapt to his feet, bowing twice and secured the animal. He then looked slowly at the three horsewomen, amazed, perplexed — two Inannas! — and the young priestess. She looked familiar. He concluded that she had probably been at the goddess's side when he was brought to the temple.

The taller of the two men — both had retreated to the corral edge — said, "Wolf! The witch did something to Helmut!"

Wolf saw Helmut grunting incoherently. "What happened to his voice?"

The goddess half-smiled. "Better for him this way."

The eidolon said quietly, "And now what —?"

"Now what, indeed. Violence from the start. Trying to frighten our horses with their spears. Overt threats. Everyone here is under-fed. All quite unpleasant —"

Anneth grinned. "And we are only strangers seeking shelter."

The goddess nodded *yes*, then turned. "Boda? Wolf? This was not our destination. We have just begun. Find horses and join us if you wish."

Boda retreated a few steps, saying, "I — I — cannot. I belong to them."

"No," the goddess said. "You are freed. Wolf as well. They are nothing. I protect you now."

Midmorning heat rose. Dry grass crackled in the light breeze, and a wind whorled in the side yards. Then what was moving stopped and the landscape was bathed in thin amber, in the viscous pool of her gaze.

Shattering the growing stillness, she said in a strange singsong, "Bring whatever you wish. We're on the move again."

Adalwolf said, "Yes, yes — on my way —"

Boda, opening the door to the house, said, "Don't leave without me!" and went in hurriedly.

The two men seemed unable to move, an unseen force pinning them. Helmut continued to groan almost soundlessly, moving in awkward circles, striking his ears. In minutes Wolf rode up pulling a second horse behind him. Boda darted from the house with a small satchel and leapt onto the animal.

The goddess raised her fist head-high, and the five turned onto the road.

They traveled without speaking for a quarter hour, passing burnt field after field. Breaking the quiet, the goddess said, "What we should expect? How far before we reach a village?"

Wolf said, "A settlement lies ahead. Another ten minutes at this speed."

"How many residents?" she asked.

"Several hundred. It's called Turnback."

"Why the name?"

Boda interjected, "Nothing good happens beyond it."

The goddess laughed. "Is that so —?"

Boda looked away, retreating again to silence. The eidolon volunteered, "Boda, are you now an official betrayer?"

"Yes, I suppose so. If they track me down ..."

The goddess hissed, "You are under my shield. No one harms you ever again —"

The eidolon spoke, probing. "Those who are here who know of Inanna ... Do they know each *other*?"

Looking up in surprise, Boda said, "We exchange rumors."

"What rumors?" the goddess said.

"One that made our hearts sing was that you would come."

Eidola said, "How many of you are here? Men and women —?"

"In the entire territory? Many, I think."

The goddess asked, "How are these rumors passed along?"

"At markets, at drinking wells, along roads when it's safe." Boda grasped the reins as if she might fall, and looked across the flat plains, finally saying, "Although he says nothing, Adalwolf knows far more than me."

The goddess turned, looking at him. "What is it you know?"

Wolf frowned, saying, "When I returned after being captive, I was elected as ... one who interprets The Lady's mysteries."

The goddess snorted, saying, "And how is that possible?"

"I am one of the few who have seen you."

"Ah, yes, I remember initiating you in my mysteries, into my deepest secrets. Didn't that happen, Anneth?"

The girl shook her head *no*. He flushed, watching their interaction. "It was presumptuous of me, My Lady. All here who believe are desperate to know ... anything."

He went on, "I am asked the color of your eyes, your hair. What bird imitates your voice. The fineness of your garments."

"You learned all that in a day as my prisoner? I suspect I should have had you killed."

He rode on, finally saying, "If you wish."

She looked ahead and saw buildings on the horizon. "Is that TurnBack?"

Boda said, "Yes."

"How many there are followers?"

The woman shook her head. "A third?"

"That many?

"Sometimes," she said, "I think far more. But who knows?"

The goddess slowed her stallion, patting its neck. Its mane was black and braided, and its eyes restless. "Shall we run?" she whispered. The horse snorted excitedly, rocking its head.

The goddess scanned the cocoa-colored landscape. A low-skimming hawk swept over a nearby field. She pointed, saying, "That old oak — we'll pull up there."

The party turned off the road and struck out over the burnt grasses toward the tree. She turned to Wolf, stating, "Everything's charred."

He nodded, pulling his horse closer. "Yes, fires last summer. Almost all crops were lost."

"Fires," she said. "Burning barley … Even at the temple I smelled grain ablaze. The smoke rolled over the mountain like storm clouds, a foul incense."

"Yes," he said. "Black smoke at first, then the fires smoldered for weeks. A fever over the land. Most of us survived."

CHAPTER 27

*Her handbag was
subordinated to carrying songs
of abandoned love.*

The oak's branches started high enough above the ground to provide them shelter from the sun. The fields were a brindle wash of burnt sienna.

Fires, she thought, *all crops gone up in smoke.*

Now, in the aftermath, their horses's hooves beat ash into long trails — dusty sockets were left at every step. *Fires*, she thought, *all crops gone up in smoke.* The animals's lower legs were gray. Only under the oak was the powder thin, hints of old sod somehow preserved from the conflagration.

They paused in the shadows. The goddess said, "Wolf, ride into TurnBack. Make contact. Bring my people out. I'll talk to those who come."

"They may not be allowed."

"Yes," she said. "I've taken care of that. For we can't have a discourse if we have no listeners. They'll come."

She hoped her brave words proved true. At this point, she was unsure of her powers. *The paradigm has to change,* she thought, *with my powers or without them.*

"Yes, My Lady." He looked grim, struck the flank of his horse and turned toward the settlement. Dust rose sluggishly behind him.

Boda whispered, "He may never return."

Anneth said harshly, "Enough of this gloom! We bring felicity. And we protect those believers —"

"I fear that when Wolf spreads the word that Inanna is here, men will come, not The Lady's believers."

The goddess smiled, dismounting. The eidolon slid off her horse as well, saying, "Good to stand. We should eat."

Anneth reached behind her, opening one of the satchels. She lifted out a thin clay jar, saying, "Honey," then took out a loaf of bread. She, too, slid off her horse and was followed by Boda. The four women broke off chunks of bread and stood eating in silence.

The eidolon said quietly, "Boda, tell us about your life —"

"What's to say? I serve. Eight men. Their faces change as they are lost or die."

"When did this begin?"

"We begin to serve at the age of six."

The goddess interjected, saying, "You describe your life as 'serving' men."

Boda responded, "I'm a woman."

Anneth sighed, "*We* are women and we are warriors."

The goddess said, "Over the valley, away from here, women are free. Their world is whatever they want. There are many women and few men."

"What do the men do?" Boda asked.

"What we wish," the goddess said. "Some maintain roads. Some build or repair homes. They furrow our fields."

Anneth giggled, "They plow our furrows."

"And," the goddess said, frowning at Anneth, "our little girls are raised to ride swift horses, speak their minds and sharpen spears."

Bowing her head, Boda said, "Goddess, it seems impossible."

The goddess touched her shoulder. "You'll see that it's not. I expect you to find a new home with us."

She lifted the woman's chin gently. "I intend to protect our way, as I protect those who pray my name."

"My people," Boda said, "have fought yours forever. How can that ever end?"

"It can never end. That, or it can be finessed."

"Finessed?" the woman asked.

The eidolon said, "She speaks of kinship, friendship. The honey we ate moments ago — Life can be as sweet."

Boda shook her head. "I take commands. I obey."

"Yet," the eidolon said, "your people want more. They hunger for what my sister represents."

To their south the low roofs of the ill-named hamlet were irregular, smoke rising from their centers. Nothing moved. Then the goddess saw a plume of dust kick up: Wolf! He led and she instantly knew these were not believers.

As the group got closer, men overtook him and she could hear their voices urging each other on — "At the oak!"

"Surround them from the back!"

"Only four!"

"Women!"

"Faster!"

"There — the witch!"

"Don't mount," the goddess commanded as the men approached. "Don't move."

Fourteen men carrying short spears ringed them. Wolf stayed outside the circle, riding back and forth.

A small man with thick jowls, cried out, "Are you the witch, Inanna?"

The goddess stepped forward, saying, "I am she. Be careful."

A bearded man beside him jeered, "You warn *us*? Whores too wanton to cover their face?"

The goddess cried out, "You encircle sacred ground. There will be no bloodshed where I stand —"

At her words three men threw long shafts. A *trinity* of spears, she thought, feeling an inexplicable elation. She watched the shafts arc up, then plummet toward them in slow motion. As they fell the goddess made the spears fragment. Bits drifted down into the ashes in the fields.

"No more of that," she spoke. "A land that mistreats strangers is corrupt. You tempt disaster."

The jowled man shouted, "Let's net them —"

Several men unfolded short rope nets hanging off their backs and spun them overhead.

"Watch the twins!" he continued. "They're likely sorcerers —"

His words were too late. As she had done to Helmut, the goddess stopped his voice and that of the others. Another spear came looping in from behind her and she splintered it as well. Then the men's horses started bucking, rearing backward. Within moments they were laying in the dirt.

They writhed on their backs, unable to stand. Only Wolf remained on his horse. The goddess pointed at him, saying, "Return, Wolf, to TurnBack. This time, bring only my people. Walk them out and into the sun —"

He smiled, nodded, and swung his horse around.

ॐ

Inhabitants poured out of TurnBack — lackeys, slaves and minions, men and women, all without exception undernourished and in disbelief. Many of them danced. Others sang. There were seventy or more, walking quickly, clustered behind Wolf who rode tall on horseback. The sun was on their heads and their eyes shone.

The goddess stood before the oak, flanked right and left by Anneth and the eidolon. As the multitude quieted, Anneth raised her voice, singing,

> *O* blessèd *are those who see*
> *The glorious goddess*
> *For they are free!*

The goddess scanned the crowd, watching faces, measuring emotions and guarding against any reaction herself. She raised her arms, stopping them paces from where she stood.

A rainbow arced across the fields, its bands of color bending in the benevolence of the sun. This thing she did felt ancient. Her words felt like ones she would utter now and forever.

She glanced to her right: Anneth's hair was aswirl with red strips, ribbons twisting like snakes in the slanting light. The girl's eyes, like those of the believers, were afire.

The goddess turned back to scan the faces, absorbing the exultation.

"Greetings! I bring you long life and good health —"

For a week the goddess repeated this ritual, traveling from TurnBack to Riverbend, Red Blade to Stone Hill, Vassal to Pyrrhus. For a few days, men continued to oppose her presence and she reacted identically. Then abruptly, they stopped appearing.

At each new event, only those who had been abused and those who were unimportant appeared. The crowds grew. In the space of seven days, she spoke to more than 900. At each gathering she promised a new way.

On the last day, minutes after she had stepped aside from her last address, those who remained in the field outside of Pyrrhus began to point overhead. Thousands of starlings were swirling in a vast dance of loops, bows, half-moons, spirals and undulations.

A murmuration, she thought, each bird reflexively reacting to the one beside it and to ones far away. Their swells were perfect, their inflections impeccable. The sky darkened from their countless wings.

She felt she was seeing the cosmos sped up, stars and planets tumbling in an endless curvature at rapid speed. The birds's arcs, she thought, were those of snakes, of thousands mirroring each other through grasses.

Surely this was a sign, a good thing.

CHAPTER 28

the wave that moves like a carving scythe
like a double-bladed ax
grave in its immortal hoax,
the wave breaking where rough
riders ride forever on the reach

I o finally persuaded Timessa to spend a few days away. They randomly chose Geneva. Traveling on the cusp of spring they stayed at, a boutique inn outside the city center. Io added that great names, great personalities had walked the surrounding roads and she intoned the names of Friedrich Nietzsche, Charlie Chaplin, Coco Chanel, the watchmaker Patek Phillipe, and others. When Io elaborated on Nietzsche's philosophy, Timessa countered that he was not a philosopher at all, not in any real sense, and that besides, as Io should know, philosophy as espoused by mortals had been destroyed long ago.

She whispered, *"Philosophy, like Nietzsche, is dead —"*

They ate at cafés overlooking the water, with Timessa always in dark sunglasses, her hair under various scarves.

The countryside was full of undulating hiking trails, but the goddess was not interested. Hiking for pleasure, she intoned, was tedious. More than once she complained that Geneva was colder than Naxos, and that they were missing the violet hyacinths blooming at the estate.

Late in the afternoon of their third day they walked past a small bookstore. Timessa turned around, insisting they browse. She found herself gravitating to a section on geography and old maps.

She picked up a tattered hardback titled, *Thrace*. The land bordered northern Greece. She remembered spending months there one hot summer running deer with Artemis and some of her nymphs. Later the full panoply of Olympic gods emerged and Thrace became famous for its swift horses and fierce warriors.

Thumbing through the book she saw a chapter on Old Europe ... *Europe* ... The word hit her with a surprising dread. Then the ancient word flashed in her mind: *Europē*. Other names, words, flooded into her mind: *Euthalia, Agnes ... Aneka, Hebe ... Anneth ...* and of course, *Inanna*.

She closed the pages momentarily, caught her breath, felt her heart racing, and then, calming herself, opened the book again. There was a centerfold map, which she opened: old Europe was bordered to the north by the Danube River and to the south by the Black Sea. But that, she thought, was recent geography.

Europē encompassed a much greater land mass, and according to the book, had been the epicenter of an early Neolithic culture centered on the Danube River valley. These so-called Neolithic people flourished as early as 4,500 B.C. But there were far earlier cultures, some dating to 40,000 B.C.

Archeologists disputed dates, theories and religious beliefs. Some thought the societies were matriarchal, other patriarchal. No expert knew more than another.

She felt lightheaded, seeing photograph after photograph of natural landscapes, snaking waterways, old dirt roadways ...

Io bumped her shoulder. "Good book?"

The goddess showed her the cover. "It brought me back in time. I spent a summer there with Artemis. Many years ago."

"Somewhere I've never been."

"I think it's present-day Bulgaria."

Io smiled. "Maybe we should have skipped Geneva and gone to Sofia."

"Maybe. The country borders Greece on its southwest and Serbia on its west." She showed Io a map.

The girl shrugged, saying, "Not France. Or Naxos. Imagine bathing in something called the 'Black Sea' —"

Timessa ignored her. Although she owned no books and never read Io's, she bought *Thrace*.

Io found it immensely amusing, saying, "Are you being sentimental? And about Bulgaria?"

That evening as they ate at a brasserie, Timessa couldn't keep her eyes off Io. It was not a return to infatuation, but more an attempt to deconstruct why the girl was so fascinating. The girl's cheekbones were symmetrical, her mouth without fault, the curve of her neck flawless …

This, Timessa thought, was simply Io. Or was it after all? The candlelight flickered softly on their wine glasses and in the girl's eyes.

Io was aware that she was being scanned. The goddess was probably being objective, one of her usual tools. Io knew Timessa remained deeply unsettled. Geneva had been an attempt to reset her constant restlessness. Io pursed her lips, wondering what the goddess was imagining.

Timessa caught herself, aware that she was likely about to enter Gaia's magic province, the zone between here and there. *Thrace. Eurōpē.* Once again, she sensed Gaia's oscillations. Io's face had become vaguely transparent, yet that wasn't possible.

Then she knew: Gaia's portal, like an eyelid, was opening. As if alive, it was viewing her from a distant time. Which in return, allowed her to — no, demanded that she — gaze backward, backward.

She suspected that the blinking to and fro was reciprocal. Whoever inhabited that place must be looking out as well …

She studied Io, who seemed to have unknowingly pulled back the portal's sheath. That evening Io had tied ribbons in her hair, saying at the inn as she viewed herself, "Flouncy, aren't I?"

The ribbons were crimson, some sort of silk, and set off the simple black dress she'd chosen. Now at the brasserie, as they sat across from each other, Timessa found her unduly fascinating.

Io finally asked, "What in the world are you thinking?"

"That I've known you forever. Or at least as long as I've lived. That you've known me that long as well —"

Io laughed. "I think I'm twenty-two, almost twenty-three. And we both know you go back millennia."

"Maybe you do, as well."

"Okay, did I have a name back in the forever long ago?"

Timessa shook her head, thinking, *Anneth*, but saying, "Gaia's portal only reveals so much. There's so much I don't know —"

She reached out and took the girl's hand, yet as she did … she saw Anneth's hair aswirl with ribbons, all twisting like thin snakes in the candlelight. She and Io were no longer in Geneva, but instead on horseback, and she rode madly across green plains beside *Anneth*, her hair blown back and wild.

Later that night at the inn, Io insisted they make love. Timessa lost herself in the girl's touch, but in her mind they were on bedding in a dark temple beside a river which purred as they played through the night.

There was no longer such a thing as time. The nighttime fires she always faced remained on Naxos. *Her* night in Geneva, or in Európē, or wherever Gaia had placed her, was, on this night, full of slow constellations, planets and incorporeal promises.

She and Io must have slept in — spring sun pushed against the windows, outlining the edges of the curtains. She was aware of Io's arm across her stomach and of the girl's breathing. Then, as if she had stepped from shadows into light, Timessa found herself walking along the strand of an immense lake, the shore bright with bur reed, blue flag iris, and flowering rush.

The small path was gritty on her bare feet and ran beside a fringe where the plants sank into deeper water. A warm breeze wove between the stems and leaves and swirled up between her legs and into her hair. It was so lovely that she hardly wondered where she was.

Pausing at the lake's edge, she saw a flash of silver in the water, then another. Fish were feeding on small black tadpoles which were clustered between the submerged stems. Kneeling, she skipped her fingers over the skirted edge, scattering the tadpoles like finned coins.

A small voice said: "You were good to come."

She looked up: Gaia, in a pink bodice and soft, layered, bell-shaped skirt, stood beside her on the trail, inquisitive. "Those that survive will become frogs … and some are salamanders."

Timessa rose, smiling, then half-bowed to the young girl. "Where are we? A pleasant spot …"

"We're exactly where you wish to be."

"Perhaps if I were a water nymph."

"I chose an inland sea. In a time even before Inanna."

"Then quite a while ago."

"In-between glaciers. In a time of salamanders."

"As I saw. And our meeting? I suspect I haven't measured up."

"On the contrary. Do you remember the last week, your outreach to the barbarians?"

Timessa remembered little. The *portal*, as she thought of it, revealed shadows, reflections and mirages that backscattered into what appeared to be present time, but then were gone as quickly as they appeared.

She shook her head, saying, "The dominant sense I have is of … someone named Anneth. Io's face often mutates into hers. It's dismaying. But outreach to barbarians —?"

"Then it's time I showed you more. I'd thought you might crack the code without me, but no matter. My fault. The traces I've left have been obscure."

She made a small face, saying, "Look! My latest move —" and spun twice, her arms out and her head looking over her shoulder into Timessa's eyes as she turned.

She planted both feet and Timessa politely applauded. Gaia said, "Takes my breath away. So appealing to my sense of equilibrium …"

"Now, tell me what you hoped I'd know."

"I'll show you instead —" Gaia glowered unconvincingly, then opened her fingers suddenly as if releasing something hot. Timessa felt a shift in air pressure …

There was a moment of hastening, a flickering. Then Timessa was in an unfamiliar land, under a bright sun, a fluorescence — the fields around her scintillating, burnt, a dark-eyed hawk gliding overhead … she was astride a horse, beside two women. One looked like her. The other was, she knew at once, Anneth.

Anneth whispered, "My Lady!" Timessa could see love in the girl's eyes. She glanced at the other rider. She knew then: an eidolon of herself.

Almost as quickly, the events of the prior week began to tumble before her eyes as if she were watching cinema at an accelerated speed. The threesome rode through a valley beside a river, then emerged onto a desolate plain. She saw outbuildings, a dwelling, a corral.

She confronted men. There was a woman and a man she knew. Then they rode again. She saw a solitary oak, a rundown town, men on horses, spears, a crowd before her, promises, tears, jubilation, accusations, triumphant scenarios repeated day after day …

Gaia slowed the speed, allowing her a full minute to view a mass of starlings swirling in a dance of bows, half-moons and spirals. Then she said, "Six and a half days in a few minutes. We see your first bold step in converting nomadic warriors from bloodlust to … what you call alternatives …

"You juggled success," Gaia went on, "without having to revert to your usual cunning. No men died last week. None of the women you led were harmed."

Timessa said, "Did this actually take place?"

"What you saw at the end … ended just hours ago. You and Anneth and your double are preparing to return to the lands you protect."

"Was what I just watched a success?"

"It was a gamble without a plan. You faced either destroying men once again — which you've done for generations — or inventing an armistice. You slowed the warfare. You may have ended it. My congratulations, as I believe that's your goal —"

"Thank you …" Timessa paused, then said carefully, "Since we're talking, am I in both places at the same time?"

"Here and there?" She smiled.

"Yes, that."

"If I answered your question, I'd derail what you must yourself discover. You're the protagonist. But as you have discovered, there's no script. As there was none when you rode into that desolate land."

"Then *I'm* writing the story —?"

"Remember the tale of Tantalus?" Gaia smiled, half-bowed and vanished.

Timessa knew of Tantalus, a legend. She did not understand how Tantalus's story was analogous. He had questioned the gods's omniscience, been caught, and then eternally punished by never quite being able to reach food or water.

In the old mythologies, he was forever *tantalized*, but left unsatisfied. She though was not questioning Gaia. On the other hand, Gaia could be accused of leading her on. It was odd that she had mentioned the old tale.

She thought of the old Greek phrase, *theos ek mēkhanēs*, god from the machinery, or *deus ex machina*. That almost described Gaia, but not quite. She was real, not a representation of a god suspended above a stage on wires.

Timessa heard a noise, perhaps a sigh. Then a soft cough. Morning.

She was on her back beside Io who idly ran a finger between the goddess's breasts. Up and down, gently. She was back, a thousand miles west of the Danube River valley.

Timessa opened her eyes, viewing the girl: thin mauve gown, lace at the high neckline, hair unkempt.

The girl was smiling. Timessa said, "Geneva?"

"Yes, my love. We're still in dour Switzerland."

"Just had a long dream. One in the long, long ago."

"Eurôpē?"

"No, somewhere farther back in time than that."

"Then long before my time."

Timessa paused. "I was certain last night that we've been together forever. But I'm not as certain now. I traveled backward pretty far. Before a time of mortals."

Io frowned. "Were there dangers?"

"A lovely lake. And black tadpoles becoming frogs and sala-manders."

The girl nodded as if she completely understood.

CHAPTER 29

The woman scooped emptiness
from a vase,
holding nothing in her palm
and saying, "See?"

Over breakfast before they returned to Athens, Timessa teasingly asked Io, "What's the one thing desired by all?"

They sat outside at a cafe along the boulevard. Timessa wore no makeup and her blouse hung loosely. The girl could not see the goddess's eyes through the dark lens.

"Happiness?" Io submitted.

"Happiness, pleasure, elation … all those things are desirable, but they spring from something. What is it"

Io squinted. "I'm hardly awake and you're grilling me."

"Go on," she prodded. "You've had two coffees. What's the end game?"

Io lowered her voice and said, "I know you know."

"There was a time when I would have said 'love.' But I'm not so sure anymore —"

Io paused. "Love can mean many things. But if the ultimate is not love, what is it?"

"Remember I dreamed last night —"

"Yes, you were in the long, long ago."

Timessa smiled. "I saw a flock of starlings. Hundreds of them all wheeling overhead. There's a word for what they do, but the word itself isn't important ...

"What *is* important is their dance. Each bird reacts perfectly to the one beside it, and to ones far away and to ones even farther away. They swirl and loop and arc in vast, rippling curves —"

"Yes! I saw that once," Io said. "I was thirteen or fourteen. Endless birds rolling overhead. My mother said it was choreography."

"Watching them," the goddess said, "you realize that for these birds, there's no angst, or reluctance, or coercion ... No *is* or *maybe*. None of that. They just dance as one. It's a performance at a level of perfection that I find illuminating."

"But we started off talking about happiness."

"I asked you to name the one thing that's desired by all."

"That's greater than love?"

"Possibly ... I'll just say it: it's *belonging*." Timessa shrugged. "Isn't that what gives the birds such freedom? You spoke of happiness. They don't think in those terms — they just *are*. They never argue, or squabble about turning left or right. They simply soar. Together. Belonging allows that strange perfection —"

The goddess's threesome returned through the valley beside the river to Broken-Hearted Way. Boda and Wolf elected to remain behind, believing, however optimistically, that they could play a role in maintaining the momentum she had created.

As promised, warriors led by Nastka waited, whooping as the three approached. The goddess slowed and raised her fist. "Six days. No one died ... A few men humiliated ... Many of the inhabitants saw unveiled women for the first time."

Nastka smiled broadly. "You accomplished much."

"We cracked the stone. I may return. Not all there were convinced."

"But some —?"

"Many, I think," the goddess said. "And when doubt infiltrates a people, unity is not possible."

"My Lady," Nastka asked in mock surprise, "you sowed division and disbelief?"

"I sowed the possibility of an *alternate* belief, Nastka. But we must not let our guard down. I may have sown sunlight for many, but many — particularly the men — seethed at my words."

"Yesterday at dusk we caught an outrider slipping through the brush."

"A single man?"

"Yes, trying to bypass this outpost."

"And —?"

"Aneka and I and a few others confronted him. He turned to flee and was surrounded. I regret to say that his body washed down the river. We did retrieve his horse."

"I see. They were probing. I was away and they hoped you were easy pickings."

"Yes, he was probably sacrificial. That is, if he returned, they'd send a larger party. If not …"

"Make no assumptions. Eyes open." She glanced over the dozens of women. Raising her voice, she shouted, "I'm proud to be among you!"

Timessa sauntered through her gardens, observing the proliferation of flowers and the change in season. Hyacinths were fragrant, their flower spikes tightly clumped. In the orchards, olive trees burst with hard buds.

The waters of the Mediterranean now reflected aquamarines rather than grays. Migratory birds winged north, stopping in the new grasses on the island. Even Aetos seemed more alert as it soared off the promontory under Delia's watch.

Perhaps it was all attributable to spring, but the goddess,

following her encounter with Gaia, felt less troubled. What she thought of as Naxos time seemed normal enough — the chronology of minutes and hours were what she had always known.

She supposed that more *Európē* episodes were pending, but none had occurred since her return. After Gaia had re-exposed her to Inanna's trials in that desolate land, Timessa was anticipating more.

Io had said that morning, "It's as if you're expecting a phone call. One that's important. Someone's promised, but the phone never rings …"

"The call will come. Gaia wouldn't have had that last rendezvous otherwise."

"In the meantime," Io said, "you're not really here, you're in suspension. You're in misery, dragging around with a lightning rod over your head, waiting to be struck."

Timessa was aware of Io's critique and that she must be boring to everyone around her. Io knew. The nymphs knew. Everyone watched her askance. She was far more involved in decoding the mystery of Európē than in the reality of Naxos.

She was also restless and impatient. She remembered Artemis saying years ago, "There is no greater crime than not being content. Being content, you will always have enough."

Yet how could she be when Gaia herself was constantly confronting her with … she couldn't escape calling them *provocations*. As it was, she couldn't anticipate the next challenge, or as she was beginning to think of it, her next trial.

On hearing Artemis's comment many years ago, she had said, "But why would I not be content?"

Those were simpler times. She now had enough of everything but was still unsettled. Timessa wondered if she could flip the goddess's axiom: could one have enough and be discontent?

It seemed an oxymoron. But who knew? She now admittedly lacked confidence about anything she analyzed. Gaia always appeared, it seemed, with exquisite timing leaving her teetering. *Oscillating*.

And what would Artemis think now? Here she, Timessa, had returned from an endless millennia of being known and worshipped as The Lady, the Great One, The Divine Mother, Inanna, Ishtar, Cybele, Lemnos … No divinity was comparable.

Her powers, she thought playing with her words, were *incomparable*. Yet … what she now experienced changed day to day. Her powers had not extinguished the volatility. Or apparently, her vulnerability. And even her powers vacillated.

The insecurity she felt came from Gaia thrusting her into hostile environments. It wasn't so much, she thought, that she was exposed to physical attack. Rather, her apprehension came from being ripped from Naxos and Io and thrust into *this other world*.

She had no handbook, no guide. Events simply occurred. Inanna appeared randomly, Anneth erratically and the nomads when their appearance suited Gaia.

Being content, you will always have enough. She smiled to herself: *ah to be an eidolon — to have no scruples, no inner voice.*

She caught herself: *Why did this dissection of hers always return to morality?*

As she continued to wander through the lower orchards, she stopped.

She'd rejected morals long ago. They were like sea-wrack, sea-run tides: shifting, fluctuating, always impure. That conclusion remained constant.

A movement overhead caught her eye: two black hawks over her right shoulder, sweeping in winged formation over the sea toward Delos. An auspicious sign.

Hawks: yes, always a propitious sign. *Then she knew.*

She would no longer *wait* for events. She would *create* them. She would do as she wished, when she wished. As Io might say blasphemously, *To hell with Gaia.*

Why couldn't she enter the here-there portal whenever she wished? Why did she await Gaia pulling some golden lever? By waiting she ceded her own authority.

And wasn't entering the portal like entering a séance? Of course: she was contacting the dead.

Then she caught herself again. Was she wrong? Was it like that? Did she reach out in her travels for the dead? Was Inanna a phantom, a divine grandee who had been erased long ago? Wasn't it as likely that Inanna was simply in another time?

Timessa knew now — she was convinced — that Gaia had not returned her to that dimension in more than a week because she expected Timessa to find her own way. Perhaps, as it was with so many things, leverage was solely a matter of exerting oneself.

Waiting, one would never be content. As Artemis had implied, never being content was abhorrent to divinities. She had been guilty, but never again.

Io met Timessa on the trail that wound out of the old vineyards. The twisted ancient vines on either side of them dated back to Dionysos, or so the natives on the surrounding estates claimed. These were the original grapes used to make the first Greek wine.

The god had introduced wine as a gift to mortals. Juice from the grape pressings at that time was so dense that it had to be cut with water — the act itself treated as a ceremony and a thanksgiving. Io knew these things. They were repeated unquestioningly by the nymphs and affirmed with pride by those whose families had lived for generations on the local slopes.

When the girl found Timessa, she said simply, "A long walk."

"A good one."

"I'm glad."

"I've resolved a few things," Timessa said. "You'll be happier as well."

"I'm always happy around you."

"No, you've been concerned. But you're sweet to say otherwise."

Io took her hand. "Were you returning to the house?"

"Yes. Time for coffee. I'm imagining something thick — burnt beans, bitter, Arabic, stirred over coals in a cheap, tin coffee can." She smiled.

"Tin coffee cans are a scarcity. You're looking for a kickstart."

"A reward for making headway."

Io squeezed her hand. "So, my goddess, what have you resolved?"

"That waiting and cowering before Gaia was a mistake."

"Oh … and your alternative?"

"I've been looking for Gaia to open a door, to say, 'Step in.' Stupid of me. Counting the days for the next encounter was a blunder."

Io paused. "Do you have a choice?"

"I realized that she's been waiting as well. Standing by, so to speak."

"For what?"

"For me. To take the initiative," Timessa said. "I hesitate to say take command. But that's it. I have immense power. But I've always been ambivalent about using it …

"It's not lack of confidence," Timessa went on, "as much as being half-skeptical. Wondering what it's for. Wondering why. Does any of that make sense?"

Io skipped as they walked, saying, "I guess. But I still don't see what you've resolved."

"Gaia's no longer going to open doors. She's shown me the portal. And she wouldn't have done that if I wasn't intended to enter. I'm to step in. When I want."

Io stopped and looked at her intensely. "Bring me along?"

Timessa smiled slowly. "No. You're too precious to put at risk."

CHAPTER 30

Light emerges, rainlight null,
desire opening through slick
apertures, idyllic:
the whir of the double-ax,
the dull blade that strikes the bull.

Timessa drank coffee. The nymph Erato had followed Io's direction regarding consistency and taste. In minutes she emerged from the side kitchen onto the patio, saying, "Your drink, goddess."

The coffee had been brewed down to a heavy syrup. Timessa thought: tar pits, boiled black paint. The precise poison she sought.

As she sipped she looked out over the Mediterranean toward Delos and Mykonos. Dozens of islands hovered to their west, each a volcanic hump with an incised harbor, almost all overrun with history. Dionysos, when he was fleeing Hera as a young man, had made pilgrimages to all, finally spending more than a decade on the very soil where she sat.

He'd abruptly abandoned Naxos after Ariadne's death, heartbroken and calling Artemis out as a murderer. As Great Goddess, Timessa had been able to reunite the two, who were now living in Eleusis.

She had listened a year ago as Ariadne had asked Dionysos, "What will you do with yourself in that small town? You of all people!" and he'd replied, "Make a living loving you."

They too had entered a portal and … What had happened? She sipped her coffee, thinking, *They'd made discoveries.*

To Ariadne's shock, Dionysos was still alive, and he learned that his beloved had been brought back to life within hours of being killed. Yet, neither knew about the other. Not for over a thousand years. She, Timessa, had brought them together.

Dionysos had dared walk through the gate she'd provided. And Ariadne had demanded justice, ripping down the barrier between them, at first oblivious to what might follow. In the end — rather than playing the role of avenger — Artemis had shrugged and said the gods forbid double jeopardy. And one of the great love stories of all time resumed.

Timessa refilled her coffee from the tin, smelling its acidity, idly watching steam rise from her cup. Closing her eyes, she sensed her own portal. It lay somewhere down below the rose-gray glow of her eyelids. It yawned seductively.

She'd expected she might find a black hole, something frightening. But no, the gateway was unremarkable. A pale light leaked from its edges. She thought she saw glimpses of a lapis lazuli sky. All she had to do was drop down as easily as slipping feet first into a lagoon, letting herself descend into warm, blue waters …

Io suddenly spoke from her side. "Goddess, you must be hungry. I know I'm starved. Would you like me to ask the nymphs make some food?"

Opening her eyes Timessa observed the girl, the house, the sea before her, the orchards falling downward in green terraces toward the water. All appeared in a crystal lucidity, crisp and limpid.

Erato stepped from the house and waited expectantly beside the door. Smiling, Timessa said, "Have them reheat the couscous and lamb from last night. Perhaps some wine and baklava when we're done …"

Io turned and went into the house. Erato followed. Timessa sensed a slight buzzing as if a fly was nearby, then it passed. She had an overwhelming sense of calm. Io reappeared and said, "I haven't seen you so tranquil in a year."

"Yes, I think I shattered some barrier on my walk. Or fell into a pool of serenity. Everything's untroubled."

"It *is* a beautiful day."

Timessa gestured for her to sit at the table. They'd eat and chat. She felt utterly at ease, her faculties alive. Some great stone had been rolled aside. Light flooded into the grotto where she'd been skulking for too many months.

Whatever, she thought. *Wherever and whenever: I seem to have decoupled from the grinding captivity.*

After they ate Io went to her atelier. Content, ready, Timessa closed her eyes and effortlessly slipped away. She dropped like a diver into the warm opening. Then as she had guessed, she emerged.

She stood beside the basalt slab that was stained blood-red between its veins of olivine — the altar stone, awaiting a next offering. She was *Inanna*. An obsidian knife, scalloped along its edges, lay at her right arm, ready for use.

Four girls, each holding a wicker basket containing a single dove stood before her, their heads bowed. And as if inevitable, Anneth stood to her left, her arm joined with the goddess's.

Timessa felt herself and Inanna speaking as one, their words rolling from a common tongue. The sounds were strange, yet she understood them completely.

"Remove the birds."

The girls began singing as they opened the lids and reached inside —

Blesséd is the Goddess,
Blesséd are those who see her light …

The doves's wings were tied with leather thongs. As the girls laid the birds on the slab, Inanna nudged Anneth, saying, "You, my priestess, shall conduct today's sacrament."

The girl nodded, and the goddess turned and ceremoniously walked into the temple. Moving past the dark monolith, she went into the private rooms. There, she pushed open a massive rear door which overlooked the river behind it.

She was alone and the sun was high. Even at a short distance she could see rounded black pebbles shining in the river bottom. The water ran ankle high.

Aware that she was unattended, the goddess stepped onto the mossy bank and pulled her gown up over her head, hanging it off a branch. Golden light fell upon her. Spangles of green reflected off the fresh leaves onto her arms and belly.

She took a footstep into the river, then another. The clear water sung in an almost subvocal softness, mimicking the girl's slow voices from the temple: *blesséd, blesséd, blesséd,* winding over stones and rubbing against the undercut banks … *blesséd, blesséd, are those who see the light —*

She remembered the previous night, laying on the temple bedding, owls hooting in the woods, a crescent moon low on the horizon and Anneth astride her with slow kisses. The girl wore a silver necklace the Goddess had given her — from it hung an vulval-shaped disc. The pendant replaced the lapis lazuli amulet.

The Goddess had said as she presented the gift, "Let no one see this."

Anneth had whispered, "Except you —"

"Remember to touch the disc and whisper *Belong* if you need protection. If there's danger, you'll be safe." The girl smiled indulgently. The Goddess wondered if she'd even heard.

They played at leisure, pleasing each other, occupying themselves almost until dawn. Then she allowed the girl to sleep, waking her thirty minutes before the midday ceremony, saying, "Up, my blackbird. Get dressed and do your eyes. You must look the part."

Now Inanna stood in the river. She washed her arms and thighs, purifying herself for what was to come. Moments after she'd risen at dawn, she'd had premonitions.

Today would be an uncommon day. She felt no disquiet. Rather, it was apprehension: something that was unexpected should be expected. Some *thing* would appear. Or perhaps occur.

Then it happened: a trembling, a small shiver. She had half expected someone to take shape on the opposite bank. Instead, what she experienced was a merging, a coalescence. She stood open in the flooding sun, aware that another being had stepped into her, merging with her bones and skin and hair.

She felt no threat. Deep warmth. Lightness. This was no twin like her eidolon. Instead, a new bright intelligence, a joining of essential cells. The two were now one. She felt the river doubly embrace her in its flow.

Who are you? Inanna whispered.

— Not a stranger.

But you are to me.

— Once. No longer. Are we separated?

No, there is muchness.

— There is more than muchness.

Are we not both great?

— We are.

Is there still a you and me?

— Do you know the saying, 'I and I'?

It's one I use when I refer to my eidolon.

— I use it as well. But we are much more than that.

How much more?

— We are not one plus one. We are One.

Inanna said, *I have had glimpses.*

— I as well.

Why this now?

— The time was right for you to know.

You know more than me.

— Perhaps. Once. But I am chaste like you.

Chaste of knowledge or of men?

— Both. But I use the word as in, I am the future.

Then I am the beginning and future, too?

— You and I are I and I.

You called yourself no stranger.

— We go forward and backward in time as one.

How can that be?

— I seek answers as well.

Inanna followed, *Will we now always be like this?*

— As one. As we are now.

Have you always been a goddess?

— I am you, but what you became many years later.

How many years?

— It will make you dizzy.

How many?

— Thirty-five or 40,000 years.

I see … Do your memories stretch that far?

— No. You were one, then you were extinguished.

Why?

— There was failure, chaos. You lost these lands, watched as all these women were captured, raped. You turned our back on them. You shamed yourself. Peace was lost. War became customary

Elaborate.

— You drowned in sorrow. Drowned in the constant deaths. Then disappeared.

You know all this and yet are here. Why?

—Gaia has given you a second chance through me.

A grand statement. My emancipator.

—There is no more you and me. You know that in your bones. If there is to be liberation, *we* are the liberator.

The goddess stood in the river, aware of her tears, of her desire to embrace herself in this madly enhanced persona she appeared to have become. She thought, *What do we do next?*

Then she heard a sound and turned: Anneth. The girl stood on the bank, barefoot and laughing. "Should I take off my clothes as well?"

The goddess shook her head, saying, "Are we alone?"

"We are," Anneth said.

"Take off your gown. Shake out your hair. I need kisses. I need your hips against mine."

The goddess was aware that she had never spoken so ... so coarsely. Or desired Anneth as greatly. Her words had always been oblique. But now she waited naked in the river, watching the girl undress. The silver necklace, the sacred gift, glinted between her breasts.

Come to me, she thought.

CHAPTER 31

Skirts in coils and folds, slips exposed, slanting
hems, gold snaked into necklaces of fire,
chains, chicanes, artificial turns, cones, chariot
wheels burning in a slow and silken smoke.

As if an inevitable lover, Timessa had softly filled Inanna. The Naxos goddess had not planned a coupling. Yet now, by virtue of their joining, she was no longer a peripatetic visitor to an ancient past. Together the two encompassed the past, all that was alive and all that would flow forward in time. They were no different than the river in which they stood.

Inanna immediately saw with Timessa's eyes, forward into unimaginable times. At first she was overwhelmed.

She could also see backward. Because Timessa had realized that time was not linear, Inanna saw that the past she had allowed could be amended.

They were longer *mysteria*. They were *I and I*. The two had not as much fused — given that they were already one — as coalesced in a cosmic riptide.

In their wonderment they shed all pretense of logic. Reason could not be applied, they agreed, to what had been mysterious — or to what had been temporarily forgotten: assembling puzzles was impossible without visualizing the completed image — which neither could have done before.

Being in two places at once was a new concept to Inanna. Timessa on the other hand, had been aware of Inanna, but had not dared to consider her real. The snapshots of *Eurṓpē* and its archaic inhabitants had rarely seemed more than cinematic.

Timessa had half-attributed her flashbacks and portal flights to some bizarre deception on Gaia's part. Now she understood that they were not. Be that as it may, the two goddesses had become one — they were now the *Great Goddess* of Eurṓpē ...

Inanna, Timessa: in this renascence — this revival — neither name was appropriate. Theirs had become a nexus of authority, of dominion and of caring, a new thing, a mélange that annulled the individuality of Inanna — and that unexpectedly sanctified the awakening Timessa had years before. There was now *belonging*. *Belonging*.

The new Great Goddess became aware of her surroundings: the living river, the sacred grove. A pair of broad-winged crows soundlessly swept down the river's corridor. She looked overhead, following their passage until they rounded a bend far downstream.

The river itself sang as if its music was a that of panpipes. She was conscious in her joining of all being coupled, twinned. She thought of *I and I* as a sun and moon in coitus — but they were more than that.

A movement caught her eye: Anneth beginning to wade.

Entering further downstream than usual, the girl waved happily, stepped deeper, then lost her balance, just catching herself, laughing. She skirted the knife edge where the shallow riffles turned to fast rapids.

Knowing Anneth could not swim, the goddess cried out, "Get up here! It's slippery there —"

"Give me just a minute —"

The girl turned toward her but side-stepped with one leg into the faster water. Her arms flailed for balance as she cried out, "No!"

She appeared to right herself and bafflingly, as if making a small balletic movement, threw a small silver piece into the air. The Goddess knew instantly: it was the necklace she had given her. The oval glinted as it spun.

Its polished face was bright, then the piece fell in a slow, silvery arc. Time stopped. Anneth paused, watching the pendant spin down, her face impassive.

Then events accelerated. She lost her footing again, stumbled into the deeper flow, fell backward and was consumed.

"Anneth!"

"Goddess —"

The girl's voice was lost as she was carried downstream, twisting and struggling in the flow, an arm or shoulder appearing and disappearing in the roiling black water. The entire incident took seconds.

Bolting, the Goddess climbed the bank, sprinted around the rear of the temple, crying out for help as she tried to outrun the current. The flow easily outpaced her and within moments she knew the girl was lost.

She stood bracing herself against a tree, infuriated that she, of all beings, had not been able to prevent the accident.

What do we do? she whispered.

— Stop the river.

It's too late. Can't you see? She's gone —

— We'll find her.

I can't sense her anywhere.

— She may be caught in some obstruction —

Yes, we have to know —

— Reverse the flow. Carry her back!

Too late, too late …

Within a short time the Goddess organized a search team. Women on horses and on foot began to work both sides of the river. Occasionally, to no avail, one would wade into the flow to examine a suspect object.

She rode on horseback beside the scouting party, mystified that she could not feel the girl's presence. What had happened to her old senses? She was aware of snakes at thirty paces, rabbits in deep grass and distant nomads slipping into her valleys. Yet Anneth had disappeared.

The searchers went hours downriver to no avail. More women joined them. The pursuit broke up at dusk and resumed before dawn the next day.

Hours later on the second day the Great Goddess ended the hunt, tearfully thanking everyone, returning quietly to her temple to light fires and supervise sacrifices. Several of the younger girls dared to publicly hope Anneth had somehow survived.

That evening when she was alone, she stood in the rear of the temple. Moonlight illuminated the river. It shimmered, shivered, a living, silver ribbon — a river of betrayal.

— Could this be Gaia's doing?

Gaia?

— A name for Nature. Ge. The greatest of all divine powers. She appears rarely but … is known as the Great Mother.

Yes, I see. I was not aware of her as that. She's a young girl.

— You were sown by Gaia. She was your instigator.

And your point?

— She's a deceiver as well. She may be behind all of this.

Why?

— She set it in motion. In the beginning. You have always been in her sights.

You as well?

— We are the same.

Yes, I know it now.

— There was once a time when I dismissed you and even these lands as being possible. I thought Eurŏpē was some grand deception on her part, that she was playing me.

A moment ago you asked if Anneth's death could be Gaia's doing …

— We don't know that she's dead.

How can you say that? We both saw it happen.

— We haven't found her body.

You're saying this is some trick? If it is … what cruelty. Why would anyone do this?

— Gaia acts in inexplicable ways …

The following morning three columns of men invaded the valley. The Goddess could anticipate the attack, waking well before dawn with a vision. She sent Nastka to intercept them.

Her orders were that, although the killing would end, she was to appear before each column with force, then mercilessly employ what to the men would view as witchcraft. Every counter-offense would confirm their belief about Inanna.

"It will appear as enchantment," the Goddess said with distaste.

Nastka was empowered with songs that, to deter one column, would conjure a hail of stones. Before the middle column her chants would conjure storms and, before the third, create the illusion of a great beast which would set upon the men.

The Goddess implied that, if necessary, she might invoke other actions. The men would be foiled, their clumsy attacks stopped.

In anticipation, the Goddess positioned herself on horseback atop a small hillock that overlooked the battleground. The horse-women were split into three groups. All were fully armed with multiple javelins tipped with the Goddess's sacred *snake*. They knew to hold fire under all but the most extreme circumstances.

As the first column of men poured down from a mountainside trail, Nastka's voice echoed over the plain, her strange words rising and falling in a sliding glissando. To the men's horses the words were an alarming howl.

Then the sky darkened with thousands of falling stones. The barbarians frantically covered their heads. Skulls were shattered, arms broken. They turned their horses and fled.

Nastka prepared as the second column, unaware of what the first column had encountered, flooded into the plain. They were only seconds out of the woods when they heard Nastka's voice and slowed. The morning sun was low and the sky cloudless.

As they emerged, spears high, the sky darkened and thunder

rolled over the plain. A deluge began, the rain in a sideways squall, winds so high that the men clung to their horses to stay astride.

The torrent turned the dirt beneath them into a slurry and all became blinded in the storm. Hail struck. Above it all, Nastka's voice wailed like multiple women in mourning. The entirety of the column fled.

None saw the mass of armed women waiting on horseback in ranks along the plain. There the Goddess's warriors remained in sunlight, watching, then cheering as the barbarians retreated. The unforgiving tempest followed the soldiers as the trail conditions worsened.

The Great Goddess raised her fist high, crying out, "Hold your positions! A final group advances on your right!"

New men poured from the woods and into bright sun. As they entered the plain, it was as if an eclipse had suddenly struck. Utter darkness fell and the men stopped their horses, muttering and calling out to each other for reassurance.

From a distance, yet close enough to be heard, Nastka began to sing. Her voice seemed to be coming from all directions. At times it was guttural, and at others, it wove among them like the whisper of a young seductress.

Many of the men put their hands to their ears, moaning. But those who remained aware saw a great beast slowly rise before them, its height four times that of a horse. Its eyes glowed.

Mimicking — even mocking — Nastka's voice, it raised its arms and swiped a hand at the darkness, as if raking at the stars. Without advancing it swayed before them.

Then to their horror, the entire column of men heard the beast utter, "Inanna ... judges ... each of you. Flee ... before she takes what's hers ... your arms, your legs, eyes, tongue ..."

In the dark several of the men lifted their long spears and threw them angrily. The beast swatted the shafts away. More men did the same.

The beast's eyes went dark and with it all light disappeared. Men a pace apart could not see each other. They knew they were among other men only by the sounds of ragged breathing, of horses shuffling and snorting in fear.

The deep voice was now sing-song: "Flee … before … she takes … your very souls …"

The trail behind them leading into the woods like a steep tunnel was suddenly flooded with light. The men pulled up in shock, then turned and started toward it at a gallop.

As quickly as they had come, all were gone. Moments passed. The sun returned. In the ensuing silence Nastka raised her fist, crying out, "*Aiiieeee!*"

In response, the women circling her cried, "*Aiii!*"

Without reacting the Great Goddess wheeled around on her horse. The temple and the river were thirty minutes to her west. She struck the animal's flank and lowered her head as it broke into a run! The riding, she knew, would clear her head.

And, too, the distant river coaxed her on. Its waters would cleanse the chicanery, her cheap deceptions. There, at the river, she would purify herself near the spot where Anneth died.

CHAPTER 32

*"What girl theatre," you said. "What royal
pastimes where waiters serve vintage
wine, bread with finger bowls of salt and olive oil.
Where the loyal are rewarded; the disloyal
are branded amoral."*

The Goddess felt an overwhelming need to purge herself. There had been no deaths, but her guile had felt almost asinine. Falling stones, rain, and a beast! Puerile, fatuous.

The drama had worked, of course. And the theatrics had solved her dismay at the constant killings. But it all felt unclean.

At the temple she duly oversaw sacrifices. A dozen fat sheep were offered in thanks for the victory. The Goddess watched as her assistants butchered animals and roasted meat. Ceremoniously, she took the first piece, then gave away the rest.

Hundreds of women attended the afternoon event. Hours of dancing and ritual songs ensued. Throughout, she felt restless and disconnected, yet observances were mandatory.

These formalities, she thought, *increasingly feel … primitive, if not inappropriate.*

I and I had changed her. She now knew that the mortal world would, in time, turn its back on this sort of ritual. She knew too that she was a figurehead, and of the worse kind: she suddenly saw the banality of it all …

What was this? Nomadic males invading a peaceful culture … Slaves … Resistance … Acquiescence … Deaths … Famine and plenty … Fires burning summer crops … Constant incursions … And now, chicanery on her part to maintain stasis. Yes, an immense success: her warriors had not thrown a single spear.

When the celebrants left, the Goddess embraced each of her young assistants, kissing their cheeks and sending them home. The mid-afternoon sun was warm. Willow leaves along the riverbank had opened like green eyes weeks before, watching, alive and bright.

She disrobed, hung her garments on a branch, then opened her arms to the trees, saying, "*See?*" She stepped into the water: it was disarmingly benign.

She stood mere paces upstream from where Anneth had gone down. The Goddess paused, studying the narrow slot of rounded stones that had caused the girl to lose her footing. Preventing misfortune, anticipating catastrophe was her strength. Yet she had not foreseen a moment of it. Perhaps it was a freak mishap, but she knew she was rationalizing. She could no longer count on her powers. *Gaia?*

Then she saw movement downstream: a standing figure Anneth's height. Sunlight struck the woman's shoulders. The face was obscured by shadows. Her heart beating madly, the Goddess took a step downstream. "Anneth —?"

A cloud shifted and the sharp distinctions, the crisp outline of a girl's body waned. A bleached boulder stood in the riverbed where the Goddess had seen a girl. A tree limb cast shadows, a flickering silhouette, a face that wasn't.

A songbird shivered on a nearby shrub, then lifted off with a cry. *Twit too. Twit too.*

She squinted, took a deep breath.

Stupid of me.

— Neither of us was sure.

The goddess turned and stepped upriver a dozen paces. Clouds passed and the sun, unhindered, burnt off a somber wash of silver-gray.

She refused to look downriver and began her bath in the transparent water. She thought, *Limpidity. Clear eyes. I must unearth the old purity I once knew.* Squatting in the flow, letting the water stream over her thighs, she splashed herself, scrubbing off all evidence of sacrifice, of animal fat and smoke.

As she was about to rise, she noticed something gleaming on the river bottom: it was only a flicker, something silver flashing in the pulsing water. Then she knew: *Yes, it was.*

She reached down and touched the necklace, slipped her fingers around the disc and lifted it out. *Anneth's pendant.*

Anneth had thrown it overhead as she slipped, as if releasing a songbird, a mortal soul before she herself was lost.

Anneth. Now her presence filled the river from bank to bank, up and downstream. *Yes, yes.* And now the goddess, quieting her thoughts, bathed in the river's flow, washed in its sacred waters. The stream, she knew, would be forever sanctified by the girl's breath and blood.

Her body had still not been found. The goddess had sent word far downriver to be alert.

Standing with the necklace in her fist, the goddess stepped from what she now thought of as *Anneth's River.* The sun warmed her loins, her ribs.

Alone — she would be forever alone, she thought. She slipped on her robe. A snake, spiraling into a coil, was embroidered on its back.

If she stayed in Európē she could see the continuum before her — skirmishes, deaths. Leaving for the Cycladic islands, however briefly, seemed imperative. Európē was becoming an endless quagmire.

Side-stepping into the future. She imagined dancing, shuffle steps, a small turn that would return her to Naxos. She needed to reactivate the portal, whether it was the entry to a parallel time or something else.

To get to Eurōpē from Naxos, she had simply closed her eyes. Was it as easy in reverse? To go from here to there she would sway sidelong, slyly, glancing sideways as the portal's light pulsed in a golden circle. Beckoning, coaxing to her to come.

She would do so.

On the afternoon of her decision, she took a walk through the plain near the temple. Barley shoots had broken ground. The soft stalks stood ankle high.

Timessa said, stepping carefully:

— I've protected you from events.

We're one. I see what you see.

— I'm hiding what became of us.

What I see is that we go on forever.

— No, we chose something different. We crashed.

—We, or was I alone?

— I correct myself: we had not yet found each other.

What did I choose that ended so badly?

— You chose to walk into a chasm.

How could that have happened?

— There were a cascade of deaths. Your warriors and the nomads …

Can you tell me more? Or just let me see what you've seen?

— You could have prevailed. Defeating the invaders is a simple thing. But something changed inside you. Something snapped. Gaia says it was the constant deaths.

It's true that mortals always die. Once, I took pleasure in the skew of numbers. But I'd grown … disgusted. I never want to see another of my warriors fall. I had hoped the barbarians would change.

— A naïve idea.

You're saying it didn't work?

— You're making me say it twice.

I want to make sure I understand.

— It all fell through. Gaia says you believed you had so much blood on your hands that you couldn't wash it off. You just quit. Your shame at earlier deaths made you withdraw. Your people were swept away in a great storm of strife. But your retreat gained nothing.

When you turned your back on it all, you brought massacres. It was as if the sun was blacked out throughout Európē …

Then what happened?

— Your powers collapsed. You disappeared. Gaia, I suspect, stripped you of authority, even of your ancient divinity.

But I've always been immortal.

— Each of us has limits.

So you wanted me to know this?

— Things are seen differently on Naxos. Here in Európē we look ahead. In Naxos, we know what happened in the past.

How long before my people are lost … before I walk away?

— Soon. These lands, these women, this paradise — all of it was lost within a generation.

The Great Goddess stopped. A small party of women met her on the path and fell to their knees when they realized who she was.

She smiled, saying, "Stand. Look around. Today we are blessed. Tomorrow, who knows?"

They stood slowly, one of them saying, "In your light, Goddess, we are always blessed."

Her face remained inscrutable. Then she half-smiled. The women stepped aside to allow her passage. Hours remained before dusk. Sadness pressed itself into her.

Shame. The word described her days to come. Although nothing had changed she felt indescribable loss. It was as if her sacred river had abruptly run dry.

Anneth lost. Now this.

CHAPTER 33

... no sun comes to rest me in this place,
And I am torn against the jagged dark,
And no light beats against me, and you say
No word, day after day.
— Ezra Pound, *The Tomb At Akr Çaar*

T*o belong is the one thing desired by all. By all.*
    The Great Goddess spent the last hour with two of her assistants, explaining that she would be gone briefly — no more than a week. One of the girls was to check on the temple in the morning, the other at dusk.

Her twin, the eidolon, would remain but not conduct ceremonies. They might see her on the grounds. They understood, eager to please.

Nastka, too, had received her orders quietly: nothing was to change at the outposts and with the patrols. The goddess assured her that any probes beyond the usual were unlikely. Due to the recent spectacle, an attack would not be repeated for weeks.

When everyone left and the temple was closed, she retreated to the back of the building and stepped quietly to the river's edge, listening to the water brush its banks and move against boulders and branches.

Her reaction was more clinical than indifferent. A dove moaned downriver. The sacred grove was a living thing. She knew it well and knew she could watch it with objectivity while loving it.

Timessa said:

— You've spent many years among these trees, beside this river.

My home-waters. I can't count the centuries.

— We'll return soon enough.

Yes, now take me away.

The Goddess closed her eyes. The portal performed. They were gone. *I and I.* Time was only theatrics. Darkness moved her forward, onward, in spirals for what felt like an eternity as she moved neither forward nor back. *Silence without tranquility. Stillness and secrecy …*

Then time returned, or at least her consciousness of it. She sensed a precociousness — steps propelled her forth as if she were on a surefooted horse. She felt an insolence, then an odd lightness. The movement ceased. *Then there was music:* a flute.

It was late afternoon. The Great Goddess opened her eyes onto the patio overlooking the listless Mediterranean. Hyacinths bloomed, the sea lapped the cove however imperceptibly and one of the nymphs stepped forward. *Delia.*

"Goddess," she said giggling, "I think you napped again. May I get you a drink?"

"Napped? For how long?"

"I don't know exactly. Ten minutes?"

Timessa smiled, then laughed. "Everything's fine. Yes, a drink would be perfect."

She scrutinized the girl a moment. "And you look happy."

Delia nodded, saying, "Yes," as she left.

Yes, Timessa thought, the most evocative word in any language. *Yes* is an opening. It welcomes entry and celebrates access. It gives and grants. *Yes* is malleable. She imagined a sultry *yes*, a happy *yes*! She played with the word's alternatives: *alright, by all means, of course.* None were as succinct as *yes.*

Delia reappeared with a tray, a glass and a bottle. "From your vineyards, Goddess."

She smiled. "Dionysos's great gift."

"Oh, by the way, Tyro thinks she saw him in the cove."

"What?"

"While you were napping." The goddess said nothing and Delia continued. "He stepped from the waves onto the shore. She says he wore … nothing."

"And —?"

"He handed her what appears to be a pendant."

"That's all?"

"He dove back into the sea."

"Send Tyro to me. Immediately."

Delia nodded and rushed into the house. In less than a minute Tyro emerged, bowing and looking tentative. The goddess said, "Tell me what happened in the cove."

"I had just finished a swim. A man stepped from the waves and walked up to me."

"You did nothing?"

"I knew immediately that it was Dionysos. I remember him visiting a year ago."

"Go on."

"He stopped, hesitated, then handed me —" She reached into her pocket and pulled out an oval disc. "— this."

Taking it Timessa fingered it quietly. "He said nothing?"

"No, Goddess." Tyro smiled benignly. "Was it a present for me?"

The pendant was beaten silver, ancient in appearance and vulva-shaped — and identical to Anneth's.

"Gods are not prone to giving gifts to nymphs. Unless they want gifts in return."

The girl nodded and handed the pendant to Timessa. "Oh. Of course —"

Standing and smiling, Timessa said, "Do you recognize what it represents?"

Tyro blushed. "It could be a squinting eye on its side."

"Or not."

Delia said happily, "I think it's an amulet. To ward off the evil eye. μάτι."

Timessa laughed. Here on Naxos everything seemed lighter now that she'd returned. "I think not. I think it's what it looks like … is a portal into happiness."

She flipped it in the air and caught it in her palm, closing her fingers. "But why?"

The amulet burned in her palm, vaguely insistent. She dismissed both nymphs and set the piece on the table. It glinted softly in the low sun. Reaching around her neck, she unhooked Anneth's pendant from inside her gown and set it beside the one from Dionysos.

They were identical. Anneth's had a light scratch along its right edge, probably from a stone in the riverbed. A tiny pearl winked from inside the upper silver lips of both.

She, as Inanna, had commissioned the piece from a local silver-smith, a craftswoman whose reputation was known valley wide. The woman had said cleverly, "Silver vulvas are popular today. I'll be subtle. As befits a priestess, My Lady —"

Still standing on the patio, Timessa closed her eyes, scanning the area for any man, particularly Dionysos. She detected no one. He and Ariadne had not visited in more than a year.

Presuming the man *had* been the god, why would he come the old way, out of the sea? Then it occurred to her. Somehow he knew of *Eurōpē*. The pendant was a sign. If Dionysos knew enough to duplicate something so intimate, Artemis and Athene, too, must know.

More *mysteria*. Then she thought of Inanna:

— Welcome to my other world.

Naxos?

— Yes … And that is the Mediterranean, which lies a six or seven day horseback ride south of the sacred grove.

The being you think has made a double of Anneth's pendant. You refer to Gaia?

— You may meet her here. She comes when she wants.

And this Dionysos?

— Use my memory. He is one of the Olympic gods.

Yes, I see him now. A handsome man.

— Be careful not to open too much of what I know. The memories will drown you.

Timessa sat. The two pendants shone in the yellow light. Absent-mindedly, she put the original back on, hooking it carefully, then smoothed her gown. She was aware that the garment she wore was from Eurŏpē and might look unusual.

Delia appeared and poured wine.

"Delia, is Io still in the atelier?"

"She is, Goddess."

"Ask her to join me."

The nymph half-bowed and left. Shortly after, Io arrived, saying, "I haven't seen you in over an hour! Lonely?" She sat beside Timessa.

"You've changed clothes," she continued. "Have I seen this piece?" Io tentatively fingered the sleeve. "I'm guessing it's vintage. The weave is unusually loose and the material —?"

" Lambswool."

"Of course! Is it something new?"

"To you. I thought I'd surprise you."

"A local weaver? It looks like it came off a loom."

"Io, have a seat." She gestured broadly. "And if you must know, yes, I missed you —"

She looks dismayingly like Anneth.

— I hoped it wouldn't upset you.

The same eyes and mouth. And her voice …

— We have a similar taste, you and I.

Her hair falls in the same waves.

— Please, no more about the girl. Not now.

Delia brought Io a glass and fresh bread. She poured retsina. "We have tsoureki, if you wish."

Io said, "Sweet bread?"

"Elissa made it this morning. Or there's cheesecake from the village shop."

Io shook her head. "Maybe bread in the morning." She looked to Timessa for confirmation and received a small smile.

Delia giggled at the exchange, saying, "Consider the cheesecake. It's like a sugar bomb."

Io waved her away. "Enough! I'm just here for a moment —"

When they were alone Io said, "She's rarely in such a good mood."

"It seems infectious. I, too, have this happy sensation."

Io noticed the pendant lying on the table. "You're full of surprises, Goddess. I leave you for a few moments to catch up with work in my shop, and you change clothes and find new jewelry."

She picked up the piece and examined it. "Old?"

"Tyro says that Dionysos appeared in the cove this afternoon and handed it to her."

"We had visitors?"

"For only a moment. She said he emerged from the waves, then returned without saying a word."

"She's sure it was the god?"

Timessa nodded. "It would have been a typical trick on his part."

"But what does it mean?"

"Look at the image."

Pausing briefly, she said, "Genitalia?"

"Of course. Isn't that blatant?"

The girl hesitated. "Beautifully done."

"It would make a perfect gift from one girl to another." They laughed.

Io asked coyly, "Then, for me?"

Timessa shook her head. "Normally, yes. But this amulet serves some other purpose. I'm not sure what."

"Then we'll set it aside."

"I wonder why would he appear without warning? Springing out of the sea —"

"Maybe he was hitting on Tyro."

"No, a god like Dionysos wouldn't waste his time with a nymph."

"Was there a god who didn't chase nymphs?"

"He's in Ariadne's thrall. He's hers. Nothing's changed."

A soft sound chimed to their left and they turned. At waist high the air was charged with gold and silver sparkles. Within a second a small girl materialized, standing ten feet away.

She wore black leggings and an oversized sweatshirt, her eyes red.

She shook her head unhappily, saying, "You sit around like a tourist. Did I call you back?"

Timessa stood slowly, turning to Io. "Better that you go."

Io looked between them and nodded. "I'll be in my shop."

Gaia walked to the back of the house. Timessa followed. Closing the door Gaia said, "You come back as two. Joined at the head."

"At the hip."

"Don't be glib with me."

Timessa said nothing, watching Gaia for signs. "I wasn't being glib."

Gaia hissed, "So … Naxos's newly minted fairy goddess has merged with Inanna. Isn't she the bygone Inanna who's about to muck up her mission in Európē? The new and the old — both of you stumbling around. A lovely coupling, if there ever was."

"You're being critical."

"Scathing is more accurate."

Timessa shook her head. "We've done a lovely thing. We help each other."

"All of this without permission."

"Permission? You wanted me to take the initiative. Remember? Not wait for you to always point the way —"

Gaia stomped her foot and the marble floor shook. "*Think, Timessa! You've … come back … But there's* nothing *for you here*. What are you doing? Sitting around drinking wine and smirking about pendants! I gave you a simple quest: to find yourself. Instead, you ran from what you did and what you were. Now you dare merge with the one being who failed me utterly. By doing so *you've* failed! And I had such hopes —"

"Always my fault!" Timessa cried out. "Never my yours. *I think not!*"

"I should destroy you as I did her so long ago! But you've altered events."

"*Oh dear*. Have things not gone the way you planned —?"

"Unfortunately, to end one of you I have to end you both!"

Timessa said slowly, "You once attacked my compassion, Gaia. You said it 'felled me like a lamb.' You also told me not to be differential again. Not to you, not to anyone —"

Gaia scowled. "You took me literally —?"

"Yes. But now I won't! I suddenly know that — unlike all the other divinities you spawned — I alone see with your eyes! Like you, I see birth and death, fertility and destruction —"

"Be careful with your words."

"Threats! You always brag about bringing down Zeus? I am greater than he ever was! And admit it: you never loved him as you do me!"

"You're full of yourself."

"Yes, and I and Inanna are one! You want to end us both? Go on! To hell with all of this! And to hell with these supercilious games!"

Gaia smiled. "*Supercilious*? I create mysteries and you mock me? Yes, to hell with all of this!"

CHAPTER 34

Tannic leaves and carbon seeps
staining gowns with a sullen woe woe woe
(languid current moves her clothes
back & forth, a dead woman's waving arm —)

*B*elonging is the one thing …
Timessa woke in the grass behind the temple on her side, her arm bruised and her hair snarled. The river sang gently. Crows complained far away.

She had no sense of time and knew instantly that this was Gaia's doing. Slowly sitting, she gazed around. The temple door was closed. Her gown was torn in front.

She looked at her arm again: impossible. A dark bruise ran from her shoulder to her elbow. Injuries were inconceivable. She touched it lightly: it throbbed.

Standing, she felt lightheaded, and immediately dropped to her knees. She now wanted to know whether minutes or days had passed. Her unsteadiness was unique.

Surely it would pass. She'd pushed Gaia too far, but what did

Gaia intend with this affront? A clear rebuff. A humiliation. But an injury?

Then she thought of what she'd said. *Zeus*. She was the greater. They both knew it was true. As the goddess knelt she remembered Gaia telling her years before about the god, how he'd become "too godly," that he had "flaunted his omnipotence."

Even then Timessa knew it was a warning. Gaia had said, "I blinded him and stripped him of his powers. Then, I took away his precious immortality, and sent him into the Peloponnese to wander as a supplicant. A pack of hounds found him within a week somewhere east of Corinth."

Stripped him of his powers.

She listened to the crows at a distance. They could be easily silenced. A mere thought would end their cacophony. She closed her eyes: the discordance continued, perhaps louder than before.

Irritated, she turned slightly, eyeing the river. Reversing its flow was an old trick. Anneth months before had gasped at the stunt. She flicked her right hand: nothing.

Gravity was clearly stronger today than her artifice. Her *dominion*, as she liked to think of it, appeared erased. Gaia had sentenced her to Zeus's undoing.

Her first reaction was contempt. What a juvenile stunt. Then she felt annoyance, which became scorn. Would she too now be forced to wander until she met her end? She could hear voices in the front of the temple. She stood and walked unsteadily to within listening distance while remaining hidden.

Nastka was speaking rapidly to the eidolon, her voice rising. The apparition stood impassively on the temple steps

The warrior said, "I don't understand where she's gone. She said days. It's now been weeks!"

"I've had no contact."

"I can't wait," Nastka said loudly. "We're almost at a point where we can't stop them."

"Neither of us is empowered to act."

"Nor were we told *not* to act."

The eidolon asked, "Can you delay them?"

"Hundreds of men? You know nothing about war!"

"I don't. But then why are you here?"

"I hoped you'd been in touch."

"Something's happened. She's always good to her word. I'm waiting like you —"

Nastka turned, mounted a horse and rode off without a word. The eidolon spread her legs slightly, raised her chest and face and, eyes closed, stood quietly in the sun. The goddess watched, debating whether to signal her return.

To her surprise, the eidolon slowly turned and said, "I sense your presence, sister."

The goddess stepped into the sun. The eidolon looked at her quietly, finally saying, " You return."

"Not on my terms."

"Rough journey?"

"Indeed. I appear to have stumbled through brambles."

"Nastka would have appreciated your advice."

"I overheard part of your conversation."

"Another invasion," the eidolon said. "Hundreds of men."

"A pity. That should not have occurred."

The eidolon stepped down and walked closer. "What happened to you?"

"Not sure. I was there and now I'm here."

"We should clean you up. Scuffed knees. And what's that on your arm?"

"It appears to be a bruise."

"Impossible."

"I suspect I've been stripped of immortality and the rest of it."

"That conclusion from a bruise?"

"I can't expect you to know. You're just an apparition."

"Yes, and a perfect mirror of what you were."

The goddess startled. "Nothing's changed? You're the same?"

"I am still exactly what you created."

"I'm not sure what I am and what I'm not … I should probably bathe and find another gown."

"I'll help. Wading may not be easy."

Nodding, feeling half helpless, the goddess turned and started toward the river. As she reached the back the eidolon opened the rear door of the temple and came out with a new gown. She quickly stepped beside the goddess and took her arm. "The water's pleasant today. I wouldn't go too deep."

The goddess paused. "Anneth's River."

"I'm so sorry."

"No reports while I've been gone?"

"No, My Lady. Nothing."

The eidolon set the gown aside. They stepped onto the bank, and then went together into the water. Her double seemed to steer them toward the center of the stream, and the goddess said, "No, no — to the right where it's shallow."

"Yes, My Lady," but they continued on the same path, the water becoming deeper with every step. The eidolon held her firmly, clearly the stronger of the two.

The goddess pointed left and said, "The rapids! That's where Anneth went down."

"Then we'll steer clear of that, won't we?" Yet contrary to her assurance, the apparition maneuvered her into deeper water.

Her grip increased and she said, "It's not as dangerous as you think. I've investigated every foot —"

"I can see the drop-off ahead! What are you doing —?"

The eidolon gripped both of her arms, twisted her sideways in a violent movement and threw her downriver with shocking force. As the goddess went in face first the eidolon said in a whisper, "The river runs forever to the sea —"

The body plummeted like an old dolphin entering a wave. No struggle.

A light effervescence rose from the dark slot where the goddess had gone headlong into the rapids. Then all signs of the savagery disappeared. The river ran quietly, its music muffled in the soft golden light of the late afternoon.

Azures, ceruleans, smoke-green lenses like jellyfish. All rushing by. She sensed she was being propelled through a narrows that rifled her in blue spirals over and over … She felt herself occasionally bumping hard objects, then sliding by in the silence of the river. Breathing had become an embellishment, no longer a necessity.

She left her eyes open, the viridescent-blue-orange glaze of rushing water softly kaleidoscopic. Driven head first through the rapids she lost all senses, her arms back like folded wings, fingers pressed against her outer thighs, her lips pursed. Eyes squinting, irises black.

In the silence she was aware of an immense hum, a constant murmur as if young girls were hurriedly exchanging secrets. *Shared secrets*. A belonging. Ribbons of algae were caught in the bank under-cuts. Light flickered.

She saw fish skewing away. And enchantingly, she felt exhilaration; a thrumming powered her forward into deepening, darker water. She'd never imagined death would be like this —

Then there was sky, a lapis lazuli. She was on her back on a sandy rise in a flat. She coughed: river water, slightly alkaline.

She smiled, then laughed. Was she Timessa? Or Inanna? Or even alive? She rolled over onto her side, thinking vaguely, *The sky is the color of sky — sapphire, a thin cerulean, a sky-colored firmament …*

Another voice within her — the I and I of Inanna:

Enough. Where are we? What have we become?

She paused, still vital.

— We took a journey. And are apparently alive.

I rue the moment we joined.

— Your ride was coming to an end. I've just hastened whatever was to be your fate. If not now, then …

Gaia was obviously furious. This is your fault.

— You heard her confirm that you would fail.

Ah, so you saved me years of shame

As they bickered, a shadow blocked the lapis sky, the sharp sun. She twisted her head and saw a tall man standing over them. He wore nothing. His black beard was cut in a long cone the length of his neck. He sounded weary, saying, "You were coming down so fast I almost had to net you."

His voice, his musculature: Dionysos.

She said, "Where am I?"

"Downriver of where you were."

"How can you be here? You're not yet alive."

"I've saved you and you're asking the time of day."

She said, "No, the millennium. You and the other gods were birthed 30,000 years from now."

Dionysos smiled. "This is my time. This is my river. I sensed you spinning down —"

She sat up, aware she too wore no clothes. She covered her breasts with her hands. "My gown?"

"You were like this when I caught you in the flow."

"Where are we?"

"The river's delta. A hundred paces from here its waters spill out on the Thracian Sea north of the Aegean."

"South of where I was?"

He said, "I don't know where you were. I just know you came from up there." He pointed.

"I was in Eurṓpē."

He shrugged. "Macedonia?"

She looked around. She sat atop a dune where the river spilled into a sea, the waters braiding and flowing in smaller rivulets and thin channels that turned into brine and shallow waves. "How did you know I was coming?"

"Artemis. She said you'd crossed Gaia. I didn't follow it all, but she said I was to find you."

"Why this river?"

"It seemed most likely."

"Why not another river?"

"The girl came down in the same way a few weeks ago."

" '*The girl*'? What girl?"

"Anna," he said.

The goddess struggled to her feet and he stepped away, watching. "What? A girl named *Anna*? You mean *Anneth*?"

She felt something around her neck and touched it: the pendant, Anneth's offering at her death.

Had she ended up here as well? Nothing made sense. Nor was this convergence likely to be Gaia's doing. Some other entity or divinity had intervened.

"Dionysos, do you have any idea what you're saying?"

He smiled. "A bit. The girl first, you somewhat later. Resurrection, awakening. You saved me a few years ago. I am honored to reciprocate."

"Had I drowned?"

"Can fish be drowned?"

"No riddles, Dionysos."

"It appears that, when you began your journey downstream, you were immobilized — but still immortal."

"In other words, wounded," she said. "but not mortally."

He shrugged. "Is mortally wounded possible for an immortal?"

She shook her head. "Words … I asked a moment ago about this girl. You said 'Anna.' Did you mean Anneth?"

"She calls herself Anna, a priestess of In-*anna*, a local goddess. An attractive girl."

"You saved her as well?"

"Artemis forewarned me. The girl was half-dead, but salvageable. She says she knows you."

The goddess paused, then said quietly, "Dionysos, what part does Gaia play in all of this?"

"You mean Artemis?"

"No."

He squatted and opened an old leather satchel that was nearby. "Here," he said, "something to wear. From Ariadne, who thought it might fit."

Smiling in appreciation, she slipped the gown on. The garment was white and pleated and fell to her ankles. A wide red band was sown an inch above the hem. "Thank you, Dionysos."

He nodded. He was choosing his words carefully, sharing what he could, but no more. And as preposterous as it seemed, the journey downstream had apparently shifted her through time as well as territory.

Still, she thought, that fit her theory: time was not linear. It was layered, multi-dimensional, parallel, reversible, manipulable. As astounding, it looked as if Anneth may have lived.

CHAPTER 35

Dionysos led her upland and to the east. They walked a few minutes. A small bluff appeared as they turned on the path. In its center she saw a low golden roof with white columns around a small structure. A long altar rose before the portico. All of it looked new.

He stopped and turned to her. "She insisted on a temple to this Inanna. She holds ceremonies daily at dawn and dusk."

"Is this building your work?"

"Artemis and Hephaistos'. She knew what she wanted, and they understood."

"Who comes — locals?" the goddess asked.

"Those who adore this Inanna, I suppose. I've never attended." He half-bowed. "There are guest quarters in the rear. Ask her forbearance. Perhaps she'll honor you as a guest. I'll leave you here and return tomorrow."

"What if she refuses me shelter?"

"Strangers are never refused in Thrace." His look was stoic. "And if things go poorly, I recall that you can take care of yourself."

She watched him return down the trail toward the river. The warm breeze moved her pleated gown. She felt the pendant on her chest. From the sun's angle she guessed the time was late afternoon. Her river descent had taken minutes.

The bright temple lay ahead. She pushed her hair back, her heart beating hard. Anneth, Anna: a temple priestess for Inanna? No, she thought, Anneth is dead and has been for weeks. Perhaps I am as well. Neither of us could have survived the river for long.

She reflected that she had no idea what lay beyond the living world. A phantasmagoria similar to this could exist, the dead surrounded by phantoms, ghosts who imitated those they had known during life. But was it possible? Dionysos grabbing her as she was swept downriver —?

The incident was beyond belief. Add to that the lovely climate she found as she woke, being revived by an old god that she'd known for millennia, and now, hearing that apparently Anneth had survived as well. Assuming nothing, she walked closer.

The architecture of the building was impressive. She knew from constructing her own temple that such a structure would take months to build, and multiple craftswomen. Or men. Paces from the altar, she stopped, listening. Time, as it now seemed to exist, slowed further.

Then the heavy doors swung open. She saw no one, but the low sun illuminated a statue inside: a lifelike, life-size image of herself sculpted in silver, ivory and gold. *Inanna*. The sculptor must have been Hephaistos, the divine artisan. No mortal could have created such a piece.

Hephaistos? she thought. He, like Dionysos, should not be alive. All of the Olympic gods appeared long, long after she ruled in Eurōpē. Time in this place seemed to have been jumbled, shifted around in an interweaving of eras. And was she really in Thrace?

A girl stepped from the temple onto the marble deck. She wore a gown similar to the goddess's; her right breast was uncovered, her gaze was impersonal. The goddess thought: *emotions deliberately obscured*. What was the old term? The girl's gaze was *anodyne*.

The girl quietly scanned the goddess, then lifting her chin, said, "Your purpose here?

Anneth, the goddess thought. Indisputably. She replied, "I come, I believe, to celebrate your goddess. May I ask her name?"

"Inanna, the Divine."

It was Anneth's voice, her hazel eyes. The girl continued, "You have come to the Temple of Inanna. There will be a ceremony here at dusk."

"And who, if I may ask, attends these ceremonies?"

"You will be the first."

"There are no others?"

"None."

"Have you spread the word that a grand new temple has arisen in this land? One that glorifies a great goddess?"

"There is no one here to know."

"You are alone?"

"I have my goddess."

"You maintain a temple yet no one attends?"

"I am Inanna's priestess. I do my duty."

The goddess paused, watching the girl. She saw no recognition in her face, yet there was tension in every word she spoke. "You built this temple?"

"I ordered it so."

"By whom?"

"Other gods who acknowledge Inanna's greatness."

"You are, indeed, an admirable priestess ... if I may ask, if there are no living persons here, why did you order it built?"

The girl spread her arms as if welcoming the sun at dawn. Her eyes bore into the goddess's. "Because I knew that *you* would come."

The goddess saw a flicker of a smile. Hesitating, she whispered, "Anneth —?"

"Yes, My Lady?"

"Come here."

The girl ran down the steps and into her arms, giggling, crying. She burrowed her face into the goddess's neck and hair, running her hands over her back. Whispering nonsense, she kissed her cheeks and lips. She sang temple phrases — *blesséd, blesséd* —

Over the next hour they talked about the last weeks, how the goddess had believed she'd never see Anneth again, how the days had seemed endless. Finally, the goddess said to her "What happened on the river when you went in?"

"Slippery stones. I had this impulse to feel them against my feet. Stupid of me —"

"And the necklace?" The goddess pulled it from under her gown, showing her. "You tossed it as you fell."

"I had meant to put it on. Then as I went down I knew I was lost — and tried to throw it to you."

"I found it and have worn it since." She smiled, saying, "And are you now Anna?"

"The name," she said, eyes wide, "glorifies you, My Lady. I am the Anna as in *In-anna*."

"Of course — and I'm honored."

They spoke in rushed, whispered words, the goddess once again stunned at the girl's resemblance to Io. She could now see both through all eras. Finally the portal's filters were down. Each woman from each era — Anneth, from a forgotten time and Io — was laid bare.

Ignoring her pleas, Gaia had obfuscated and obscured. Her reasons for doing so were as unclear as her actions. Somehow though, as the goddess had shot down the river's channel like a block of wood, the veil had been ripped aside: the two girls were now indistinguishable — were, for all purposes, impeccable counterparts — as were the distant goddesses Inanna and Timessa. They too were the same, conjoined over time (as if, she thought, time was even relevant).

The goddess and Anneth reveled in their reunion, but had not spoken of the river, how it had taken them both to this foreign place, how they had survived … The goddess presumed that the girl knew. No mortal could be turned over and over for hours underwater down rapids and lived. Yet she had.

Further, Anna had rendezvoused with divinities that she not known existed, who had found and revived her and had built this temple on the shore of the Thracian Sea. The goddess guessed this was in fact Thrace, but nothing was certain.

Let it suffice, the goddess thought, *for now. Let it suffice that we are together again.*

❧

At dusk Anna conducted a ceremony that both knew by heart, one she had taught the girl a year before. They stood side by side, their backs toward the temple, speaking together, until the final chant when Anna cried out,

Bless us, Goddess, with your milk and honey!
Bring us fertility and love!

In the dark beside small torches clustered in the temple, they ate quietly, glancing at each other. The food was elaborate, much of it freshly cooked. The goddess, unwilling to probe too deeply too soon, said, "You're alone, yet we have food."

"It appears twice daily."

"Who brings it?"

"The gods, I suppose. It's always just here —"

On the second day of the goddess's arrival, Dionysos reappeared, rising from the sea's edge as the two women stood together. He bowed to the goddess, falling to one knee, before she said, "Dionysos, please."

"Is Anna honoring you as her guest?"

"She is."

"Good … Artemis will come by in a few days. She offers apologies for being delayed."

The goddess was not surprised that she might appear. "Tell her we have much to discuss."

He nodded. "She tells me that you should know that things are going poorly in Eurōpē."

"Be explicit, Dionysos."

"She says that battles are seesawing. Many losses on both sides."

She hesitated. "Is it possible for me to return?"

"I cannot say."

"A back-and-forth battle is one thing. An impasse is even better. But eventually every standoff crumbles. When will the momentum shift?"

"I only hear the news."

"So you don't know —?"

He nodded. "Artemis follows it closely."

"I see. Thank you for telling me what you know."

He glanced at Anna, exchanging looks. "This girl swore to me that you would come. I see that she is pleased." Then eyeing the goddess for confirmation, he fell to his knee again, bowing his head.

Without waiting for her to release him, he rose and turned back to the sea. Then, as if having a second thought, he looked back at her and said, "There is so much we don't know."

She smiled. "*Mysteria*."

He laughed heartily. "Indeed," then dove into the sea.

Days went by. The two fell into a routine, waking before dawn, conducting the sunrise ceremony, then bathing in the cold river before walking hand-in-hand to the sea. At dusk the sunset ceremony would be conducted. Then in the evening they would share a meal and talk.

But always, the goddess thought about her time away from Naxos and of events in Eurṓpē. And that she seemed, as much as ever, caught in-between.

CHAPTER 36

Phragmite grew along
the beach, pottery shards
washing up from the sea,
cobalt, indigo, coughed up
from the crimson waves.

Artemis had not visited. And Dionysos had not returned. And so, enchantingly, the idyll continued uninterrupted. Frequently, after their sunset ceremony, the goddess and Anna would retreat to her private quarters and make love without restraint.

Sometimes their play would begin midmorning or midday. There was clearly no one near, wherever it was they were. No one could hear Anna's cries and their voices echoing through the sanctuary. There were no apparent obstacles to their gratification.

Just the same, the goddess was increasingly aware that Anna undressed could easily be Io. In Europē the goddess had been Anna — Anneth's — lover for months and knew her intimately. Now, disturbingly, the girl often moaned like Io, mounting her during foreplay and increasingly imitating Io's mannerisms.

Once while the two indulged themselves, she remembered one of Gaia's last comments during their confrontation. She had basically said, "I find you sitting around smirking about being seduced!"

Yes, true, she thought. But the goddess dismissed the similarities: everything in this land was an amalgam of compressed times and overlapping territories. Why *shouldn't* Anna mirror Anneth? And Io as well?

One morning after the sunrise ceremony, she took the girl by the hand and led her down to the broad river. They sat on a dune overlooking the delta and the goddess asked directly, "How did you survive the journey down this river?"

The girl radiated naiveté. "I don't know, My Lady. I drowned, then un-drowned."

"Mortals can do no such thing, my love."

"The god pulled me from the water."

"What do you remember?"

"I remember cold water. Being suddenly yanked out. Being tired. Being in his arms. Not breathing, just watching. I remember him walking from the stream …

"I remember knowing I was dead. Yet a goddess waited on the shore. I remember her hand on my heart as I lay on my back. Breathing again. The sky overhead."

"And the goddess's name?"

"She called herself 'Artemis.' A goddess I did not know."

"How were you certain she was a goddess?"

"She said, 'Wake! I am the goddess Artemis.' Her eyes were flashing colors and I believed every word she said."

"Did you identify yourself?"

"They knew my name. They said they were expecting me."

"How could that be?"

"I don't know. It all seemed so real. As I gained consciousness, I corrected them about my name — I said I should be called Anna."

"I see."

"The goddess asked me if I needed a temple to oversee. I said, 'Of course,' that I was your high priestess."

" 'High priestess,' huh?"

Anna nodded. "I am. And she said they would start that day to build the temple because you would be arriving soon."

"They seem to have anticipated our every move."

"Or planned them ahead of time," the girl said.

"That had occurred to me," the goddess said. "So clever. So neat. So … Artemis. Planning all of this would be just like her."

But why? Timessa thought. She knew that love, the most difficult sentiment to divine, dominated her now. Anna had become bewitching. Slowly Gaia's challenges — her portals, fires and provocations — increasingly appeared absurd, her issues portentous.

And Gaia's fieriness at their final meeting struck her now as an act, something even haphazard. Sending her to Eurōpē like a bird with broken wings was a pointless trick. If it were meant to be a lesson, what had she learned? *Nothing*, she thought.

Yes, Gaia had similarly banished Zeus and, by doing the same to the goddess, had erased her dominion over things … but only to a point. Here, in Thrace, her intended undoing felt quite different. It was instead liberating.

Here Timessa could luxuriate in Anna, in her cool skin and hazel eyes, in her adoration — and in the peace of the river and the land. She had, effectively, for the first time since she had emerged as the Great Goddess, dodged Gaia's obstacles and objections.

Still, she could not ignore the immense harm that had come from Gaia's anger. The eidolon, her double, had found her wounded, sympathized, then literally wrestled her into the rapids. And Io: was she waiting on Naxos? There, on the island, had minutes gone by or the days experienced by the goddess here in Thrace?

Could the goddess ever return to Naxos? And as Dionysos had briefly noted days ago, the conflict in Eurōpē was — if he was to be believed — going poorly. What part, if any, was the eidolon playing there? Further complicating matters, Artemis appeared to be competing with Gaia in some unexpected way.

As glorious as the past days had been, she was increasingly conscious that the splendor, the peace in Thrace, could inevitably change.

Before dawn the next day the goddess and Anna woke, playing sleepily. They dragged out the minutes as light flooded the temple, then dressed to begin the morning ceremony.

Midway through their ritual, a woman in her early twenties walked quietly to the altar, bowing briefly and watching. Like Anna and the the goddess, she was dressed in a white gown. Her gaze was dispassionate, detached.

Each ritual ended with Anna crying out, "Blesséd is Inanna!" which she did as usual. The woman responded, "Blesséd is Inanna!"

The goddess locked eyes with her and said quietly, "And blesséd is the divine Artemis."

"Timessa," she replied. "Or are you now Inanna?"

"Neither," she smiled. "We joined as one."

Artemis said. "I will call you Goddess."

"Have you come a long way?"

"Time and distance?" asked Artemis. "They appear to mean so little."

"As do the old terms, drowning and death."

Artemis cocked her head. "Indeed."

"Once we were certain of ourselves," the goddess said.

Artemis shrugged. "Dionysos is busy by the river. Will you join me there? We can talk."

"And Anna?"

"Leave her here. She understands."

"Does she?"

Anna's face had become impersonal. She said, "Yes, see you soon," and half-bowed.

The goddess stepped around the altar and walked with Artemis down the path. She could see Dionysos near the bank, bending over.

When they were closer she saw a marble bench he had apparently just erected. It was wide enough for two. He looked up, ran his hand over the polished surface and said, "If you wish, Goddess."

She smiled, motioning to Artemis to sit first, then joined her, facing the river. Then Dionysos squatted before them, saying, "We hardly act alone. Athene, Hephaistos and Poseidon are aware as well that you are here."

She watched him warily. "And Gaia?"

"Do you agree that none of us individually is as strong as she is?"

"I do."

"Those of us I mention have had lengthy discussions. In the end Athene concluded that together we were stronger. Far so."

She laughed. "Are we discussing a rebellion?"

Artemis remained stoic. "We are discussing a shift in power. Perhaps she overreached."

Timessa was stunned. No one had ever challenged Gaia. "Did she?"

In the silence that followed, she asked, "What precipitated this?"

Dionysos smiled. "The two of you had a confrontation. Io told me shortly after."

"She saw nothing. She had already left."

"Yes, but she watched from the side while the two of you spoke."

The goddess said, "I see … The encounter was … so unlike Gaia. She seemed furious."

He nodded. "Io says you were upset yourself."

"Yes, Gaia's criticism became too much."

Artemis said, "You're into your second or third year of it."

"The last thing I remember," the goddess said, "was shouting, 'To hell with all of this!' Then I was lying on my side in Európē."

Artemis smiled. "Yes, it was at that point … that we decided to take action."

Timessa had been under Artemis's wing for millennia. As a nymph she was acknowledged as the most brilliant of the many girls who ran with the Olympic goddess. When Gaia tapped her to become a vessel for the spirit of the goddess known as Inanna, there was skepticism among the remaining Olympians. But in the subsequent years they had developed a deep caring and respect for her.

All watched her struggle — and watched as Gaia erected constant barriers, pushing her relentlessly. Most dismaying to Artemis was the suffering Gaia imposed on Timessa. That imposition particularly seemed cruel as the girl had always, up that point, been happy.

Now she lived in grief for errors that were never hers, and worse, was restricted from discovering how to escape the pain.

Artemis and Athene concluded that the *challenges* had become mere entertainment to Gaia. When the merged goddess, Timessa-Inanna, finally resisted, Gaia banished her as she had done others. And that act turned the other divinities from cautious observers into subversives.

They had been monitoring events for some time. When Anneth slipped in the river, Poseidon instantly appeared, insuring she would survive as she plummeted downriver. Similarly, Dionysos awaited the girl's arrival at the river's end. Artemis was on hand to revive her. They proved to be kind and Anneth welcomed their generosity.

It was Athene who had anticipated Gaia's outburst on Naxos. She declared that if Gaia's actions became intolerable — if she finally cast out her prodigy — the other divinities would step in. Which was exactly what had occurred.

Eurṓpē became Gaia's dumping ground. Athene theorized that Gaia presumed that a powerless Great Goddess would soon fall to attackers. And that the Olympians would forget Timessa — or accept that bringing back the ancient goddess had been a failed experiment. They would, as usual, cower before Gaia's decision.

Neither Athene nor Artemis could accept such a finale, yet by themselves could not prevent the outcome. Both were pleased to confirm, upon sharing their concerns, that there were others who would join them. Only Aphrodite, Hestia and Hera had asked to be exempted.

The others — particularly Hermes, Apollo and Hekate — had voiced support and stood ready to help. The resistance organized, coalesced and had to bide its time only briefly. When Gaia erupted in anger, they quickly moved to save the goddess.

The active leaders were Dionysos, Poseidon, Artemis and Athene, and they had succeeded by saving both Anneth and the goddess. Now as Artemis sat beside the river, she explained some of the recent events to the goddess

"Dionysus makes it sound simple. But we have to presume that Gaia will discover us. When that occurs, we believe that together we can resist — and protect you, as necessary."

Timessa spent some moments looking over the river. For a quarter mile it fragmented into multiple channels, braids and shallow passages. They could not afford to become similarly divided.

She said, "Gaia has never been challenged. Do we know the extent of her powers?"

"We have observed her for countless years," Artemis said. "The thunder-god Zeus collapsed before her. He miscalculated. None of us have her raw power."

"I do," the goddess whispered. "Or I did. Once. But at the temple in Eurōpē I seemed to have been stripped of it all."

"You're sure?" Artemis quietly asked.

"Certain. I'm grateful you saved me, but I'm a shell of what I was." Then she laughed. "I've been returned to nymph-hood, which I suppose could be considered a blessing."

Dionysos stood. "There's an alternative."

The goddess half-smiled. "A way to salvage my descent?"

"Your necklace —" he said.

"Anna's necklace?"

"Yes," he said. "Remember you empowered the pendant?"

"How could you know?"

He paused. "Anna told us."

She nodded. "Yes, saying a certain word would trigger it. That, and touching the pendant at the same moment."

Artemis nudged her, saying, "You're wearing it —"

Guardedly, slowly, the goddess smiled. "I am."

She pulled it from her gown, holding it out, saying, "And what do you see on the amulet?"

Artemis looked carefully, then said, "That which is most sacred. Αἰδοῖο θήλεος."

"Yes. And I remember the word which I burned into the silver itself."

"The energy-word," Artemis smiled. "That which rescues, which activates."

Timessa grasped the amulet between her thumb and first finger, saying, "The word is *Belong* —"

Fire ensued.

It began in her throat and descended to her thighs. A molecular firestorm. All of it in compressed time, her eyes burning. She inhaled sharply. Both Dionysos and Artemis could see the re-echoing of power playing across her face.

As the flames dissipated she felt ordinary, but she knew. All this time, the pendant had been imprinted with a nugget of the cosmos, the fire of the stars — stamped with the full force of her old authority.

Her power had been embedded there, implanted so that Anneth might survive some imagined siege.

Timessa stood, finding Dionysos's eyes. "Thank you … What I was in the past I appear to have become again."

He bent at his knee.

CHAPTER 37

The portal had not been sabotaged. Closing her eyes she could see it. Gaia must have seen no utility in erasing it. Slipping into it was still, as it was before, like stepping onto a bridge that led to wherever a traveler wished to go.

She was its sole traveler and now wished to return to Naxos. Shortly after her meeting with Artemis and Poseidon — and after assuring Anna she would return — Timessa steeled herself to go.

Artemis then told her that the estate in Naxos had been shuttered . Her nymphs had been sent away to work with Artemis's girls. Io was missing. The estate, however, was being maintained to the goddess's standards: the orchards and vineyards were cared for and security remained unchanged. It would look like every other boarded up estate in the Cycladic islands.

The goddess had to see for herself. Particularly, she had to see if Io had left her any sign that she would recognize. Too, she hoped that the days she had been missing would be mere moments on Naxos. Those hopes were crushed. Artemis stated that the days in Thrace had been the equivalent of weeks on the island.

Timessa also had to shake her recent suspicion about Anna: the girl had assumed too many of Io's mannerisms, her peculiarities. Hearing that Io, her most intimate confidante, was gone seemed impossible. After all, Io witnessed Gaia banishing her. She would have waited on Naxos, trusting that Timessa would return.

The portal worked. The goddess materialized beside the marble blocks, the remnants of Dionysos's mansion. The windows and doors of her house were secured. Io's atelier was closed. She wandered around the buildings. Her convertible was in the old garage, but up on blocks.

There was silence except for the sound of distant waves. She sat at the table on the patio. Had Gaia sent Io away? They hadn't been given the opportunity to even exchange parting words.

The goddess felt tears. *Impossible.* How long had it been since she had cried? Seven or eight hundred years, she thought, remembering a small tragedy from that time. A nymph had fallen into a deep ravine. They had been running together when Euthymia had taken a wrong step. Timessa had screamed, but not been able to save her. The crevice was impossibly deep. Later, when Artemis demanded details, Timessa had broken into tears.

Now the goddess was not here to soothe her. She wiped her eyes and smiled to herself: imagine, she thought *soothing* the Great Goddess. She'd fallen into the trap of feeling sorry for herself. Perhaps it was inevitable. There had been no time for reflection.

She looked up and scanned the Mediterranean: seabirds, a mirage of waves, the distant hump of Delos, salt mist, grass bent over along the brow of the promontory. She was alone. She stood, found the key she hidden long before and opened the house, walking from room to room.

Upstairs, she inspected their bedroom. Bedsheets had been stripped off, her personal belongings were gone, Io's clothes had vanished. The deck where she had spent so many hours was devoid of chairs.

Did Artemis have to be so efficient? Yet she had always been quick and decisive. So much was unresolved. Perhaps she had been correct. There was little to see on Naxos. She compared the stillness of the estate to the chaos where she had been.

When she stepped back onto the patio, locking the door, she saw something glinting on the table. Odd that she hadn't noticed it before. Taking a step closer she knew: the duplicate necklace that

Dionysos had presented Tyro. It had been lying there when Gaia vanished her to Európē. No one had noticed. She wore its mate under her gown. She picked up the replica. It was warm from the sun.

Belong. Anneth's pendant — the original amulet — had returned her powers. Now, pleased by her discovery, she hooked the duplicate around her neck — feeling it caress the other between her breasts — she smiled: two charms. Primordial power infused both. She would return the original to Anna and wear its twin herself.

Her expedition to find Io had failed. And Naxos offered nothing. The estate had been scrubbed clean. Even the eagle, Aetos, had been moved somewhere. She hoped Delia was caring for it. After less than an hour the goddess knew she would return to Thrace.

She thought as she scanned the property, *My retreat: magnificent, solitary, deserted.* Her sense of isolation was thorough. Here, her memories were of hyacinths, wild flowers and constant activity. But these things were now muted.

She caught herself, surprised by her cloying romanticism … yes, she felt vaguely forsaken, and knew she kept expecting Io to appear. Yet she did not.

Anna was waiting. Returning was as easy as imagining the girl's face. Or her laughter. Her long neck. Her slender waist.

And once together, once they held each other again under the Aegean sun, she would seek Artemis's consul. There were so many unsettled matters — Gaia's whereabouts, the role of the eidolon, her own future if there was to be one …

And Io? She suspected that Artemis knew. There was more to uncover. She stood, taking a last glance at her home. Its emptiness was regrettable. She expected to return. Someday. On her terms.

Taking a deep breath she closed her eyes.

A light flash, flaxen, aureate. As it dissipated the goddess appeared beside the altar at Anna's Thracian temple. The sun was high and a breeze washed the grasses in soft strokes. Seeing no one she took the path down to the river and stopped where the trail turned and the wide landscape of the river opened.

Three women stood beside the shore. Anna and Artemis stood in profile; the third woman faced the river, her back to the goddess.

Anna suddenly turned, laughing, then sprinted to Timessa, throwing herself into her arms. They held, turning rocking in the soft sand. She lowered Anna to her feet, took her hand and walked her back to the river. The third woman turned to face them, smiling. The goddess's heart soared: as she hoped it was Athene.

Two years had passed since their last meeting. The two goddesses half-bowed.

Artemis spoke first. "I apologize for what you must have found in Naxos."

"You warned me." Timessa studied Athene, then said, "I'm honored to be in your presence."

"As am I in yours." The divinity paused. "I trust you approve of our recent actions."

"Your 'recent actions' appear to have saved my life."

"We couldn't have you go the way of Zeus."

Timessa nodded. "I'm grateful … Speaking of Gaia, no one has spoken of her fate."

"Fate," Athene said, "may be overly dramatic. We simply defanged her. Her obsession with you needed to be deflected."

"How was that done?"

"Once you were banished to Eurōpē, we veiled you from her sight."

Veiled, unveiled, hidden, exposed. All traces of her vanished, then revealed again. The veil ripped off. She was tired of the cycle.

"And at this moment, do I remain hidden from her sight?"

"We believe it so. To her you no longer exist. Our contrivance has taken immense energy. Thank Hephaistos for the machinations."

"And at some point I will reemerge?"

"Perhaps," Athene said. "None of us know how this will play out. We presume she'd be infuriated if she knew."

The goddess looked overhead. Crows were rising and falling in arcs as they skimmed the riverbank on the opposite shore. Their cries were, as always, constant. Without reflecting she silenced them with a thought.

The birds flew toward the sea as if nothing had happened, yet were now without voice. Her second thought was: *straightforward, effortless, as easy as it used to be …*

Putting her arm around Anna's waist, she said to Athene, "You say I no longer exist. I presume you mean to Gaia. Am I invisible to anyone else?"

Artemis interjected, saying, "Thank Hephaistos's ingenuity. He's hidden you from *her*. When she looks, if she does, it is as if your very atoms are scattered to the stars. Not one has your name. To Gaia there is no longer a detectable Great Goddess. You're gone. Or at least so he says."

"But to others —?"

"To others you're plain to see."

Anna smiled, "You're rather obvious to me, My Lady."

"So we operate, as if I'm concealed from only her. Otherwise, all is normal."

"If complete chaos is normal," Athene said. "There are a few things to resolve. That is, if you wish."

To resolve upriver, Timessa thought. The bloodlust of Eurōpē where the aggression of the nomads had accelerated. "You speak of the invasion?" she said.

"Yes, as one of many things. There have been many casualties among the warriors there. The defense of your lands is going poorly. That must be sorted out."

"Together we can do so easily."

Athene shook her head. "You can return there with a mere thought. We cannot."

"The portal works for any of us."

"No," Athene emphasized. "Gaia crafted it for you and Anna alone. It reads DNA, doublechecks helixes. It operates only for you and the girl."

Artemis said quietly, "We believe that either or both of you can freely go back and forth. Poseidon went upriver once, under our power, but the effort almost killed him."

"I'm on my own if I return?"

"As you have always been," Athene said. "Gaia filled you with all that was Inanna. We can hide you from her, but not reverse what she has done."

Timessa pulled Anna against her, kissing the girl's forehead. "Wherever I go she comes."

The others said nothing. Anna said loudly, "I remain the high priestess in Eurōpē. And My Lady wields all power there! Ending any invasion is easy. I have seen her do amazing things. Why are all of you so concerned?"

"Because," Athene said, "unlike the rest of us, your goddess has developed a conscience."

The girl said, "I don't understand."

"Killing," Athene said, "is 'easy' when you view men as numbers, things, as annoyances like those crows. Shut them up, take them down. Those nomads — they're half-human.

"But one of the viruses Gaia planted when she transferred the ancient debris into Timessa is a virus with a sense of moral right. It was the ancient Inanna's downfall. It lives on. Its curse is to weigh right and wrong …

"Your goddess," Athene continued, "believes she knows better — she knows morality is as inconstant as a butterfly's flight. But still, she's burdened by an inner voice. It counts the dead and announces the numbers. It whispers, *Wrong, wrong, wrong.* It's its own enemy."

Timessa added, "She's saying, Anna, that I have to resolve my qualms about destroying those who wish to destroy."

The conversation halted. By an unspoken consensus they watched the river as it fragmented, braids rejoining braids, channels mysteriously disappearing before they reached the sea.

After a few minutes Athene said, "The river reminds me of Poseidon. Once he and I were enemies. He wanted whatever I had. He terrified me, but never dominated me. Millennia passed and we slowly began to respect each other. Now we're friends … Gaia, like Poseidon, at times is terrifying, but she hasn't broken you."

"I always loved her," Timessa said. "But I can't imagine being friends."

Athene said, "Yes, as you saw, what she can raise and glorify she can as easily crush. I flinch when you say you loved her."

Timessa smiled. "It's difficult not to love a charming nine-year-old."

Athene placed a hand on her shoulder, saying, "Who without a second thought would kill you. Worse, think of this: she has cursed you with a sense of morals, yet has none herself …

"You had become a mere distraction for her, a passing sport. So many of the things she has created so gloriously, she has destroyed."

CHAPTER 38

Small cakes for the blessed.
Candles carried down stone
alleyways in Mykonos where once
workers carried baskets
trembling with fish from seas
where the fish are gone.

Upriver. It was what Artemis meant when she referred to where Poseidon had been. It was where she'd left the eidolon, Nastka and hundreds of warriors. Now, so much of that felt absurd. Spears, believers, horsewomen, nomads with slave-women, falling stones, blinding rain and a beast that towered over battlefields. What she remembered of it felt half-farcical.

Athene left Thrace shortly after the discussions about trusting Gaia, leaving before Artemis, too, quietly departed. In their absence Timessa stood holding Anna beside the river, neither speaking once they were alone.

Anna pushed away, took her hand and led her to the temple. They climbed the trail. A torch burned beside the altar. The girl opened the temple doors and walked her into the back where she slowly took off Timessa's gown. "Say nothing," she said. "We stay here tonight. I know we leave tomorrow, but tonight be mine."

In the morning they rose and conducted the sunrise ceremony. No one attended. When Anna spoke the final words, she lifted her arms to the sun and cried out, "*Aiii!*"

Her voice echoed for a moment, then there was stillness. Timessa said, "Let's go down to the river for a moment."

The girl nodded. "Yes, I love the sound."

In moments they stood in the sand on the bank holding hands, both dressed in pleated gowns cinched loosely below their breasts. Each wore an identical necklace tucked from sight. The goddess smiled as a fat crow glided toward them from an opposite bank. It wheeled overhead, then landed several paces away, its head bobbing rhythmically, its eyes orange.

Timessa cried out loudly, "Ah, you alone, crow, have come to bide us farewell."

The bird watched. Anna whispered, "it's one of the ones you silenced yesterday."

"Oh, then I'm mistaken. It's come to retrieve its voice."

"Yes," the girl said.

With a languid gesture, the goddess raised her hand and turned it slightly. The crow blinked, lifted off, banking low, cawing noisily into the light breeze that blew downriver.

As Anna smiled a winged shadow crossed between them and the river. The goddess looked up: an eagle, the first she'd seen in Thrace. Its flight was languid, measured. Everything about the bird screamed *Aetos*, which was an impossibility. She watched its leisurely track — its path paralleled the river. In seconds it was gone.

Aetos? she thought. *Unimaginable …*

Anna said abruptly, "Take me home."

Inanna's temple in the sacred grove beside the river stood as she had left it. The rear door was closed. "It remains as before."

"Of course," Anna replied. "Only its maker could unmake it." Her voice was muffled. At Timessa's insistence, Anna was veiled.

There were voices. Two of the young girls who maintained the temple walked around from the front. One of them — Euthalia — said, "Oh, My Lady. We thought you were still asleep."

She paused. Timessa said, "Say hello to my guest, *Anna*."

Euthalia smiled and nodded. Seeing her veil, she said, "You're a foreigner."

"Yes, she has come from Thrace. You must welcome her as if she were one of us —"

The girls said together, "Welcome to Inanna's sacred lands."

Anna nodded, saying nothing.

"Now, Euthalia," Timessa said officiously, "have you seen my sister?"

The girl gasped, shaking her head. "My Lady, you told us a week ago that she slipped in the river and was washed away. You've been in mourning since —"

"Have I? Yes, of course. All this grief, all this fighting …" The girls looked down. Timessa continued, "Has Nastka appeared this morning?"

"She is on the front lines. Isidora was here at dawn and reported on casualties. But My Lady, you were here." Euthalia giggled nervously. "You listened. You gave commands and she left."

"I did. Indeed … How long have you both been on duty?"

"Before dawn, My Lady."

"Let's make today special. We all need a break. Go home. Too much pressure. I'll watch over things till morning —"

They nodded like small birds. "Should we return tomorrow?"

"Yes, tomorrow."

They bowed deeply and left. Timessa said to Anna, "We appear to have a sleeping goddess in the temple. And however we solve our puzzle in the next hour, we don't need observers."

"I'm confused, My Lady."

"I suspect that when I was thrown downriver, my sister, my trusty eidolon, saw an opportunity."

"For what —?"

"To step into my shoes. I think when we see her, we'll be seeing the new Inanna."

"Oh my."

"Yes, she's gone rogue."

"Your twin," Anna said. "Seeing her no one would guess."

"Not if she pretends she's me. Which would be easy enough. I transferred many of my memories to her. She knows the rituals as well as I."

"What do we do?"

"Replace the pretender. Remember she's just an apparition, however ambitious." She paused. "I could do so from where we stand. But I'd rather confront her."

"You say she's a ghost. But you're speaking of her as though she's real."

Timessa laughed. "Yes, that's how I'd begun to view her." She nodded her head toward the front and said, "Let's."

They walked around the building, stopping at the long altar. The fields were bright with the new barley and the sun was at high noon. The obsidian knife lay to the side of the stone slab. There were signs of a recent sacrifice. Both temple doors were open but there was no movement inside. Short shadows were as sharp as the knife's edge.

Taking Anna's hand, Timessa said, "You will be the one to announce our arrival."

"How, My Lady?"

"Your war cry. She will know in an instant."

Anna nodded, stepping back. With a glance at the goddess, she howled, "*Aiiieeee* —!"

The cry echoed against the sacred oak trees and over the plains. If the eidolon had been asleep, she would be no longer.

ॐ

They waited. The goddess wasn't sure if she could execute her plans. Inanna would have done so easily, but she was now something else, a combined goddess, Inanna and Timessa — what Anna called her Great Goddess. Still the question of Gaia's impact on her powers remained.

She touched the pendants between her breasts, removing the original. She placed it over Anna's head.

"Now step back," she warned the girl. "I intend to become the snake."

She focused a second, then like Gaia when she would disappear, lost substance in a golden flash. A massive black snake replaced her, half-coiled where the goddess had stood, its head the size of a large boot turned upside down. Its eyes flicked as rapidly as its tongue.

Anna couldn't help but be repelled. As she watched she heard a voice in her head: *Howl. Again —*

Anna nodded, turning toward the temple and screamed.

As the snake wove and dipped restlessly, the eidolon stepped out. The snake — the coiled being the eidolon had never seen — hissed. The eidolon drew back to the temple doorway, proclaiming, "Stop! I am the goddess Inanna!"

The snake darted up the temple stairs, forcing Eidola against the wall. A second flash occurred, illuminating the entire front of the temple: the snake was gone. The goddess herself now stood before her double. "You don't *belong* here."

She raised her arm and flicked her wrist counterclockwise. It was the eidolon's trick turned on her, the veiled crone's artifice when she had been attacked by dogs in the east. At that time, the ground had boiled, scalding the dogs.

Now, the eidolon shivered, speechless, silent, becoming increasingly transparent, then vanished with a prolonged 'Ahh' as she half raised a hand.

Belong. You no longer belong.

She turned to Anna and said, "Remove your veil."

Hesitantly, the girl pulled off her veil. As she did so the two girls who performed afternoon temple duties appeared. They bowed upon seeing Inanna, saying in unison, "My Lady." Then they glanced at Anna, gasping.

"Ah," the goddess said, "you see our lost priestess."

"But she's —"

"Not dead. A friend of mine found her downriver, revived her from that state. This very day as I stood beside the river, I saw her walking toward me in the flow, smiling. Look, now she's back among us!"

Anna smiled at the two. "It's true," she said, opening her arms. "I'm tired, but no less for the wear —"

The two appeared stunned, but slowly, in disbelief, walked into her arms.

After a moment they heard hoofbeats and a horsewoman pulled into the clearing. Timessa signaled for her to remain on the horse. "Do not dismount! Go back and get Nastka. Tell her there's been a change of plans. She's to come immediately —"

The warrior half-bowed, her legs tight around the horse's sides, a spear in her hand. "Yes, Goddess ..." She turned the animal and left at speed.

As she waited on Nastka, Timessa inspected the inside of the temple for traces of the eidolon: she found nothing. The specter had left no mark. Now she was erased.

Timessa took all blame for misestimating her, well aware that the apparition was nothing more than a reflection of herself. She thought, *Lucidité poétique*. What goes around comes around. Lucid and unexpected insights ...

An hour before dusk three horsewomen appeared. Hearing hoof-beats minutes before the three arrived, the goddess waited beside the altar, her arms crossed, her face expressionless. Anna stood at her side, unmasked, her hair tossing in the light wind.

Nastka led the group, a thin leather cloak tied at her neck. Her javelin was azure and hung at her side. Multiple blue stripes were painted on her face from her hairline to her collar bone. The other women were similarly marked, one with white and the other with green and red stripes broken only by their sunken eyes.

All appeared sleepless, troubled. Nastka brought her horse to a stop and raised her hand, saying, "Goddess."

The Great Goddess said, "You no longer dismount in my presence?"

"You told me not to do so."

"Did I?"

As she spoke, Nastka shifted her gaze to Anna. She pointed, saying, "The dead rejoin the living?"

The goddess said, "Yes, she has been revived from the Underworld. Get off your animals, genuflect. After you apologize, welcome your sister."

The three slipped off their horses, made obeisance and stood. Nastka looked the priestess over and said, "Anneth? It's really you. I don't understand."

The girl half-smiled, saying, "Miracles. Inanna found me in another world. I return to serve the temple as before."

To the women the goddess said sharply, "I did not call you here to gawk. Enough of this. I want a full report about the war. Everything about the last week. Hold nothing back."

Nastka shook her head. "For days you have simply said, 'Take care of things yourself.' "

"Do not waste my time. That was then —"

"Yes." She bowed again.

"Facts, Nastka. Numbers, all of it."

Nodding, she said, "Six days ago seventeen men came down the trail along the river. We intercepted them east of Broken-Hearted Way. All died, no casualties on our side … The next day another group came through, this one larger. There were forty of them. Again we took all down —"

"How?"

"As if indifferent to death, they simply rode into our wave of spears."

"Go on."

"The third day, more came. This group was larger than the last—now fifty-five men. I'd increased our force. Who knew what they'd throw at us next —?"

"And the outcome?" the goddess asked.

"The same. The riders came faster. Mindless. I think they thought that they could charge through Broken-Hearted if they rode fast enough."

"But they failed."

"Yes. We threw up another wall of spears!"

"Over a hundred dead to that point."

"Yes."

The goddess shook her head. "None of the men escaped?"

"No, My Lady. Our spears were tipped with *snake*. No one survives."

"And today?"

"Nothing. The last foray was around midnight. We stopped it as well. Then silence under today's bright sun."

The goddess smiled gently. "You look tired, Nastka."

"Many of us have not slept in days."

"Go home. Rest," she said. "There will be no more assaults. Maintain all outposts. Start the smoke signals again as we did long ago. For now, the raids are over."

"My Lady —?"

"Yes?"

"How can you be so sure?"

"Things occur, things do not."

The woman half-smiled. "Perhaps, My Lady, I am too tired to understand."

"Of course. And when you bathe, wash off those stripes. They're something new."

Again, she looked confused. "You demanded that we paint ourselves."

The goddess said, "I've changed my mind."

CHAPTER 39

Your eyes flamed, the necklace stopped
at your breasts.
White blouse, pearl earrings.
Black pigeons fought in kaleidoscopes
of beating wings
in the sloped streets.

Time after time the next morning, as the goddess and Anna strolled the temple grounds, she saw Io and Anna as one. Perhaps they were. The two women stopped at the riverbank. Smoke and fog hung on the stream.

Anna said, "We need a breeze to blow away the mist. You own the fog, My Lady. You own the wind! Make the sun shine —"

"No wind is a goddess's wind," she said inaudibly, then more clearly, "The sun will appear."

Black, soft water ran in the stream. There were flickers of sunlight through the trees. She expected water nymphs to appear, but she knew she was too early in time. Or that such half-immortal girls simply didn't exist in this land.

The shallow, eddying fluid, the forked branch tips — all demanded her attention. Swallows were crying overhead. She thought: *Where are my crows …?*

And where is Io? Selected by Gaia, primed by Artemis … Io, her lover for the last three years. Now, rather, there was Anneth, or Anna, the Eurōpē priestess and warrior, still very much a girl, one who had arisen from the dead. A girl who had arranged their dark rendezvous at the river's wide delta beside the Aegean.

Yes, instead, there was Anna, who had contrived to erect a temple there. Who had been furtively adopted by a half dozen Olympic gods … But why? And now she was certain that Gaia had not been as much overthrown as sidestepped. It was arrogant to think otherwise.

What had Athene said? *We can hide you from Gaia.* The concept seemed bizarre. Gaia was like an all-seeing eye, like Helios who saw all things in his daily arc through the sky. Yet Athene was saying that she, Timessa, no longer appeared to Gaia, whether she was in Naxos, Thrace or here beside the dark river.

The river had proven to be a time machine that drove minutes forward as it plummeted downhill, its water carving through millenniums as if through stone. The channel began in one era and ended tens of thousands of years later, an aqueous portal that drowned beings, then brought them back to life …

She thought, *If Artemis and Athene can conceal me, Gaia can conceal Io.* Had she? Was that it, some sort of crude revenge? Perhaps when Gaia realized that the goddess had been hidden from her sight, she snatched Io, veiling *her* from view.

Mysteries, *mysteria* — veils, masks, Anna's veil, Nastka's stripes. Even the eidolon had ventured east under disguise. Then she caught herself: words, words. λόγος. They lead one away from the truth as quickly as they point toward it.

Was her Eurōpē nothing more than Gaia's ingenious construction — an assemblage as new as Anna's Thracian temple, a mere theater set designed for some obscure purpose?

Standing with her arm around Anna's waist, she thought, *Priorities.* One was liberating Io, unveiling her, for the goddess was sure she wasn't lost. Another was disentangling herself from Eurōpē.

Yes, Gaia had embedded the old Inanna's griefs and errors into her consciousness. She could escape Gaia, but not the virus. The women here — who included Anna — seemed as real as those anywhere, in any time. She could leave at will but knew now that she could not leave them behind. Inanna had once done so, but she would not.

And she was apprehensive. Eurốpē remained Gaia's creation, a forced destination.

The goddess took Anna's hand and led her to the temple's front — they abruptly stopped paces short of the altar. *Odd*, she thought, *I've such a sense of premonition. The air feels thin, as if there's been an omission … something's missing, or something's coming to fore …*

Then the majestic bird that had passed over them in Thrace shadowed them again. They looked up as a massive, orange-eyed eagle dropped from overhead. Its descent was silent. It hovered a moment, its wings beating backward, then perched on a post at the clearing. The bird shivered its wings, its claws sunk into the post, watching the two. The goddess saw a telltale nick on its beak and knew: *Aetos.*

Lazily, the bird rose from its post, hung in the air, then flew to her. As she extended her arm Aetos landed, its claws soft, swiveling its head, the black irises of its eyes unblinking. Anna backed away.

"How are you here?" the goddess whispered.

The bird was not likely to have broken free. Not purposely. Delia guarded it well. It could only have come as an augury, its presence startling, a strange and marvelous thing.

And if it was a harbinger, then of what? *Mysteria* … It, like the goddess, had to have crossed the thin film of time …

She looked at Anna, saying with a faint smile, "An old friend."

"Such birds can be trained?"

"There are places in the world where certain birds are symbols of power. Athene, whom you met, often carries an owl."

"Yes, I saw it once."

"I worked with this one for many months. But I admit it was not the bird that was trained."

Anna smiled. "It was you —?"

"Yes."

"Why have I not seen it before?"

"It lives in a place beyond even Thrace."

"How is it fed?"

"It hunts as does any wild thing."

"It looks as if it could take whatever it wanted."

"It can." The goddess gently ran a finger between the bird's eyes and down the back of its head. "We have to know why Aetos has traveled so far."

"Is it because you're here?"

She shook her head. "Perhaps —"

"My Lady, I'm certain that's it … this hawk is here for you."

At Anna's conclusion — and as if on cue — Aetos lifted off the goddess's arm, hovering briefly before soaring over the temple. As they watched, the bird screeched in its tight arc, rising without apparent effort. Gaining altitude it gyrated lazily.

In the years she had hawked the bird, the goddess had never seen it circle. In the past it had been an utterly efficient pilot; now it appeared to serve a different purpose. She felt lightheaded as it orbited, her thoughts purged by the bird's girdling geometry.

Then as suddenly, it broke the halo's edge and, as if carrying a great weight, drifted eastward over the plain, rocking its wings against invisible thermals, against the fierce sun, flying in the direction of the distant terraces.

The goddess fought dizziness, then felt a shocking clarity.

She exhaled, hyperaware of each extraordinary moment: without warning, in complete cognizance, she was breathing out all the years of torment, all the old questions of morality and extinction. Her sense of lightness was remarkable. Then she knew.

"The bird has carried away the flames," she whispered.

Anna said, "What?"

"Aetos. The bird has inhaled the fire. It's all gone. I never imagined —"

Epiphanies are sudden and absolute. She knew now: Aetos had carried away the firestorm that had lingered for so long in the back of her eyes … It seemed almost madness to accept — yet she could not deny — that the eagle had, consciously or not, extirpated Gaia's foul brew.

She knew at the same moment that the bird had been a mere catalyst for her understanding.

Laughing, she recognized an irony: Gaia's work had been defeated by a bird. And the truth was simpler still: Aetos had swept in, observed, and swept out — leaving her crystalline.

She rung with clarity. The awakening was hers. Inexplicably, she remembered a Viennese fashion show years earlier. The theme, as the designer had envisioned it, was ancient Japan.

Timessa had led a dozen models out onto the catwalk. Musicians dressed like Samurai had struck bronze gongs to announce the start. Lights had clicked on overhead like wondrous suns.

She had stepped out before the fashionistas, the gongs still vibrating through the floors, the air … *oscillating*. She had felt the throbbing bronze through her veins, behind her eyes. Gloriously alive, she remembered smiling at models who stood behind her, and having them smile back. All of them felt the same thrum of the gongs …

❧

Aetos had winged toward the terraces, the eastern forest, the burnt plains. The goddess was reminded of Nastka: she had promised the warrior that the invasions would pause. Yet she hadn't acted. Now she would.

She pictured the smoke and fog that Anna had observed over the temple's stream, imagining it miles to the east, tripled in density, cloaking the no-man's land that buffered her lands from the nomads'.

She would block the long connecting trail with a miasma — with a firestorm's bitter fog. The mix would become impenetrable. The trail that joined here and there would disappear. Men who dared to enter the film would lose all sense of sight and sound. The only smell would be fetid, that of marsh gas and strange animals that had lost their way and died along the riverbank.

As quickly as she visualized it, she spread the vapor like a tree-high blanket just east of the farthest outpost. No nomad would ever slip through. Every rider's horse, however stubborn, would rebel on contact. Only the fish in the meandering river would slip through unhindered from west to east, east to west, traveling underwater, unaware except for the darkness of a barrier overhead.

❧

The scrim of time had worn away. Increasingly, it seemed only a patina, a thin glaze separating one era from another. She had suspected that time's supposed linearity was a fraud. Gaia had teased the concept.

Mortal beings aged. Birth and death drove creation and destruction. Gaia's vast cycles turned. The Grand Wheel turned. But, she knew, these processes might be occurring simultaneously, separately, side by side with other places and peoples.

Her portal from Naxos to Európē might not transport her backward into the past, but rather sideways or even forward, the veneer between one and the other easily penetrated. If so, Európē was real.

On the other hand, the river — Anneth's River — served as both a real waterway and a miraculous portal. For those who plunged into it, there had never been deaths. She and Anna proved its utility: they had merely slipped from Európē to Thrace, then back again.

Yes, she thought, just pull back the veil … that was how she, Anna and Artemis, Dionysos and Poseidon, had slipped into Thrace, shifting, swimming or shimmering in a simple flare from one place to another.

There was no *mysteria*. That was Gaia's deception. There was only the fraud of linear time put forward as fact to obscure what was … She paused, thinking, *Yes, what was no more than a fusion of countless events … countless phenomenon occurring simultaneously.*

She remembered Artemis hunting deer in Sicily, white hounds leaping around her. And when the hunt was done, she fed the hounds raw meat. Then, Artemis, a half dozen nymphs and the satiated dogs boarded a craft and launched into the sea.

Timessa said as she watched green, pale water unfold before them, "What a beautiful time."

Artemis had said, "There *is* no such thing."

CHAPTER 40

T<i>ime.</i> The aether gathered a beautiful light about it. Salt-bright under the sun. Young girls dancing in the sand, beside the green sea — the west shore of Delos, Artemis's birthplace — their feet tapping out the Dionysiakos, all wearing thin gowns.

In those days the village held few mortals. She recalled an old woman, dressed in black, an apron tight around her belly, wandering down to watch them. The woman sat on a bench and grinned, toothless, her eyes black.

Filly, one of the nymphs, turned to Timessa, asking, "Will we ever look like that?"

"Her time," Timessa said, "is running out." They accepted death, although it rarely touched them.

Their dance, naïvely salacious even at their age, was one they'd learned from Dionysos, who had taught it to his maenads. As they danced they sang,

Crime, crime, crime —
Bedtime, daytime,
Any time's the right time,
Noontime, nighttime,
Love's a crime, crime, crime —

They giggled, sang louder, reached their arms up higher than before in their silliness. The old woman had joined them at the beach's edge, swaying her hips to the beat, grinning with them in the sun.

There was no old woman watching now where the goddess stood beside the temple's river. The water flowed as if an eternal thing. Anneth's River. She had spoken its name to only one being, the eidolon, who was no more. Not even Anna knew.

The girl slept in one of the temple's back rooms. In the last half hour of their lovemaking the goddess had slipped, calling her Io, but the girl had only moaned. At first appalled at her mistake, then curious, the goddess called her Io a second time minutes later. Eyes closed, Anna had said, *yes yes*. She fell asleep, a small smile on her face. Covering her the goddess went out the back door to watch the sun drop below the oaks.

She heard voices in the front and turned. No ceremonies were scheduled. Yet on occasion worshippers would appear to ask favors. She pulled a hood over her head and went forward. Standing by the altar were four girls. All looked familiar and she stepped closer.

Seeing her they gasped and dropped to their knees, heads bowed. She spoke, saying, "Rise and identify yourselves —" and knew as they raised their faces: Delia, Kalypso, Tyro and Elissa, four of her nymphs from Naxos.

She stepped closer, frowning. "And how," she said quietly, "do you find yourselves here?"

Before they could respond, she scanned them, their thoughts transparent: Artemis had sent them. There were no complicated motivations. They were her girls, and they were simply eager to see her again.

Delia said, referring to Artemis, "The goddess said we could spend a day or two with you. With your permission."

"Did she?"

"She said you were in a land of women."

"Yes," the goddess said. "Strong ones, brave to the bone. This is Európe and you stand before the Temple of Inanna."

"A local goddess?" Elissa asked.

"Here," the goddess whispered, "*I* am Inanna."

"Oh … You're not Timessa?" Delia asked.

"No. I am known as The Lady, or the Great Goddess …"

The goddess looked them over. All wore seamless wool gowns that would not pass for local garb. Too, their hair was braided.

"You can't go around looking like you do. I have clothes in the temple. You'll find gowns hanging in the rear. My assistant is in the back. Be quiet — she may be asleep. Change and come back out."

They bowed and as they started toward the wide doors of the sanctuary, the goddess said, "And shake out your braids. Here, horses's manes are plaited, not girls's hair."

The usual evening shift of local girls appeared at sunset. They brought food. When they were introduced to the goddess's guests, two of the attendants left on horseback to bring more. Before light was gone, they were back with baskets of barley cakes, nuts, bread and vegetables. The goddess invited them to stay.

Anna had waken earlier, and now eight young women sat on blankets in the rear of the building, torches illuminating their small party, the river singing quietly nearby. Far downriver doves hooted in the dark.

The goddess could not remember being as lighthearted in years. Nastka had reported earlier that incursions had ceased. The trail east of the farthest outpost was impenetrable. Even her own warriors feared entering The Lady's miasma.

Nastka's stripes were scrubbed off, her hair tied in ribbons. With her smile she looked younger. The goddess had invited her to join the gathering, but she had declined. She had outposts to check before sleeping and would be up early. Still, the warrior looked happy as she left.

Now as the goddess sat with the temple attendants and the nymphs, Kalypso nudged her, smiling knowingly and nodding at Anna. "She looks like Io."

"But," Kalypso said, "she isn't."

Anna spoke for the first time, saying, "My Lady, tell them to stop."

Delia interjected with a sparkle, "But you're an *Io* lookalike."

Anna said blankly, "And who is 'Io'?"

The goddess smiled, looking at the nymphs, "Enough. I trust you haven't come all this way to torture my priestess?"

The youngest of the attendants said to the four visitors, "Anna is our greatest warrior. And now with great honor she serves Inanna as her priestess."

Kalypso said, "We, too, serve a goddess. Doing so brings us joy."

Anna raised her hands head-high and, like Io often did on Naxos, fluttered her fingers with a half-smile, saying, "Please. No more. It's warm tonight. And look! I've started the winds —"

A breeze swept downriver, brushing their shoulders. The goddess startled. Hands overhead, fingers fluttering. Even "I've started the winds —" was familiar. She looked at the girl and Anna smiled.

Everyone grew silent. After a moment Delia enthusiastically said, "We should go swimming!"

One of the attendants giggled. "In the river?"

"Uh-huh."

The youngest girl said, "It's too dark."

"We'll bring torches," Kalypso said. "It'll work!"

The goddess's eyes went from girl to girl, finally settling on Anna. She said, "And you?"

Anna shrugged, saying, "Of course. But let's stay on the shallow side." She pulled off her gown as she walked toward the river. Her small breasts shone in the torchlight and her pendant glittered.

A pink birthmark showed on her left collarbone. The goddess wondered how she had not noticed — Io was marked identically.

"Okay, girls," Anna said with authority. "You, too."

Each removed her clothes and hung them off branches at the bank. Several began to wade yet several hesitated.

Anna took one girl's hand and led her out. "Stay to the right," she said. "It's deep downriver."

Within minutes seven girls were calf-high in water, their voices giggly. Torchlight flickered off the moving film. The goddess watched from the bank. She alone remained dressed, half-vigilant but relaxed.

After a quarter hour the goddess clapped her hands and cried out, "Party's over. Everyone out."

They dried themselves and talked. One of the local girls passed around figs and almonds. As the evening ended, the attendants said simple goodbyes and rode home on their ponies. Candles were blown out, curtains were pulled shut and the temple grew quiet.

The goddess whispered to Anna, "Silence tonight. Not a word."

The girl smiled, loosened the goddess's gown and let it fall. "*Yes,* My Lady."

'*Yes,*' the goddess thought, the word, the *yes* that gave and granted. *Yes yes*, to whoever this being was.

CHAPTER 41

Timessa hadn't slept. Leaving Anna in bed, she rose before dawn, slipping out of the temple's rear door. Delia and Kalypso stood on the riverbank. They turned, saying cheerfully, "Good morning, Goddess."

She smiled and joined them. "It's a pleasant river, isn't it?"

Delia said. "There's nothing like it on Naxos."

The goddess watched the golden water roil over the gravel and polished stones, bubbling, purling as it wound toward Thrace. "It's a stream," she said. "that carries dreams. Perhaps it carries the drowned to the Underworld. Who knows?"

"But not all the drowned," Kalypso whispered. "Some are washed ashore and resurrected."

The goddess looked at her sharply. "You never told me how you found your way here."

Delia smiled. "Artemis said she thought Gaia had designed the portal only for you and the girl. But Apollo was there and said, 'No, that only the *pure* may step from there to here.' He looked at us and said, 'Like them,' So we tried and it worked."

There to here, the goddess repeated to herself. Her phrase. She asked, "Was it effortless?"

"It was," Kalypso said. "Artemis touched each of us, saying 'Such guileless, silly girls —' and we were here."

"She told me," the goddess quietly said, "that she, Athene and Dionysos could not come. That there was a barrier —"

Delia said, "They're not like us. They're not gullible."

Kalypso giggled again, clearly amused. "They're not *ingenuous*."

"Yet … *I* am here," the goddess said.

"Of course!" Delia said. "Can I tell you something without getting into trouble?"

The goddess nodded. "Go on —"

"Elissa calls you The Incorruptible."

"I see." She took a deep breath and slowly exhaled. The girls quietly stood beside her. In the silence the rear door of the temple opened: Tyro and Elissa.

Delia called out, "We're over here —"

An orange sun wove through the oaks. Amaranth and acanthus were blooming in shallow beds around the temple. The goddess heard swallows overhead and thought of the hyacinth she'd planted on Naxos. It, too, would be blooming soon. Inexplicably, she imagined she could smell Anna's hair.

As Tyro and Elissa joined them, Delia said, nudging Elissa, "Isn't it true?"

"What?" the girl said sleepily.

"That you call the Goddess incorruptible?"

Elissa froze. The goddess laughed and took her into her arms, stroking her hair.

"It's nice," she said, "to see all of you again."

The goddess knew the dawn ceremony would begin shortly and waited in front. Anna appeared in her sacred robe, nodding solemnly to the goddess. She stepped to the altar, wiping its surface, preparing for the ritual.

The goddess stepped beside her and said, "Anna, before we begin, come with me."

"Yes, My Lady …?" She followed the goddess into the temple and watched as she closed the doors.

"What is it?" she asked. The goddess pushed her against the door. As Anna gasped the goddess pulled her robe back, exposing the birthmark.

The goddess hissed, "Open to me: are you Io or Anna?"

"I am Anna, Inanna's priestess …"

"And if I were to say, *No, you're Io* —?"

"I would be Io," she whispered.

The goddess shook her head. "No more evasion. Who are you?"

"Io," she whispered.

"How can that be?"

"Gaia. It was Gaia. Never my idea —"

"Then you've misled me for months."

"Not me. Gaia. She threatened to destroy you if I didn't play along."

"Was I that easily fooled —?"

"Don't you see? Gaia sent me here each time you came."

"But why —?" The goddess slipped a hand behind her neck and gently drew her close, whispering, "Was I that blind —?"

"You are honorable, admirable. All of us love you …" The girl began to cry.

The goddess released her and stepped away. "So, you have been Io, Anneth, Anna …"

In the girl's silence the goddess abruptly asked, "Do you confer with Gaia regularly?"

"No, not in months." After a moment she said, "My Lady, I should hold the morning rites. We have visitors."

She stepped back into the goddess's embrace, looking into her eyes, then slipped away.

❧

Nastka arrived after the dawn ceremony with her daily report. The goddess, Anna and their visitors listened as the warrior recited: *No attempted incursions … Defenses remain high. …*

"The fog," she said, "the dirty yellow *thing*, lies in place across the river, woven among the trees, its claws deep in the trail —"

Making a face she said, "It's a smoky, half-alive, half-snake."

The goddess dismissed her with a wave. "No, not alive. It's just fog. Keep up your vigilance."

Nastka nodded, mounted her horse and left at a gallop.

"She'll continue to think of it as a snake," Anna smiled. "It *is* appropriate."

Delia asked, "Why a snake?"

"Because here," Anna said, "Inanna appears as both goddess *and* snake."

Elissa said, "Like the snake on your robe?"

"Yes."

Kalypso turned to the goddess, asking, "But why a snake?"

The goddess turned to Anna.

The girl said, "They terrify mortals. To the barbarians, the Goddess is either The Witch or The Snake. It works quite well."

CHAPTER 42

That evening the goddess dreamed of Gaia. Had she ever done so before? She doubted it. Her sleep was choked with impenetrable images. Bewildering dialogue. Abstruse articulations. Then it ended with a revelation.

But before that revelation Gaia had worn masks — one of a fiery sun, one of a hawk. At the end, barefaced, while the two wandered down a cobblestone backstreet in an ancient city, the little girl had said, "What, Timessa, have you been chasing? What is the one thing you cannot grasp?"

Timessa had tried to speak, but could not. Gaia had smiled mysteriously, saying, "Unable to say the word? It's *belonging*. It's all that lasts."

Belonging, she thought as she now lay on the bedding beside Io, her arm around the girl's waist.

It underlies all. It is the fire that drives life, the invisible matter that powers the cosmos, the force that binds all.

When missing it's desired; when found it fills the finder —

Belonging, she thought, *is acceptance. It is the manifestation of love.*

Timessa remembered her argument with Gaia on Naxos. Timessa had dared to say, 'Unlike all the other divinities you spawned — I alone see birth and death, fertility and destruction —'

Gaia had replied with a warning. She had sent her tumbling backward to Európē. And there, finally, the remnants of the old fires that had ravaged her for years had been extinguished. When Aetos appeared, she suddenly understood.

All the maddening vacillations stilled. Her sense of lightness became extraordinary.

Yet … Had she solved Gaia's dream riddle which was, simply, to recognize what she was missing? Having to ask, she knew she had not.

She imagined a confrontation at the gates of a city she wished to enter, one guarded by a mighty sphinx.

Says the sphinx: *What is love?*

Timessa: Isn't it all *mysteria?*

Sphinx: *Questions cannot be answered with questions, nor riddles with so-called* mysteria.

At this impasse, she would not have been allowed through the city's gates. What was this sphinx? She reminded herself that nothing happened randomly when Gaia was involved.

Dismissing her annoyance she rose from beside the sleeping girl — a sleeping Io, who could still be mistaken for Anneth or Anna — and changed from her nightgown. Dawn was close. She imagined that from inside the temple, she could hear the river. It would be meandering slowly, then quickening toward Thrace. Io's breathing, she was sure, echoed the river's soft song.

The goddess stepped out the back, walking to the riverbank. An almost imperceptible light had begun to show in the east. Breathing the cool air she closed her eyes. She heard distant hoofbeats — no doubt one of her warriors riding to join others on a daily patrol.

Hoofbeats. Then she remembered another dream:

Nastka rode hard with the goddess at her flank. The horses relished the speed. The two were riding east. Occasionally Nastka would turn to catch the goddess's eye and grin. Blue javelins glistened at her knee. The women ascended a terrace and entered a mountain trail. In minutes they had arrived at an outpost.

Looking down the trail she could see an ochre-colored miasma blanketing

everything. It was heavy upon the terrain, pressing its fingers into the earth. A
hundred paces short, she turned her horse into a clearing.

She slowed, then stopped. A golden light infused the space. It was as if a
globe of burning plasma hung overhead.

Nastka whispered, "The light pours down for you —"

☙

A noise from the river interrupted her recollection. A deer? A small
herd of four does and a fawn had crossed the day before. The light
was dim and she squinted.

Then she saw a small figure standing in the gentle flow: a girl
whose back was to the goddess. She wore a simple gown that fell
below her knees.

One of the attendants, the goddess thought, *probably Euthalia*. The girl
shook her hair and turned.

Not Euthalia: Gaia.

Gaia! Her face was inscrutable. Vacuous. Then her eyes slowly
sparkled. She lifted her arms gracefully, paused — her words
echoing over the water and through the oaks — and said, "Ah,
Timessa."

Timessa stepped back a pace. "You found me."

"Oh, I've always known your whereabouts. It's Artemis whom I
haven't allowed to know I know."

"I'm no longer who I was on Naxos."

"No?" Gaia laughed and stepped closer. "I'm aware that I had to
return you to this place once again."

"To become who I now am?"

Balancing in a balletic movement, the little girl whispered, "Yes,
indeed … So, Timessa, *who are you now?*"

"Asks the sphinx?"

"Questions," Gaia said smiling, "cannot be answered with
questions."

Feeling remarkably lighthearted, aware she could finally be facing
her demise, the goddess replied, "Stay where you are. I'll join you
there."

Gaia held out her hand — it was an unusual offering. They had rarely touched. The goddess took a dozen steps through the water and stopped before her.

"You ask who I am … And I would answer that, now, the light in my eyes —"

"— is that of a comet," Gaia said.

"Yes! But my understanding came not as lightning, but as a soft flash."

Gaia reached up and touched her cheek. "In time, for the lucky ones, all is revealed. My wait has been rewarded."

"I should have known," the goddess said, "there were *never* questions. I've wasted years."

"If you know that, then you know as well that there are no gates."

"Nor a sphinx that blocks the way."

The little girl blinked. "None of that."

"And," Timessa said slowly, "no fires. And no guilt for Inanna to drag around."

"I left you clues."

" 'Clues?' More like cruel challenges," Timessa smiled. "My suffering seemed endless."

Gaia laughed quietly. Timessa went on, "You know that a few days ago when Aetos winged away, whatever burden I carried … disappeared."

Gaia said, "Call it purged."

"I was freed."

"From what, Timessa?"

"From wanting to know what you wanted …"

"Now you just *are*?"

"Yes," she said. "Wondering about the past ended. Worrying about the future became … a distraction. Mere shadows on a wall."

"Timessa, those who worry about what once happened, about what might occur … are only half-alive," Gaia went on. "They are not *here*."

Timessa caught her breath, pausing. "Like apparitions."

"Like ones who are not present. Is there a greater crime?"

"*That* was Inanna's error, wasn't it? Lamentation blinded her."

"Grief," Gaia said, "occurs when something is lost. And of course, if something is lost, it no longer exists —"

"Your point?"

"What can be gained, Timessa, by grieving? Not the return of what has disappeared …"

Timessa whispered, "Those who mourn become lost themselves."

Minutes passed. The river's passage seemed immutable. The two stood in its flow, aware of each thing within Eurōpē.

Gaia broke the silence, saying, "This, Timessa, is being present."

"Yes, I see. One can know nothing by sifting through ashes."

"Or by practicing clairvoyance."

Timessa said, "Knowing these things …"

"… is to know the eternal," Gaia finished her sentence. "That which is everlasting appears, thrives and goes on — until it doesn't."

Timessa hesitated. "You're saying that the everlasting is and is not … *and* there is nothing eternal?"

Gaia watched her quietly.

"Is there anything," Timessa asked, "that lasts?"

"Only love," Gaia said. "It fills the cosmos. But even that's not all of it. Love constantly seeks the whole … which is *belonging*. You waited on me to open your eyes, while *I* waited on you to see."

Gaia had withdrawn with a half-smile, a slight transparency, a shift which became a lazy flash. Golden sparkles drifted for moments over the river, then dropped one by one into the flow, glowing in a soft phosphoresce as they drifted downstream. Timessa stood in the water, then slowly turned to look up at the first trace of a rising sun.

She walked from the river, seeing Io on the temple's back steps. The girl wore a linen shift and was barefoot. As the goddess caught her eye, Io called out, "I watched as she left. *Poof!*"

"Yes, she surprised me."

"No notice?"

Timessa shook her head. "None. She was waiting in the river."

"Well, you look pleased."

"I am. We agreed to this and that."

"Like what?"

"Things I see now that I hadn't seen before."

"So you've made up."

"I suppose." Timessa shrugged. "Do you know what she said?"

Io shook her head.

"That the light in my eyes is like a comet."Smiling, Io said, "I agree. The old fires are gone —"

"Perhaps."

"You're wrapped in delicious mysteries."

"No, not that. What's delicious is the opposite of that. The *mysteria* are gone."

Io smiled. "The sun's rising. I'll change and open the doors."

She turned and bounded up the rear steps. The goddess made no judgment as she watched her disappear. Io simply was. The two of them had been … were … and would be. She recognized now that lovers were like that.

She thought of the other beings around her: Aetos, Artemis, Dionysos, Athene, Poseidon, even the nymphs — all breathed the same air, existed under the same sun, their nuclei beating to the same primeval rhythm.

CHAPTER 43

The morning passed quietly. Timessa sensed that her time in Európē was coming to an end. At noon she sent the nymphs away, promising to rejoin them soon. The portal would take them home.

At dusk women met at the temple for the usual evening observances. The sky had turned a thin vermillion, its horizon aglow. A single, first star appeared above the gathering.

When the ceremony ended, the goddess looked across at those attending. Her custom at the end of ceremonies was to raise her hand and open her palm in a gentle sign. She saw Nastka, Hebe and a dozen village women. And this evening there was a new face.

Artemis. The goddess stood in the back.

She should not be here, Timessa thought. *There is a barrier* —

Artemis's eyes were serene, severe. Although hers was a new face, the others recognized her as someone of importance. Timessa spoke concluding words: "We meet again at dawn. Until then, go your ways." She paused. "The visitor may remain, if she wishes."

All left except Artemis and the attendants. The girls stayed to clean the altar, oblivious to the two women who faced each other.

Timessa said, "Once there was an impediment between there and here."

"Once." Artemis frowned, asking, "Am I interrupting anything?"

"Artemis," Timessa said, "is always welcome. What brings you to Európē?"

"Like many I come to see the snake."

"The snake?"

"They say there's a goddess here who becomes one at will."

"Yes … But why would you care?"

"To seek its insights —"

"Serpents do not speak."

Artemis squinted. "Are you sure?"

"How can I not be? I am it."

"Yet you use words."

"As the goddess, not the snake."

"If speechless," Artemis asked, "how does the serpent makes its prophesies?"

"You also know that it foretells?"

"Yes."

"Then you should know that it speaks through its oracle, a virgin priestess."

"The one called …" Artemis hesitated. "Anna … I've heard rumors that she loves the goddess here."

"Perhaps she does."

"Yet you called her 'virgin.' Can she be such, yet be a goddess's lover?"

Timessa smiled faintly. " 'Lover?' Did I call her that?"

"I saw how she looks at you. It's obvious."

"Then yes."

"Yes what?"

"Yes, she is that —"

"Virgin and lover: isn't that a paradox?"

"On the surface. Still, you and I know not everything is what it seems."

"Indeed," Artemis said. "As this Anna is Io."

"Names," Timessa said. "Such random things."

Artemis hesitated. "Now I wish to know whether the serpent shows itself to strangers."

The goddess narrowed her eyes. "When it wishes."

"I hear the mere sight of it is unforgettable."

Timessa raised her hands. There was a bright, violet fluoresce and Artemis covered her eyes.

When she lowered her hands, Timessa still stood before her as before. At the same moment the temple doors opened and her priestess stepped out. She wore a serpent-robe. The black garment was cinched at her neck.

The girl's face was inscrutable, as pale as a moon in fog. She held a wide, golden cup in her palms, descended the steps and stood silently beside her goddess.

Timessa took the chalice from her, saying to Artemis, "No need for the snake. Drink: an elixir. It binds us for eternity."

Taking the cup, Artemis asked, "Is there such a thing?"

"There is neither there nor here," the Timessa hissed. "Yet, as you drink you will see eternity in my eyes."

Artemis raised the cup to her lips. The liquid was honeyed, its color that of amber. As she swallowed she watched Timessa watching her.

For a moment silence fell upon them. Then the last rays of the setting sun struck Timessa's eyes. The goddess's unblinking eyes glowed, and a soft plasma seemed to burn there. Artemis was swept with … an unexpected wave of love.

"The elixir?" she asked.

Timessa nodded. "That and more."

An instant passed. Artemis thought, *For so long this same girl was caught in spirals. Seized and caught in a vortex, twisting and turning, meandering for years. Not now. Now, she has found an extraordinary certainty …*

Yet still *she burns. But not as before. Now, gloriously —*

Artemis bowed, saying, "Night falls. We should sit beside the river."

The three moved to the back of the temple, into the heart of the sacred grove where the river twisted like a lazy, lacquered serpent. Oak leaves rustled. Trout flickered like quicksilver.

Io said, "It's all sublime."

Timessa whispered, "Yes, exactly as it is."

Moments passed. Artemis pointed at the sky. A comet moved in an unhurried arc through the darkness. She said, "Once we viewed these as omens."

"Of what?" the goddess asked.

"Of some great event."

"Now they are in my eyes."

Artemis startled: Timessa knew. "Yes, it's true."

"You simply see what Gaia saw," Timessa said.

Artemis whispered. "An authentication."

"Is it not why you came? To see for yourself?"

"It is."

"Yet have we not always been together?" Timessa asked.

Artemis said, "Yes. Belonging makes for a strange perfection —"

"A perfect union," Io said.

As constellations dusted the night-sky, the goddess turned to Artemis. "Io has a proclamation."

Io nodded, saying, "I do." Waiting for the goddess's attention, she said loudly, "I declare that we're through in Európē."

Artemis asked, "Just like that? What's to become of all this lovely chaos?"

Io looked slyly at Timessa. "It was all a grand piece of theatre, wasn't it?"

"Perhaps," Timessa said. "But we are now past all of that."

Io said. " At dawn we return to Naxos —"

"The nymphs are already opening the estate," Timessa smiled. "Helios shines, hyacinths bloom. And Aetos waits to be hawked."

Artemis said. "Remember when you were young and we were on a hunt? The hounds we brought leapt about us in their joy. I still see you laughing."

"Was it when we boarded a craft and pushed off into the sea?" Timessa asked.

"Yes, and within minutes dolphins leapt about us like those hounds."

Timessa said, "But when I said, 'What a beautiful time,' you said, 'There *is* no such thing.' "

"That was then," Artemis said. "*Now* you know what you did not know that afternoon."

She paused. "Even after we have seen into all that is — as you have done, Timessa — everything goes on as it was before."

Timessa smiled. "Soon we shall be in Naxos, standing on the promontory."

Artemis's eyes were gray. "Never waiting, as there is nothing to anticipate."

Timessa nodded. "Or looking back as there is nothing to regret."

"You know now that seeing this way," Artemis said, "is not dispassion."

"Yes. This is simply seeing what is."

Timessa thought, *I'll be back on Naxos soon. But now, at this moment, this is all. There is no more. This is … all that lasts.*

❖ The End ❖

GLOSSARY

Glossary of Key Characters

All names are those of Greek divinities featured in this story.

Aetos A golden eagle hawked by Timessa.
Anna, Anneth Each an iteration of Iole.
Aphrodite The goddess of erotic love, beauty and sensuality.
Apollo The god of music, arts, and the bow; Artemis's brother.
Artemis The goddess of animals, protector of girls; Apollo's sister.
Athene A goddess celebrated for her wisdom and intelligence.
Dionysos The god of wine, excess, theatre and dance.
Eidolon Eidola, a specter or apparition, a double of Inanna.
Gaia The earliest and greatest goddess who created Earth.
Great Goddess An ancient goddess pre-dating the Olympian gods, also called The Lady, Great One, Inanna, Ishtar, Cybele, Lemnos, and numerous other divine names.
Hephaistos An Olympic god and ingenious artisan.
Inanna See Great Goddess.
Poseidon God of the sea and rivers, of earthquakes and horses.
Timessa A nymph who ran with Artemis for millennia before becoming the Great Goddess.

ABOUT THE AUTHOR

Patrick Garner is a writer, artist and podcaster, in addition to his other pursuits. He has written stage plays and cofounded the off-Broadway Bright Lights Theatre company in Providence, RI. He was honored by the American Theater Critics Association when one of his plays was selected for a reading.

He published *A Series of Days of Change* and *Four Elements* (poetry), *Playing with Fire* and *D Is for Dingley* (biographies), as well as numerous articles and reviews in national magazines. His paintings and etchings are in museums, universities and private collections. Narrator and host of the breakout podcast, *Garner's Greek Mythology*, he lives in New England.

Made in the USA
Thornton, CO
06/07/24 20:55:13

b8a331e2-8912-478e-afff-0bc7f85d5bc5R01